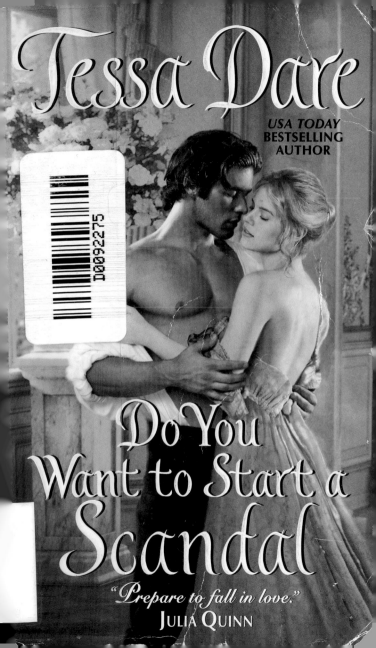

Tessa Dare

USA TODAY
BESTSELLING
AUTHOR

Do You
Want to Start a
Scandal

"Prepare to fall in love."
JULIA QUINN

these ot
from Ne
bestse

Tessa

Also Available...
**ANY DUCHESS WILL DO
THE SCANDALOUS, DISSOLUTE, NO-GOOD MR. WRIGHT
A LADY BY MIDNIGHT**

"You mean to kiss me?"

"I believe that's what I just said, yes."

"Here. Now."

He nodded. "That was the idea."

"But . . . why?"

He seemed bemused by the question. "For the usual reasons."

"Persuasion, I suppose you mean. You must think me easily swayed. One dose of your masculine lip elixir, and I'll be cured of any doubt, is that it?"

He briefly stared into the distance before returning to meet her gaze. "I'm going to kiss you, Charlotte, because I expect to enjoy it. And because I expect you'll enjoy it, too."

His low voice did strange things to her.

"You seem very certain of yourself, my lord."

"And you, Miss Highwood, seem to be stalling for time."

"Stalling for time? Of all the things to say. I'm not stalling for—"

He lifted an eyebrow in accusation.

"Fine." She was out of excuses. She hiked her chin, resigned. "Very well. Do your worst."

By Tessa Dare

Tessa Dare

Do You Want to Start a Scandal

AVONBOOKS

An Imprint of HarperCollinsPublishers

DO YOU WANT TO START A SCANDAL. Copyright © 2016 by Eve Ortega. All rights reserved. Printed in the United States of America. No part of this book may be used or reproduced in any manner whatsoever without written permission except in the case of brief quotations embodied in critical articles and reviews. For information, address HarperCollins Publishers, 195 Broadway, New York, NY 10007.

First Avon Books mass market printing: October 2016
First Avon Books hardcover printing: September 2016

ISBN 978-0-06234904-0

Avon Trademark Reg. U.S. Pat. Off. and in Other Countries, Marca Registrada, Hecho en U.S.A.
Avon, Avon Books, and the Avon logo are trademarks of HarperCollins Publishers.
HarperCollins® is a registered trademark of HarperCollins Publishers.

16 17 18 19 20 QGM 10 9 8 7 6 5 4 3 2 1

To my three cosmic kitties—the two spinster sisters and the unrepentant rake who showed up one night to rattle their tranquil existence. Even though you sit on my keyboard and spill coffee on my desk, the snuggles and purrs more than make up for it.

Acknowledgments

Like Charlotte Highwood, I've always been intrigued by mysteries.

Thanks to my mother, for passing on all her old Nancy Drew books. Thanks to my friends and my family, close and extended, for their support and understanding when I don't have a clue. Much gratitude to my husband, who agrees our love is one mystery that doesn't need to be solved. It just is.

Another persistent mystery in my life is why my editor, Tessa Woodward, continues to put up with me—but I am so grateful that she does. My thanks to everyone else who makes up the crack Avon team. And all my appreciation to my agent, Steve Axelrod, and Lori and Elsie, who have all the answers.

Lastly, my thanks (and apologies) to Jane Austen and Stephen King for providing two iconic opening lines in fiction, both of which I shamelessly twisted for my own uses since it was not a particularly dark or stormy night.

Chapter One

Nottinghamshire, Autumn 1819

The gentleman in black turned down the corridor, and Charlotte Highwood followed.

Stealthily, of course. It wouldn't do to let anyone see.

Her ears caught the subtle click of a door latch—down the passage, to the left. The door to Sir Vernon Parkhurst's library, if her recollection served.

She hesitated in an alcove, engaging herself in silent debate.

In the grand scheme of English society, Charlotte was a wholly unimportant young woman. To intrude on the solitude of a marquess—one to whom she hadn't even been introduced—would be the worst sort of impertinence. But impertinence was preferable to the alternative: another year of scandal and misery.

Distant music spilled from the ballroom. The first few strains of a quadrille. If she meant to act, it must be now. Before she could talk herself out of it, Charlotte tiptoed down the corridor and put her hand on the door latch.

Desperate mothers called for desperate measures.

When she opened the door, the marquess looked up at once. He was alone, standing behind the library desk.

And he was perfect.

By perfect, she didn't mean handsome—although he *was* handsome. High cheekbones, a squared jaw, and a nose so straight God must have drawn it with a rule. But everything else about him declared perfection, as well. His posture, his mien, his dark sweep of hair. The air of assured command that hovered about him, filling the room.

Despite her nerves, she felt a prickle of curiosity. No man could be perfect. Everyone had flaws. If the imperfections weren't apparent on the surface, they must be hidden deep inside.

Mysteries always intrigued her.

"Don't be alarmed," she said, closing the door behind her. "I've come to save you."

"Save me." His low, rich voice glided over her like fine-grain leather. "From . . . ?"

"Oh, all kinds of things. Inconvenience and mortification, chiefly. But broken bones aren't outside the realm of possibility."

He pushed a desk drawer closed. "Have we been introduced?"

"No, my lord." She belatedly remembered to curtsy. "That is, I know who *you* are. Everyone knows who you are. You're Piers Brandon, the Marquess of Granville."

"When last I checked, yes."

"And I'm Charlotte Highwood, of the Highwoods you've no reason to know. Unless you read the *Prattler*, which you probably don't."

Lord, I hope you don't.

"One of my sisters is the Viscountess Payne," she went on. "You might have heard of her; she's fond of rocks. My mother is impossible."

After a pause, he inclined his head. "Charmed."

She almost laughed. No reply could have sounded less sincere. "Charmed," indeed. No doubt "appalled" would have been the more truthful answer, but he was too well-bred to say it.

In another example of refined manners, he gestured toward the settee, inviting her to sit.

"Thank you, no. I must return to the ball before my absence is noted, and I don't dare wrinkle." She smoothed her palms over the skirts of her blush-pink gown. "I don't wish to impose. There's only one thing I came to say." She swallowed hard. "I'm not the least bit interested in marrying you."

His cool, unhurried gaze swept her from head to toe. "You seem to be expecting me to convey a sense of relief."

"Well . . . yes. As would any gentleman in your place. You see, my mother is infamous for her attempts to throw me into the paths of titled gentlemen. It's rather a topic of public ridicule. Perhaps you've heard the phrase 'The Desperate Debutante'?"

Oh, how she hated even pronouncing those words. They'd followed her all season like a bitter, choking cloud.

During their first week in London last spring, she and Mama had been strolling through Hyde Park, enjoying the fine afternoon. Then her mother had spied the Earl of Astin riding down Rotten Row. Eager to make certain the eligible gentleman noticed her daughter, Mrs. Highwood had thrust her into his path—sending an unsuspecting Charlotte sprawling into the dirt, making the earl's gelding rear, and causing no fewer than three carriages to collide.

The next issue of the *Prattler* had featured a cartoon depicting a young woman with a remarkable resemblance to Charlotte, spilling her bosoms and baring her legs as she dove into traffic. It was labeled "London's Springtime Plague: The Desperate Debutante."

And that was that. She'd been declared a scandal.

Worse than a scandal: a public health hazard. For the rest of the season, no gentlemen dared come near her.

"Ah," he said, seeming to piece it together. "So you're the reason Astin's been walking with a limp."

"It was an accident." She cringed. "But much as it pains me to admit it, there's every likelihood my mother will push me at *you*. I wanted to tell you, don't worry. No one's expecting her machinations to work. Least of all me. I mean, it would be absurd. You're a marquess. A wealthy, important, handsome one."

Handsome, Charlotte? Really?

Why, why, why had she said that aloud?

"And I'm not setting my sights any higher than a black-sheep third son," she rushed on. "Not to mention, there's the age difference. I don't suppose you're seeking a May-December match."

Lord Granville's eyes narrowed.

"Not that you're old," she hastened to add. "And not that I'm unthinkably young. It wouldn't be a May-December match. More like . . . June-October. No, not even October. June-late September at the very outside. Not a day past Michaelmas." She briefly buried her face in her hands. "I'm making a hash of this, aren't I?"

"Rather."

Charlotte walked to the settee and sank onto it. She supposed she would be seated after all.

He came out from behind the desk and sat on the corner, keeping one boot planted firmly on the floor.

Have out with it, she told herself.

"I'm a close friend of Delia Parkhurst. You're an acquaintance of Sir Vernon's. We're both here in this house as guests for the next fortnight. My mother will do everything she can to encourage a connection. That means you and I must plan to avoid each other." She smiled, attempting levity. "It's a truth universally acknowledged that a titled man in possession of a fortune should steer far clear of me."

He didn't laugh. Or even smile.

"That last bit . . . It was a joke, my lord. There's a line from a novel—"

"Pride and Prejudice. Yes, I've read it."

Of course. Of course he had. He'd served for years in diplomatic appointments overseas. After Napoleon's surrender, he helped negotiate the Treaty of Vienna. He was worldly and educated and probably spoke a dozen languages.

Charlotte didn't have many accomplishments, as society counted them—but she did have her good qualities. She was a good-natured, forthright person, and she could laugh at herself. In conversation, she generally put other people at ease.

Those talents, modest as they were, all failed her now. Between his poise and that piercing blue stare, talking to the Marquess of Granville was rather like conversing with an ice sculpture. She couldn't seem to warm him up.

There must be a flesh-and-blood man in there *somewhere*.

She stole a sidelong look at him, trying to imagine him in a moment of repose. Lounging in that tufted leather chair with his boots propped atop the desk. His coat and waistcoat discarded; sleeves uncuffed and rolled to his elbows. Reading a newspaper, perhaps, while he took the occasional sip from a tumbler of brandy. A light growth of whiskers on that chiseled jaw, and his thick, dark hair ruffled from—

"Miss Highwood."

She startled. "Yes?"

He leaned toward her, lowering his voice. "In my experience, quadrilles—while they may feel interminable—do, eventually, come to an end. You had better return to the ballroom. For that matter, so had I."

"Yes, you're right. I'll go first. If you will, wait ten minutes or so before you follow. That will give me time to make some excuse for leaving the ball entirely. A headache, perhaps. Oh, but then we have a whole fortnight ahead. Breakfasts are easy. The gentlemen always eat early, and I never rise before ten. During the day, you'll have your sport with Sir

Vernon, and we ladies will no doubt have letters to write or gardens to pace. That will see us through the days well enough. Tomorrow's dinner, however . . . I'm afraid that will have to be your turn."

"My turn?"

"To feign indisposition. Or make other plans. I can't be claiming a headache every evening of my stay, can I?"

He extended his hand and she took it. As he drew her to her feet, he kept her close.

"Are you quite sure you've no marital designs on me? Because you seem to be arranging my schedule already. Rather like a wife."

She laughed nervously. "Nothing of the sort, believe me. No matter what my mother implies, I don't share her hopes. We'd be a terrible match. I'm far too young for you."

"So you've made clear."

"You're the model of propriety."

"And you're . . . here. Alone."

"Exactly. I wear my heart on my sleeve, and yours is clearly—"

"Kept in the usual place."

Charlotte was going to guess, buried somewhere in the Arctic Circle. "The point is, my lord, we have nothing in common. We'd be little more than two strangers inhabiting one house."

"I'm a marquess. I have five houses."

"But you know what I mean," she said. "It would be disaster, through and through."

"An existence marked by tedium and punctuated by misery."

"Undoubtedly."

"We'd be forced to base our entire relationship on sexual congress."

"Er . . . what?"

"I'm speaking of bedsport, Miss Highwood. That much, at least, would be tolerable."

Heat bloomed from her chest to her hairline. "I . . . You . . ."

As she desperately tried to unknot her tongue, the subtle hint of a smile played about his lips.

Could it be? A crack in the ice?

Relief overwhelmed her. "I think you are teasing me, my lord."

He shrugged in admission. "You started it."

"I did not."

"You called me old and uninteresting."

She bit back a smile. "You know I didn't mean it that way."

Oh, dear. This wouldn't do. If she knew he could tease, and be teased in return, she would find him much too appealing.

"Miss Highwood, I am not a man to be forced into anything, least of all matrimony. In my years as a diplomat, I've dealt with kings and generals, despots and madmen. What part of that history makes you believe I could be felled by one matchmaking mama?"

She sighed. "The part where you haven't met mine."

How could she make him see the gravity of the situation?

Little could Lord Granville know it—he probably wouldn't care if he did—but there was more at stake for Charlotte than gossip and scandal sheets. She and Delia Parkhurst hoped to miss the next London season entirely, in favor of traveling the Continent. They had it all planned out: six countries, four months, two best friends, one exceedingly permissive chaperone—and absolutely no stifling parents.

However, before they could start packing their valises, they needed to secure permission. This autumn house party was meant to be Charlotte's chance to prove to Sir Vernon and Lady Parkhurst that the rumors about her weren't true. That she wasn't a brazen fortune hunter, but a well-behaved gentlewoman and a loyal friend who could be trusted to accompany their daughter on the Grand Tour.

Charlotte could not muck this up. Delia was counting on her. And she couldn't bear to watch all her dreams dashed again.

"Please, my lord. If you would only agree to—"

"*Hush.*"

In an instant, his demeanor transformed. He went from cool and aristocratic to sharply alert, turning his head toward the door.

She heard it, too. Footsteps in the corridor. Approaching.

Whispered voices, just outside.

"Oh, no," she said, panicked. "We can't be found here together."

No sooner had she uttered the words than the library became a whirlwind.

Charlotte wasn't even certain how it happened.

Had she bolted in panic? Had he swept her into his arms somehow?

One moment, she was staring in mute horror at the scraping, turning door latch. The next, she was ensconced in the library's window seat, concealed by heavy velvet drapes.

Pressed chest to chest with the Marquess of Granville.

The man she had meant to avoid at all costs.

Oh, Lord.

She had the lapels of his coat clutched in her hands. His arms were around her, tight. His hands rested flat against her back—one at her waist, the other between her shoulders. She stared directly into his immaculate white cravat.

Despite the awkwardness of their position, Charlotte vowed not to move or make a sound. If they were discovered like this, she would never recover. Her mother would sink her talons into Lord Granville and refuse to let go. That was, if Charlotte didn't expire of mortification first.

However, as the moments crawled past, it seemed increasingly unlikely that she and Granville would be discovered.

Two people had entered the room, and they wasted no time making use of it.

The sounds were subtle, hushed. Muted giggles and the rustling of fabric.

Perfume filtered through the draperies in a thick, pungent wave.

She slid her gaze upward, searching the darkness for Granville's reaction. He looked directly ahead, impassive as that ice sculpture again.

"Do you think he noticed?" a male voice murmured.

In reply, a woman's husky whisper: *"Hush. Be quick."*

A sense of dread rose in Charlotte's chest.

The dread was compounded by several moments of soft, distressingly wet sounds.

Please, she prayed, squeezing her eyes shut. *Please don't let this be what I suspect it to be.*

Her prayer went unanswered.

Rhythmic noises began. Rhythmic, creaking

noises that she could only imagine to be originating from a desktop—one being rocked violently on its legs. And just when she'd steeled herself to endure that much—

That was when the grunting started.

The human body was such a strange thing, she mused. People had eyelids to close when they wanted to rest their sight. They could close their lips to avoid unpleasant tastes. But there was no such appendage to block out sounds.

Ears couldn't be shut. Not without the use of one's hands, and she didn't dare move those. The window seat was too narrow. Even the smallest motion could disturb the draperies and give them away.

She had no choice but to listen to it all. Even worse, to know that Lord Granville was listening, as well. He too must be hearing every creak of the desk, each animalistic grunt.

And, within moments, every keening wail.

"Ah!"

Grunt.

"Oh!"

Grunt.

"Eeeeee!"

Good heavens. Was the woman reeling with pleasure, or reciting vowels in grammar school?

A mischievous tickle of laughter rose in Charlotte's throat. She tried to swallow it or clear it away, to no avail. It must have been nerves or the sheer awkwardness of the situation. The more she told herself not to laugh—reminded herself that her reputation, her journey with Delia, and the entirety of her future rested on *not* laughing—the greater the impulse grew.

She bit the inside of her cheek. She pressed her lips together, desperate to contain it. But despite her best efforts, her shoulders began to convulse in spasms.

The lovers' pace quickened, until the creaking became a sharp, doglike, yipping noise. The unseen man released a throaty crescendo of a growl. *"Grrrraaaaagh."*

Charlotte lost the battle. The laughter erupted from her chest.

All would have been lost, if not for Lord Granville's hand sliding to the back of her head. With a flex of his arm, he brought her face to his chest, burying her laughter in his waistcoat.

He held her tightly while her shoulders shook and tears streamed down her cheeks, containing her explosion in the same way a soldier might leap on a grenade.

It was the strangest hug she'd ever experienced in her life, but also the one she'd most desperately needed.

And then, mercifully, the entire scene was over.

The lovers engaged in a few minutes of parting whispers and kisses. Whatever fabric had been shoved aside was gathered and rearranged in place. The door opened, then closed. Only a faint whiff of perfume lingered.

There were no more sounds, save for a fierce, steady thumping.

Lord Granville's heartbeat, she realized.

Apparently his heart wasn't buried in the Arctic Circle after all.

Drawing a deep, sudden breath, he released her.

Charlotte wasn't sure where to look, much less what to say. She dabbed her eyes with her wrists, then ran her hands down the front of her gown, making sure she was all of a piece. Her hair had probably suffered the worst of it.

He cleared his throat.

Their eyes met.

"Dare I hope you're too innocent to understand what just went on here?" he asked.

She gave him a look. "There's innocent, and then there's ignorant. I might be the first, but I am not the second."

"That's what I feared."

"Fear is the word for it," she said, shuddering. "That was . . . horrific. Scarring."

He tugged on his cuff. "We needn't speak of it further."

"But we'll think of it. Be haunted by it. It's burned in our memories. Ten years from now, we could both be married to other people and have full, rich lives of our own. Then one day we'll meet by chance in a shop or a park, and"—she snapped her fingers—"our thoughts will travel immediately to this window seat."

"I heartily intend to banish this incident from my thoughts forever. I suggest you do the same." He drew aside a fold of the drapery. "It should be safe now."

He went first, making the large step down to the floor. She was amazed again at how he'd managed to hide them both so quickly. His reflexes must be remarkable.

He found the cord for tying back the draperies and began to secure one side in place.

Charlotte gathered her skirt, preparing to make her own descent from the ledge.

"Wait a moment," he said. "I'll help you."

But she'd already begun, and what was meant to be a graceful step turned into a clumsy tumble. He lunged to break her fall. By the time she'd found her feet and steadied herself, she was right back in his arms.

His strong, protective arms.

"Thank you," she said, feeling overwhelmed. "Again."

He looked down at her, and again she caught that hint of a sly, appealing smile. "For a woman who wants nothing to do with me, you fling yourself in my direction with alarming frequency."

She disentangled herself, blushing.

"I should hate to see how you treat a man you admire," he said.

"At this rate, I'll never have a chance to admire anyone."

"Don't be absurd." He retrieved the dropped drapery cord. "You are young, pretty, and possessed of both cleverness and vivacity. If a few tangled reins in Rotten Row convince every red-blooded gentleman to avoid you, I fear for the future of this country. England is doomed."

Charlotte went soft inside. "My lord, that's kind of you to say."

"It's not kindness at all. It's simple observation."

"Nevertheless, I—" She froze. "Oh, goodness."

They'd been discovered. The door to the library was flung wide.

Edmund Parkhurst, the eight-year-old heir to his father's baronetcy, stood in the doorway, pale and saucer-eyed.

"Oh, it's you." She pressed a hand to her chest with relief. "Edmund, darling, I should think you would be in bed."

"I heard noises," the boy said.

"They were nothing," Charlotte assured him, approaching the lad and crouching to look him in the eye. "Just your imagination."

"I heard noises," he repeated. "Bad noises."

"No, no. Nothing bad was happening. We were only . . . playing a game."

"Then why have you been crying?" The boy nodded toward Lord Granville, who was still clutching the drapery cord. "And why is that strange man holding a rope?"

"Oh, that? That isn't a rope. And Lord Granville isn't a strange man. He's your father's guest. He arrived this afternoon."

"Here, I'll show you." The marquess moved forward, holding out the length of braided velvet—no doubt hoping to calm the boy's fears. He didn't seem to realize how unlikely it was that a tall, imposing man could pacify a frightened child who'd never seen him before in his life.

The boy backed away, shouting at the top of his voice. "Help! Help! Murder!"

"Edmund, no. There isn't any—"

"MURDER!" he shrieked, running down the corridor. "MURDER!"

She looked at Granville. "Don't stand there. We have to stop him."

"I could tackle him in the hall, but something tells me that wouldn't help."

In the space of a minute, Sir Vernon, their concerned host, had joined them in the library. Followed by the worst possible person—*Mama*.

"Charlotte," she scolded. "I've been searching everywhere. Is this where you've been?"

Sir Vernon quieted his son's hysterics. "What happened, my boy?"

"I heard noises. Murder noises." The boy leveled a pointed finger on a straightened arm. "From them."

"There weren't any murder noises," Charlotte said.

"The boy is confused," Lord Granville added.

Sir Vernon put a hand on Edmund's shoulder. "Tell me exactly what you heard."

"I was upstairs," the boy said. "It started out with a squeaking. Like so. *Eek, eek, eek, eek.*"

Charlotte slowly died inside as the boy began an uncanny reenactment of the passionate sounds of the past quarter hour. Every sigh and wail and groan. There could be no doubt as to what activity the boy had actually overheard. And now they would all conclude Charlotte and the marquess had been engaging in that particular activity.

While grunting.

And using ropes.

In her worst nightmares, she couldn't have dreamed this scene.

"Then there was a terrible growling, and I heard

a lady scream. So I ran down to see what was the matter." He turned his accusing finger to the window seat. "That's where they were together."

Sir Vernon looked visibly disturbed.

"Well," said Mama. "I certainly hope Lord Granville means to explain himself."

"Pardon me, madam. But how do we know it's not your daughter who needs to explain *her*self?" Sir Vernon looked to Lord Granville. "There has been some talk in Town."

Charlotte cringed.

"Sir Vernon, you and I should speak privately," Lord Granville said.

No, no. A private conversation would doom her. Everyone needed to hear the truth, here and now.

"It isn't true," she declared. "Any of it."

"Are you calling my son a liar, Miss Highwood?"

"No, it's only . . ." Charlotte pinched the bridge of her nose. "This is all a misunderstanding. Nothing happened. No one was murdered or assaulted in any way. There wasn't any rope. Lord Granville was tying back the drapery."

"Why was the drapery untied in the first place?" Sir Vernon asked.

"There's something on the floor over here," Edmund said.

When he held up the object for inspection, Charlotte's heart stopped.

It was a garter.

A scarlet ribbon garter.

"That's not mine," Charlotte insisted. "I've never seen that garter in my life. I swear it."

"What about this?" Edmund turned the ribbon over, exposing a patch of stitching.

The garter was embroidered with a single letter.

The letter C.

Charlotte exchanged frantic glances with Lord Granville.

What now?

Her mother spoke loudly. "I cannot believe that Lord Granville, of all gentlemen, would behave in such a shameless and shocking manner toward my daughter."

Mama, no.

"I can only conclude he must have been overcome with passion!" her mother loudly declared. To Charlotte, she whispered, "I've never been prouder of you."

"Mother, please. You're making a scene."

But of course, a scene was just what her mother wished to create. She would jump at the opportunity to cause a scandal, if it meant affiancing her daughter to a marquess.

Oh, Lord. Charlotte had tried to warn him, and now her worst fears were coming true.

"I'm telling the truth, Mama. Nothing happened."

"It doesn't matter," Mama whispered back. "What matters is that people will *think* something happened."

Charlotte had to do something, and quickly. "It isn't my garter! I'm still wearing both of mine. Here, I can prove it." She bent to gather the hem of her skirts.

Her mother smacked her hands with a folded fan. "In mixed company? You'll do no such thing!"

How could it be worse to prove that she was wearing two garters than to let Sir Vernon believe she was wearing only one?

Once again, she tried to calmly state the truth. "Lord Granville and I were merely talking."

"Talking?" Mama fanned herself with vigor. "Talking about what, I should like to know."

"Murder!" Edmund shouted. He made the word a chant, stomping his feet in time. "Mur-der, mur-der, mur-der."

"Not murder!" Charlotte cried. "Nor any other untoward activity. We were speaking of . . . of . . ."

"Of what?" Sir Vernon demanded.

Lord Granville intervened. He silenced Charlotte with a touch to her arm. Then he cleared his throat and gave the completely truthful—and utterly devastating—reply.

"We were speaking of marriage."

Chapter Two

The next morning, Piers sat at the table in his suite, nursing a cup of coffee and massaging his temples. His head was pounding.

"How exactly did this happen?" In the corner of the room, Ridley brushed down Piers's blue topcoat. "Explain it to me again."

"I'm not certain I *can* explain it. And you really don't need to do that, you know."

Ridley shrugged and continued brushing the coat. "I don't mind. It soothes me."

"As you like, then."

To the rest of the household, Ridley was his valet. To Piers, he was a colleague in service of the Crown. A trusted partner and professional peer. As usual, Ridley's purpose at Parkhurst Manor was to listen below-stairs while Piers moved among the elite.

Piers didn't like asking a fellow agent to perform menial chores.

"When the quadrille began, I went to the library," he said, trying to retrace his steps from the previous night and make some sense of them. "I was planning to start on the investigation."

The investigation. The true reason for this country holiday. Sir Vernon Parkhurst didn't yet know it, but he was under consideration for an important appointment. The Crown needed a dependable envoy to sort out the tangled, corrupt state of affairs in Australia. The vetting had been a simple enough process . . . with one snag.

Over the past few months, the man had been bleeding money. Moderate sums, at irregular intervals. A hundred pounds here, two hundred there. He'd been disappearing from Town for a few days at a time, as well. Nothing too serious, but the pattern pointed to trouble. A gaming habit or a mistress, most likely. Blackmail couldn't be ruled out.

If Sir Vernon had any secrets he'd pay to keep, it was Piers's task to discover them.

"I meant to make a quick search of his desk for any ledgers or correspondence. She interrupted me. Without an introduction, without even knocking first. I found her . . . provoking."

"And pretty."

"I suppose." There was no point in denying it.

Ridley wasn't blind. Miss Highwood was quite pretty, in fact—with lively eyes and a wide, unabashed smile. A tempting figure, as well.

"Charming, too, I'll warrant."

"Maybe."

"And she was a breath of fresh air," Ridley went on, rhapsodizing with a flourish of his hand. "A beam of innocence and sunlight to warm the cold, black heart of a jaded spy."

Piers made a dismissive noise, then sipped his coffee to end the conversation.

The hell of it was, Ridley knew him too well— and he was, to a degree, correct.

Piers had spent too much time moving through palaces and parliaments as though they were scenes in an endless play. Everyone he encountered, from kings to courtesans, was playing a role. Parkhurst Manor was just another scene—and a boring one, at that.

Suddenly, in burst this woman—a pretty young thing in a pink gown—who was the worst actress he'd ever seen. She bumbled her lines, knocked over the scenery. No matter how she tried, Charlotte Highwood was unable to be anyone other than herself.

That quality was rare and refreshing, and Piers felt like a damn cliché for being charmed, but he'd learned to enjoy a fleeting pleasure where he found it.

He would pay for that lapse in concentration.

So would she.

"I let her dally too long," he said. "We were discovered. Explanations were impossible to offer without inviting more questions."

Questions such as the reason he'd been in Sir Vernon's private library at all. Better to let his host believe he'd sought a quiet place for seduction than to admit the truth.

"Mistakes aren't like you, my lord," Ridley said.

No, they weren't.

Piers rubbed his face with both hands. No use dwelling on it now. The only thing to be done was move forward. Face up to his errors and correct them, if possible. Minimize the damage, if not.

At some point during last night's debacle, his alternatives had become plain. He could disclaim involvement and flee the "murder" scene, abandoning his assignment and throwing an innocent young woman to the dragons.

Or he could do his duty, in more ways than one.

"Naturally, you'll do the honorable thing," Ridley said. "You always do."

Piers gave him an ironic look. They both knew honor was elusive in this line of work. Oh, they chased after that shiny feeling of patriotic heroism—it was the reason they'd taken the job, after all. But they never seemed to quite grasp it. Meanwhile, shame and guilt nipped at their heels.

The best course, he'd learned, was not to examine it too closely. These days, he avoided looking inside himself at all. What little honor remained to him was muddled with deception and darkness.

This matter with Miss Highwood would be no different, and more was the pity for her sake. She deserved better than what he meant to do today.

He tapped the folder on the table. It contained information on every resident, guest, and servant in Parkhurst Manor—including Charlotte Highwood. "You've read this. Sum it up for me."

Ridley shrugged. "Could be worse. She comes from gentry. Several generations of country squires, an estate with modest but steady income. Her father died having sired three daughters but no sons. His estate passed to a cousin, and the ladies were left with middling dowries. Charlotte is the youngest. The eldest, Diana, suffered asthma in her youth, so the family moved to the seaside for her health. Here's where it gets interesting."

Piers drained his coffee to the bitter dregs. "Oh?"

"They went to Spindle Cove."

"Spindle Cove. Why does that sound familiar?"

"Before her marriage, Lady Christian Pierce spent some time there, as well."

"Violet? You're right. That is interesting." As Piers recalled, the couple were now stationed in the south of France.

"Quite the little village, Spindle Cove. Established by the daughter of Sir Lewis Finch as a haven for unconventional women. The young ladies follow a strict schedule: Mondays, country walks. Tuesdays, sea bathing. Wednesdays in the garden, Thurs—"

"Really, I don't require every detail," Piers said, impatient. "Let's return to the Highwoods. Has she any connections?"

"Good news, bad news there."

"The bad first, please."

"The eldest sister married the local blacksmith."

Piers shook his head. "I can't believe her mother allowed that. She must not have had a choice."

"The good: The middle sister eloped with a viscount."

"Yes, Charlotte mentioned that. Which viscount, again?"

There was a knock at the door. When Ridley opened it, the butler stood in the corridor.

He announced, "The Viscount Payne to see you, my lord."

Ridley closed the door, then grinned at Piers. "That viscount."

* * *

"Colin? Is it really you?"

"Now there's my favorite little sister."

Charlotte dashed across the sitting room and flung her arms around her brother-in-law, hugging him tight. "How on earth did you arrive so quickly?"

"Your mother sent an express. And I have a well-established talent for making speedy trips northward."

"I'm so glad you're here."

Colin would put this right. Or more accurately, he would make it all a shambles, chuckle in a disarming way, put any scandal to rest, and then they could all sit down for luncheon.

Luncheon sounded lovely. She hadn't been able to eat anything that morning, and she was growing so hungry.

"Please tell me you're not considering anything stupid like dueling," she said. "You know I'm a better shot than you are. Minerva would never forgive me."

"We're not going to duel. There isn't any need."

She sighed with relief. "Oh, good."

"Granville means to propose this morning, and I've agreed to allow it."

"Propose? But that's absurd. The two of us . . . We were only talking."

"Alone," he pointed out.

"Yes, but it was only when the others came in that we hid."

"In the window seat." He looked at her meaningfully. "Where you overheard a passionate tryst."

Charlotte sighed with frustration. "*We* didn't do anything."

Colin's eyebrow rose in doubt. "I'm someone who's gotten away with a great deal of mischief. I won't believe you didn't do *anything*."

"There was nothing, I tell you. Not between us. Don't you believe me?"

"I do. I believe you, pet. But unless these mysterious lovers come forward to take the blame, no one else will. And to be honest, the mere truth—that you were caught alone with him in such close quarters—could be enough to harm your prospects. It wasn't very prudent of you, Charlotte."

"Since when do you care anything for prudence? You're an inveterate rascal."

He held up a single finger in contradiction. "I *was* an inveterate rascal. Now I'm a father. And let me tell you, while Minerva might contest the old maxim that says reformed rakes make the best husbands, she would be first to agree that we make the most overprotective fathers. I used to enter a ballroom and see a garden of flowers, ripe for the plucking. Now I see my daughter. Dozens of her."

"That sounds disturbing."

"Tell me about it." He shuddered. "My point is, I know all too well the untoward thoughts that lurk in men's minds."

"There is nothing untoward in Lord Granville's mind. He has the most toward mind I've ever encountered."

Even as she spoke the words, however, she wondered. She recalled the thumping of his heart in that window seat. The way he'd held her in his arms. Most of all, his sly teasing.

I'm speaking of bedsport, Miss Highwood. That much, at least, would be tolerable.

Heat swept over her skin.

"I'm just not ready to settle down," she said. "Yes, I wanted the amusement of a London season, but I had no plans of considering marriage this soon."

"Well, there's something they say about best laid plans of mice and men. I'm fairly certain it's in the Scriptures."

"It's from a poem by Robert Burns."

"Really?" He gave a remorseless shrug. "I seldom read either. And by seldom, I mean never. However, I do know something about love, and how it laughs in the face of one's intentions."

"There's no love involved here! We barely know each other. He doesn't want this match any more than I do."

"Oh, I doubt that."

"Why?"

He tilted his head. Lord Granville sat in an armchair at the other end of the long, narrow room. She hadn't noticed him come in. Had he been sitting there the entire time?

"Because the way he's been looking at you makes me want to bludgeon things."

"*Colin.* You're not the bludgeoning sort."

"I know! Believe me, I'm just as disturbed by these changes as you are."

"What wretched timing, too."

Colin put his hands on her shoulders. "Hear him out, pet. Considering what hangs in the balance, you owe yourself that much. I'll support you in any decision you make. But you must be the one to make it."

She nodded.

When he married Minerva, Colin had become the man of the family. However, he'd never been much of an authority figure. And as much as Charlotte prized her independence, she had almost been disappointed.

She'd never known her father. In her youth, she'd longed for a steady, male presence in her life. An older brother, an uncle . . . even a cousin would do. Just a man who could sweep into the room, with wisdom and command and only her best interests at heart, and say—

Go upstairs and rest, Charlotte. I'll take care of every-thing.

"Go upstairs and rest, Charlotte." Lord Granville rose and crossed the room. "I'll take care of everything."

No, no, no.

That was the wrong man.

And why was he addressing her as Charlotte? As proper as he was, he ought to know better. That degree of familiarity was reserved for family.

Or couples who were betrothed.

She stared at the carpet. "We are not engaged, my lord."

"I suppose not. But that won't take long."

Colin kissed her on the cheek. "I'll leave the two of you alone."

"Don't," she hissed at him, reaching for his sleeve. "Colin, no. You can't leave me."

But her efforts were in vain. Her brother-in-law escaped her clutches, deserting her.

Left with no other choice, she turned to look at the marquess. Judging by the weariness around his eyes, he hadn't slept any more than she had last night. He had, however, found the time to bathe and shave, and change into a dark blue morning coat, paired with immaculate buff breeches and polished boots.

Charlotte never trusted people who looked this good first thing in the morning.

She tucked an uncooperative strand of hair behind her ear. "You can't possibly mean to propose marriage to me."

"I can mean, and I do mean. I have given my word to your mother, Sir Vernon, and now your brother-in-law, as well."

She shook her head in disbelief. "This situation is intolerable."

He made no reply.

"I'm sorry," she said. "I didn't mean that to sound quite so insensitive. It's not as though you're the last man on earth I would choose to marry. I'm not stupid enough to assert anything of the sort. I always find it ridiculous when ladies say such a thing. The *last* man, truly? I mean, the world has a great many criminals and dullards in it. And even eliminating those, there must be millions who scarcely bathe."

"So you're saying I rank above the median."

"In the top quartile, solidly. But that's precisely why you deserve better than marrying the first impertinent girl who literally flung herself at you."

His lips quirked in a subtle smile. "What makes you believe you were the first?"

Oh, dear. There he went, being likable again. It was much too early in the day for his subtle humor. She hadn't readied her defenses.

"You're a marquess and a diplomat."

"But not an amnesiac. I do recall who I am."

"Then you should recall this: You need a wife who is elegant and accomplished. The consummate hostess."

His gaze settled on her in a most unsettling way. "All I truly need from marriage, Miss Highwood, is an heir."

She swallowed, audibly.

"I have no need to marry for money or connections," he continued. "You, however, could benefit from mine. On my part, I require a young, healthy bride—preferably an intelligent and good-natured one—to bear me children and ensure the succession of my line. This situation we find ourselves in, though unexpected, can work to our mutual advantage."

"So it's a marriage of convenience you're proposing," she said. "A simple transaction. Your wealth for my womb."

"That's a rather crass description."

"Is it an honest one?"

Perhaps he truly didn't need a worldly, elegant partner. Perhaps he found his needs of companionship met in other places, and all he wanted was a fertile bride without the inconvenience of a courtship.

All the more reason to get out of this.

He led her to a pair of chairs and motioned for her to sit. Charlotte's body felt numb.

"Although this is not the match you might have envisioned," he said, "I suspect you will find it a satisfactory one. As Lady Granville, you will have a fine home. Several of them, in truth."

"Yes," she said weakly. "I seem to recall the number five."

"You will also have pin money, a legacy, and entrée into the highest echelons of society. When children come along, you need not be a servant to their upbringing. In short, you will have everything you could possibly desire."

"With one rather notable exception," she said.

"Tell me, and it will be yours."

How could it not be obvious? "I would like to fall in love."

He paused, considering. "I suppose that might be open to negotiation. After you've given me an heir, of course, and only if you can promise to be discreet."

She was incredulous. "You've mistaken me, my lord. I would like to fall in love with the man I marry. And what's more, I would like to be loved by him in return. Don't you want the same when you wed?"

"Quite honestly, no. I don't."

"Don't tell me you're one of those bullheaded men who refuses to believe in love."

"Oh, I believe love exists. But I have never desired it for myself."

"Whyever not?"

He looked aside, as though he were choosing his words carefully. "Love has a way of rearranging a man's priorities."

"I should hope it does," Charlotte said, laughing a little. "If it's done right."

"That's precisely why love is the one luxury I can't afford. I have duties and responsibilities. A great many people depend on my clear judgment. There's a reason the poets say 'falling in love,' and not 'climbing.' There's no controlling it, no choosing where one lands."

She supposed he was right, in a way. But even if she could bring herself to disappoint Delia, endure the gossip, and give up everything she'd thought she wanted . . . she couldn't imagine agreeing to marry without love.

You can't eat love, she heard Mama's voice insisting. But then, she couldn't hold a conversation with a heap of coins. She couldn't find tenderness or passion in a vast, empty house. Or even five houses.

She knew herself too well. A polite marriage wouldn't remain polite for long. She would try to make her husband love her, and if that attempt failed, she would grow resentful. They would end up despising each other.

This was why—no matter what her mother schemed and planned—Charlotte had promised herself she would only follow her heart.

"I can't agree to a convenient arrangement, my lord. Your devotion to duty may be admirable, but 'lie back and think of England' simply isn't for me."

His voice became low and dark. "I cannot promise you everything you might wish, but I promise you this: When I take you to bed, you will not be thinking of England."

"Oh."

When he'd spoken of bedding last night, he'd left her speechless.

This time, he left her breathless.

She was not the most beautiful of the Highwood sisters—that honor belonged to Diana. Nevertheless, Charlotte knew herself to be pretty enough, in the standard English way. She'd known the admiration of the opposite sex—even been kissed a time or two. But those admirers were all boys, she now realized.

Lord Granville was a man.

Beneath that exquisitely tailored morning coat, he would be all sculpted muscle and sinew drawn tight. His body would be hard everywhere hers was soft. He would have dark hair scattered in intriguing places.

"Charlotte."

She jerked to attention. "Yes?"

Good Lord. She'd been picturing him undressed again.

This room was unbearably warm.

"It simply isn't fair," she said, inwardly regretting how childish she must sound. "We didn't commit any sins. Why don't you tell Sir Vernon the truth? That you went into his library to . . ." She cocked her head, puzzled. "What *were* you doing in his library, anyhow?"

"It doesn't matter."

"I suppose not. What matters is that some *other* couple had a scandalous tryst on the desk. We shouldn't be punished for it."

His gaze caught hers. "If we don't marry, only one of us will be punished. And it won't be me."

"I know."

The world congratulated men on their sexual exploits, but it was cruel indeed to women who dared behave the same. *He* could walk away from this situation unscathed. She would be ruined. Friendless. Loveless. Grand Tour–less.

Miserable.

Lord Granville must be truly decent, if he was willing to do this for her. The perfect gentleman.

He reached forward and took her hand in his. "Here is what I propose."

Please, don't propose. Not now, when my resolve is so weak.

"An understanding," he said.

She peered at him. "What are we understanding?

Or what are *you* understanding, I should say. I'm lost."

"We will assure your mother and Sir Vernon that we have an understanding. A private understanding, to be kept between us until the end of my stay. Announcing an engagement after one night would only invite more gossip. After a fortnight, however . . . no one will question it."

She laughed aloud. *"Everyone* will question it. Have you forgotten my reputation? They will never believe you proposed to me willingly. They will consider you fortunate to have preserved all your limbs."

Despite her objections, Charlotte knew this was the best outcome she could expect from the conversation. This "understanding" he suggested . . . it wasn't a true solution, but at least it bought her some time. She would have a fortnight to find another way out of this.

And she *must* find another way out of this, somehow. For the good of them both.

Colin's words came back to her. *I do believe you, pet. But unless these mysterious lovers come forward to take the blame, no one else will.*

The mysterious lovers weren't likely to come forward. But that didn't mean they couldn't be found. This was the country, not London. The possibilities were limited. If Charlotte could discover their identity and force them to confess . . .

Then she and Lord Granville would be in the clear.

Two weeks. That would surely be enough time. It had to be.

"Very well, an understanding it is." She rose to her feet and gave him a brisk handshake.

As she turned to leave, he kept hold of her hand.

She looked at his hand, then at him. "My lord?"

"They will be waiting on us, your mother and brother-in-law and Sir Vernon. I can't let you leave the room looking like that."

Self-conscious, she touched a hand to her hair. "Looking like what?"

He pulled her into his arms. "Unkissed."

Chapter Three

Charlotte looked up at him, shocked. Surely she hadn't just heard him say "unkissed." But what else could it have been? Untwist, un-hissed, un-Swissed . . . nothing else made sense.

She asked, "You mean to kiss me?"

"I believe that's what I just said, yes."

"Here. Now."

He nodded. "That was the idea."

"But . . . why?"

He seemed bemused by the question. "For the usual reasons."

"Persuasion, I suppose you mean. You must think me easily swayed. One dose of your masculine lip elixir, and I'll be cured of any doubt, is that it?"

He briefly stared into the distance before returning to meet her gaze. "I'm going to kiss you, Charlotte, because I expect to enjoy it. And because I expect you'll enjoy it, too."

His low voice did strange things to her.

"You seem very certain of yourself, my lord."

"And you, Miss Highwood, seem to be stalling for time."

"Stalling for time? Of all the things to say. I'm not stalling for—"

He lifted an eyebrow in accusation.

"Fine." She was out of excuses. She hiked her chin, resigned. "Very well. Do your worst."

The worst kiss was what she expected. That was the only reason Charlotte was allowing it, she told herself. One cold, passionless embrace would affirm the truth—that there was nothing between them. If they lacked the warmth to fuel a kiss, how could a marriage work?

Perhaps he would abandon the idea, here and now.

But it went all wrong, and long before his lips touched hers.

The simple power in his arms as he pulled her close—it sent a girlish, giddy thrill chasing through her body.

She looked up at him, unwilling to appear afraid. However, that motion exposed the wild beating of her pulse, making her feel more vulnerable still.

So she dropped her eyes to his mouth. Another

mistake. The jaw which looked stern from afar framed a mouth that was wide and generous this close.

So close.

And then, just as she was reminding herself that this was meant to be an emotionless, unexciting embrace, she panicked and made it even worse.

She wet her lips with her tongue.

Charlotte, you fool.

Maybe he hadn't noticed?

Oh, he'd noticed.

He would see everything now. Her willingness. Her curiosity. The tiny shivers of anticipation racing up and down her spine. She might as well have stood naked before him.

"Close your eyes," he said.

"You first."

She glimpsed that subtle curve of a smile.

Then his lips were on hers.

The kiss . . . oh, it was nothing like him. Or nothing like anything she'd known of him thus far. By all appearances, he was restrained and proper. But when his lips met hers, they were warm, passionate. Teasing.

And his hands were everywhere the perfect gentleman's shouldn't be.

His hand slid slowly down her back—not tentative, but possessive. As if he was determined to explore every inch of what would be his. His touch left a wake of sensation rippling through her body.

Then his hand claimed her bottom and squeezed, pulling her into his strength and heat.

She gasped, shocked by his boldness.

His tongue slid between her lips. Gentle, yet insistent. Exploring a little deeper with each pass. Goading her into kissing him back.

So she did.

Heaven help her, she did. She slid her arms around his neck and kissed him in return. Just trying to behave as if she had the slightest inkling what she was doing.

Whatever she was doing, he seemed to like it. A soft groan rose from deep in his chest. It was a heady thrill—the knowledge that she could provoke such a response in such a man. She clutched his shoulders tight.

Something within her had awakened. An awareness, a yearning . . . a glimpse of some future Charlotte she wasn't quite certain she was ready to be.

Later, when she had a moment alone, she needed to relive every second of this encounter. Where exactly did her knees go weak? How did he make her *want* these things? Most worrying of all—

When had she started to want *him*?

* * *

The wanting didn't take Piers by surprise.

He'd found her attractive at first glance, and tempting within minutes of their acquaintance. He'd felt the slight, feminine contours of her body pressed against his in the library window seat. All those mental exercises he'd been trained to use in case of capture and torture? He'd performed every last one of them behind those draperies, just to avoid becoming aroused.

Today was different, however.

Today, he needn't hold back. And once the floodgates were open, a veritable deluge of need poured forth.

No, the wanting didn't surprise him.

But the needing? That shook him to his boots.

She'd been correct; this was meant to be a persuasive embrace. He needed to convince Charlotte Highwood to accept his hand—both to preserve his sterling, upright façade and to ward off questions about his true purpose here.

Kissing her was all in the line of duty.

But work had never tasted so much like pleasure.

The muslin of her frock was worn to softness, and enticingly frail. She felt perfect against him, ripe in his hands.

And she tasted so damn good.

He never took sugar in his tea, didn't care for syrupy chocolate. But she'd been sipping something sweet. Was it treacle? Honey? Perhaps it was just her natural essence. Whatever it was, he couldn't get enough. He hungered for her.

"*Charlotte,*" he murmured. He paused a moment to gaze on her upturned face before kissing her cheek. Then her soft, pale neck.

And though it wasn't required—or even advisable—he tugged her closer still and renewed the kiss.

It had been a long, long time since he'd done anything purely because he wanted it. He'd earned this much, hadn't he? A sweet, enticing woman in his arms.

It wasn't fair to her, but life wasn't fair. Everyone learned that lesson eventually, and she would come out better for it than most—a marchioness, with wealth and rank at her disposal. Left to her own devices, she could—and likely would—do far worse.

He pushed the guilt aside.

And he sank deeper into her.

This wasn't her first kiss. He could tell that much, though he doubted any of the young men who'd kissed her had known what the hell they were doing. He felt a vague, stupid sort of rage toward them. It made him all the more resolved to make this kiss sublime. Sufficiently long and slow and sweet and deep to obliterate those embraces from her memory.

From this day forward—when she thought of kisses, she would think only of him.

He could sense the moment she recalled the world around them. She stiffened in his arms.

No, no.

He clutched her tight. She wasn't getting away from him. Not just yet.

He changed to light, teasing kisses. Brushing his lips against her sweet, lush mouth again, then again. Just one last time . . . and then one time more.

When he pulled away, her lips were swollen and rosy pink. The sight was satisfying in a deep, primal way.

She blinked up at him, looking dazed. "I . . . I'm suddenly not so certain this understanding is a wise idea."

"I'll speak to your family and Sir Vernon. You needn't worry. They will agree."

"My lord—"

"Piers," he corrected. "From now on, you call me Piers."

"Piers, then." She searched his face. "Just what sort of a diplomat are you?"

Darling, if only you knew. You would turn and flee as fast as those slippers would carry you.

"One with a specialty," he said, in all honesty. "Negotiating surrender."

* * *

"An *understanding*?" Mama followed Charlotte into her bedchamber. "You had him in the palm of your hand, and you settled for an *understanding*?"

Charlotte collapsed onto the bed. "The understanding was my choice, Mama."

"That's even worse. Have I taught you nothing? Seal the bargain when you have the chance."

Charlotte pulled a pillow over her head. She didn't want to argue with her mother right now. She wanted to be alone, so she could send her mind back through every moment of that kiss, and sort through all the sensations swirling through her. Then she would divide her reactions into two heaps: emotional and physical.

The emotional pile would be the smaller of the two—by a factor of ten, undoubtedly. The wild tumult he'd stirred in her was only a matter of bodies and desire. Hearts had nothing to do with it.

At least, that was what she hoped. But she would feel much better having confirmed it.

She could hear the footfalls as Mama paced the room. "You heedless girl. A fortnight. Do you know that's two whole weeks?"

Yes, Mama. I'm familiar with the definition of a fortnight.

"What if he changes his mind?" she wailed. "You've left him every opportunity to wheedle out of it. He could pack his things in the middle of the night and flee."

Charlotte tossed the pillow aside. "Your confidence in me is so inspiring, Mama."

"This is no time for that insolence you call humor. The marquess was engaged once before, you know. He put off the wedding for eight years, and then the girl married his brother instead."

Yes, she recalled hearing gossip about it. "That betrothal was a family arrangement. They were young; they changed their minds."

"You had better hope his mind has no further changes. If he calls off this 'understanding,' you will be ruined. This is your life, Charlotte."

"Oh, I know it is." She sat up on the bed. "And it's entirely your fault that I'm in any danger."

"*My* fault?"

"You encouraged the scandal and forced Lord Granville's hand. All that talk of him being overcome with passion."

"I might have encouraged it, but you began it. You're the one who cuddled behind the draperies with him." She sank into a chair and flicked open her fan. "For the first time, one of my daughters gave me cause to be proud. I was hoping you'd snare a duke on this holiday, mind. I thought the area was called the Dukeries, but I was grievously misled."

"It *is* called the Dukeries. That doesn't mean it works like orangeries. Did you imagine dukes would be growing on trees?"

Mama harrumphed. "At any rate, a marquess is the next best thing. You were very clever to snare him."

"I wasn't trying to snare him at all!"

"Now that you have him, you had better keep him. You must be on your best behavior for the rest of the fortnight. A model of etiquette. Watch your posture. None of that slang, or wit. Talk less, smile more."

Charlotte rolled her eyes. No amount of smiling was going to make her into an ideal bride for Piers.

"Find every occasion to be alone with him. Sit near him at dinners and in the drawing room. Ask him to turn pages for you at the pianoforte. No, wait—don't play the pianoforte. That will drive him away." She smacked her thigh with the fan. "I always *told* you to be more diligent with your music practice."

"Mama, stop this. If this 'understanding' does become a betrothal"—*and I will make sure it does not*—"it will have nothing to do with my accomplishments or manners, and everything to do with Lord Granville's character. My charms weren't what caught him. It's his own sense of decency that has him snared."

Mama exhaled her breath in a huff.

"He's an honorable man," Charlotte said.

She refrained from adding, *One who kisses like an unrepentant rake.*

Her mother seemed to think on this. Then she stood and made ready to leave the room. "Just as insurance, we will lower the necklines of all your frocks. I'll speak to the lady's maid about it directly."

"No." Charlotte leapt from the bed and blocked her mother's path. "Mama, you can't. You can't tell anyone about this."

"But—"

"You mustn't breathe a word. Not to the servants, not to Lady Parkhurst. Not to the neighbors, your correspondents, or even the walls."

"I don't talk to the walls," Mama protested. "Often."

She knew her mother all too well. If left unchecked, she would drop hints at luncheon. Insinuations at teatime. By the time they gathered for after-dinner sherry, she would be boasting of the imminent marriage and writing letters to all her friends.

There would be no escape, once that occurred.

"Lord Granville has asked for the understanding to be kept private," she went on. "He is an important man, and he values discretion. He would be most displeased to be the subject of gossip." An idea came to her. "In fact . . . I wouldn't be surprised if this is a sort of test."

"A test?"

"Yes, a test. To see if we can be trusted. If you speak a word of this to anyone, he will know. And then he is likely to withdraw his suit altogether."

Mama gasped and bit her knuckle. "Oh, Charlotte. Perish the thought."

Charlotte put her hands on her mother's shoulders. "I know you can do it, Mama. All your years of encouragement and mothering, hoping your daughters would marry well . . . It has all come down to this. You must hold your tongue. Bite it. Cut it out, if need be. Everything depends upon your silence."

"Yes, but it's only—"

Charlotte cut her off with a look. *"Silence."*

Mama whimpered, but sealed her lips.

"Good," Charlotte said, patting her mother's shoulders in praise. "Now go to your bedchamber and rest. I have letters to write."

She herded her mother out of the room, then latched the door behind her and collapsed against it.

Oh, dear. Who could tell if her warnings would last a full two weeks? She needed to identify the true lovers, and quickly.

She went to the small writing desk and dipped her quill in ink. She hadn't been prevaricating; she did have letters to write.

One letter, to be accurate.

The letter C.

With a bold swoop of the pen, she inscribed the letter on paper and sat back to ponder it. She had a mystery to solve, and this was her first—perhaps only—clue.

Chapter Four

$\mathcal{P}$iers leaned forward, closed one eye, and lined up his shot.

Billiards—like so many sports—was an exercise in applied geometry and physics. If the equipment was standard and the playing surface smooth, the only element of variation was the player's skill.

Success was all about concentration. A narrowing of focus. Dulling the senses, ignoring emotion, weeding out any human frailties—until all that remained was one's body, a target, and intent.

With a swift pump of his arm, he made the shot, sending the white cue ball cracking into red, both balls spinning across the green felt in perfect, predictable trajectories.

Most of his life, he had managed people in much

the same way. Not because he had disdain for them, or an inflated sense of his own importance, but because emotion could too easily skew his shot. Detachment was key—and it had never been a struggle.

Until now.

Until Charlotte.

She had his mind and body spinning out of control. He couldn't cease thinking of her. The sweetness he hadn't ceased tasting. The perfect fit of her body against his. The way she'd breezed past his defenses, slipped under his skin.

Yes, she was young. But Piers had learned to take the measure of people quickly, and Charlotte Highwood was more than she appeared. She possessed the sort of honesty that required confidence, and a keen awareness of herself and others.

Damn, this was dangerous—but perhaps danger was what he'd been craving. Yes, that must be the answer. She had his blood pumping and his mind on alert just like his most perilous assignments had done during the war.

That kiss had made him feel alive.

"Ouch."

Something long and sharp poked him in the arse. Then in the side.

Edmund Parkhurst stood between him and the doorway, brandishing a billiard cue. The boy's brows gathered in a scowl, and he jabbed the point right under Piers's lowermost rib—like a diminutive cannibal holding his captive at spear point.

"I know." His voice was as menacing as an eight-year-old boy's could be. "I know what you did in the library."

Bloody hell. Not this again.

"Edmund, you were mistaken. I'm a friend of your father's. No one attempted any violence. We've discussed this."

"Murder." *Jab.* "Murder." *Jab.* "Murder."

Piers let his cue clatter to the table. Where were this child's parents? Had he no nursemaids? Tutors? Hobbies, playthings, pets?

"I am not a murderer," he said, firmly this time.

And he *wasn't* a murderer. Not technically—so long as one employed the same ethical acrobatics used to absolve soldiers and executioners from their bloodier duties. No court in England would convict him of the crime. He felt less secure about escaping divine judgment, but . . . only eternity would tell.

"I know what you did. You're going to pay." The boy lifted the billiard cue and swung it like a broadsword.

Piers dodged the blow, backing around the table. "Edmund, calm yourself."

He could have disarmed the lad easily, but he could only imagine the scene that would result if he so much as bruised Edmund's little finger in the process. The boy would be running down the halls shrieking not only "MURDER!" but "ASSAULT!" and "TORTURE!" too. Probably adding "FAILURE TO PAY TAXES!" for good measure.

Edmund stalked him around the billiard table, swinging again—harder this time. When Piers ducked, the blow struck a pheasant trophy mounted on the wall, knocking the bird from its perch. He could have sworn he heard the thing squawk. An explosion of feathers filled the room, twirling and drifting to rest on their shoulders like snowflakes.

The emotions on Edmund's face underwent a swift progression—from regret at destroying one of his father's prizes, to anticipation of punishment, to . . .

Pure, concentrated fury.

The boy lowered the cue like a lance, hunched his shoulders, and bore down on Piers in a full-speed charge.

"MURRRRR-DURRRR!"

That, Piers decided, was quite enough.

He grabbed the cue with one hand, holding both it and Edmund in place. He spoke in a low, stern voice. "Listen to me, lad. Bashing one another with billiard cues is not the way gentlemen settle disputes. Your father would be most displeased with your behavior. I am losing my patience, as well. Stop this. At once."

He and the boy regarded one another, warily.

Piers released his grip on the billiard cue. "Go to your room, Edmund."

There was a long, tense silence.

Then Edmund stabbed him in the groin and dove under the billiard table, leaving Piers gasping for breath.

"You miserable little—" He doubled over, pounding a fist against the green felt.

That was it.

Today, Edmund Parkhurst was going to learn a lesson.

"May I put this down yet?" Charlotte asked, her voice strained. "I think I'm getting a cramp."

Delia didn't look up from her sketching board. "Just a few more minutes. I need to finish roughing in the folds of your toga."

Charlotte tried to ignore the twinges in her arms. "Which of the Grecian goddesses holds a silver tea tray, anyway?"

"None of them. It's standing in for a lyre."

There were very few people in the world for whom Charlotte would stand in the morning room, draped in bed linens, holding an increasingly heavy tea tray for hours on end—but Delia Parkhurst was one of them.

After the *Prattler* had made her a social outcast, Charlotte had given up on full dance cards. However, moping wasn't in her character. When scorned by the gentlemen, she looked about for new friends.

She found Delia.

Delia was warm, witty, and also an unwilling wallflower at balls, having been born with a hip that didn't sit quite right. They conspired in the corners and invented games like "Spot the Wooden Tooth" and "Rake, Rake, Duke," and folded their unused dance cards into paper boats for a Punchbowl Regatta.

That was, until they began putting the time to a better purpose:

Plotting their escape.

"Next year, we will be a thousand miles from here," Delia said. "Free of our families, and far from anyone who reads London scandal sheets. I will have Renaissance marbles to sketch, and you'll be exploring temples and tombs, and in the evenings we'll be surrounded by *comtes* and *cavaliere*. No more tea trays."

Guilt crept over Charlotte. After that scene in the library, their plan to tour the Continent was in dire jeopardy, and Delia didn't even know it.

It was going to kill Charlotte if she had to disappoint her friend.

Delia set aside her pencil. "There. I'm finished for today."

Charlotte lowered the tray, unswaddled herself from the linen, and shook the knots from her arms and legs.

"Dare we broach the topic of our journey today?" Delia asked.

"Oh, no. Not yet."

Not while your father believes I lifted my skirts for a marquess in his library.

"Why not?"

Charlotte tried to be vague. "I haven't had nearly enough time to prove myself to your parents. Much less your sister. Frances looks at me as if I'd lead you into ruin at the hands of the nearest roué."

"Frances is protective, and she pays too much mind to gossip. At least I don't have any older brothers to object. Only Edmund, and he's easily persuaded."

I wouldn't be so certain about that, Charlotte thought.

"What's holding you back? Is it Lord Granville?"

The question took her by surprise. "How did you know?"

Delia shrugged. "You left the ballroom as soon as he arrived, and I know how your mother thinks. But I wouldn't worry about her angling for the marquess's attention. He might as well reside on the moon, the man's so far out of reach."

That's what Charlotte had thought, too. Until she'd found herself not only within reach of him, but clasped in his embrace. The memory sent a shiver down the back of her neck.

She sat down and took Delia's hand. "There's something I must tell you. I'm worried about how you'll take it."

"Charlotte, you're my dearest friend. You can always confide in me."

A lump formed in her throat. Would she still be Delia's dearest friend once she told her the truth?

A small crash from down the corridor drew their attention.

Then a larger crash drew them to their feet.

She and Delia hurried out of the morning room and followed the sounds of broken pottery to the entrance hall, where a shamefaced Edmund stood next to the remnants of a vase.

Accompanied by none other than Piers.

Each of them clutched a billiard cue in his hand.

Lady Parkhurst rushed down the stairway to join them, her cap askew and slightly breathless—as though she'd woken from a nap with a jolt.

"What on earth . . . ?" She took in the scene with a quick sweep of her gaze. "Edmund. I should have known you'd—"

"Forgive me, Lady Parkhurst." Piers bowed. "The fault is mine. I was giving Edmund here a few lessons in the art of fencing."

"Fencing? With billiard cues?"

"Yes. We were too enthusiastic, I'm afraid. Edmund is a quick study. My parry knocked over the vase." His gaze slanted to another pile of broken bits in the corner. "And the cupid."

"And the pheasant in the billiard room," Edmund piped up. "That was him, too."

Piers cleared his throat. "Yes. All my doing. I hope you can forgive my clumsiness."

Charlotte bit back a smile. Clumsiness? As she knew well from their encounter in the library, Piers possessed lightning reflexes and full command of his strength. He was merely taking the blame for the boy. Just as he'd taken the blame for her.

"I will, of course, replace all the broken items," he told Lady Parkhurst.

"Oh, please don't," Delia said. "They were dreadfully ugly."

"Delia," her mother said.

"Well, they were."

Lady Parkhurst gave her daughter a look of motherly warning. "I will fetch the downstairs maid to sweep. Kindly take your brother upstairs."

Delia obeyed, taking Edmund by the shoulders and steering him toward the staircase. The boy dragged his feet in protest. Before he reached the top of the stairs, he looked over his shoulder and whispered at Piers, "This isn't over. I have my eye on you."

She looked at Piers. "What does that mean?"

"Don't ask."

Charlotte knelt in the corner and began gathering the pieces of the cupid statue. It wasn't so thoroughly demolished as the vase. Perhaps it could be reassembled.

Piers joined her, crouching low and reaching for the cupid's plaster base and replacing it on the pedestal.

"You shouldn't help," she said quietly.

"Why not?"

"Because you're a marquess. Marquesses don't do this sort of thing."

"Why not? If I make a shambles of something, I clear the mess away. That's as it should be."

She reached for a section of cupid feet and stacked it atop the base. "You don't believe that. If you did, Edmund would be piecing this thing together. It was obviously his fault."

"Not entirely." He added the cupid's plaster ankles. "Sparring requires two participants."

Charlotte handed him the next piece of the statue—a pair of white knees and chubby cupid thighs. As he took it, his fingertips grazed the back of her hand. Just that mere brush of contact, skin on skin, electrified her.

She dropped her gaze, reaching for the rounded cupid bum and placing it atop their growing reconstruction. Her fingers must have been trembling. No matter how she swiveled it, the bit of plaster wouldn't settle into place.

"Perhaps there's another piece missing," she said. "I can't seem to make this one fit."

"Allow me." He took the piece from her hands and inverted it. "I believe it goes this way."

Oh, Lord. She'd been holding the backside upside down, stubbornly trying to force it in place. All the while, the cupid's stubby little penis pointed upward like a clock's hand chiming midnight.

She ducked her head, mortified.

"And I believe the next bit is over there, behind your knee."

She reached for it too hastily, then dropped it again when a sharp edge bit into her fingertip. A drop of blood welled at the site.

"You're hurt," he said.

"It's nothing."

But he'd already taken her hand in his. After a quick appraisal, he lifted her injured finger to his mouth and sucked the pain away. The action was efficient, not wicked—but it sent her wits scattering just the same.

Then he cupped her hand in his, holding his thumb pressed against her tiny wound. His eyes, however, never left her face. Her heart pounded as though it was determined to keep her finger bleeding; as though it never wanted this moment to end.

She could grow accustomed to being looked after.

"Really, my lord . . ."

"Piers," he corrected her.

"Piers." She looked to the corridor for salvation. "The maid will be coming. We're huddled on the floor, holding hands, surrounded by naked plaster. It wouldn't do for us to be seen together like this."

"On the contrary, it would be perfectly appropriate. We will be announcing a betrothal in less than two weeks."

"That's just what I'm trying to say. We won't."

His eyebrow arched. "Have you forgotten the events of the past few days?"

"No."

She hadn't forgotten his sly teasing. She hadn't forgotten his strong arms around her. She certainly hadn't forgotten that searing, passionate kiss.

She withdrew her hand from his. "What happened in the library was my fault. I should never have followed you there."

"I should not have allowed you to stay. Sparring requires two participants."

Charlotte melted inside. He was trying to do right by her, and she appreciated that more than he could know. But it only made her more determined to do right by him in return.

"I made the mess, and I'm going to clear it away." She gathered the courage to smile at him. "I have a plan."

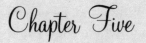

Chapter Five

*S*he had a plan.

Piers had noticed these impassioned statements of hers were falling into a pattern.

Don't be alarmed.

I'm here to save you.

I have a plan.

She kept vowing to protect him. It hadn't seemed to occur to Charlotte Highwood that he might be better placed to rescue her, rather than the reverse.

He couldn't decide if she was purposely obtuse or sweetly deranged.

He abandoned the task of piecing together the cupid and helped her to her feet. "You have a plan."

"Yes." After a cautious glance about the hall, she lowered her voice. "I'm going to find the lovers. The ones who really had a tryst that night. Once I present the proof to my mother and Sir Vernon, we won't have to marry at all."

This was her grand idea? There were so many things wrong with this plan, Piers didn't know where to start.

At the sound of the approaching maid, he waved her into the empty music room, where they could speak in private.

"I'm quite good at investigations, you know." She drifted away from the open door. "When my sister Diana was accused of stealing things at the rooming house, I almost solved the mystery."

"Almost."

"Yes. I had the responsible person puzzled out. It was only her accomplice that took me by surprise."

This record of almost solving a rooming house mystery didn't particularly catch Piers's interest. He was too busy noting how the room's large windows and mirrored panels bathed her in sunshine. Golden light limned her delicate profile and set loose tendrils of her hair aglow.

Good God, listen to him. Golden light and loose tendrils of hair. He'd be scrawling verses of poetry next.

This wasn't infatuation, he told himself. It couldn't be. He'd cultivated a keen attention to detail, that was all. Sensitive information. State secrets. Loose tendrils. It all made perfect, rational sense.

"It's simple," she said. "Someone—or rather, two someones—had a torrid tryst in the library. We know it wasn't the two of us. We just have to learn who they were and make them confess."

He looked at her with skepticism. "Whoever had a torrid tryst in the library, they will not want to be found out. Much less confess."

"Then we'll compel them somehow. Or catch them in the act." She made a dismissive gesture. "We have a fortnight to work that out, and I'm getting ahead of myself. First we need to learn their identities."

"That's not possible."

"It's quite possible."

"We were behind the drapes. We never caught even a glimpse of them."

"No, but we have all sorts of other observations. To begin, we heard them. If not their voices, at least their . . ." She made a face. "Noises."

God. It was too close to luncheon to be reminded of that. "I'm not certain what grunting and squealing could tell you."

"Well, at least it gives us reasonable certainty that the lovers were a woman and a man. Rather than two women or two men."

He found himself at a loss for a reply.

"Am I not supposed to acknowledge such couples exist?" she asked. "Cupid parts notwithstanding, I meant what I said the other night. I'm innocent, but not ignorant."

He waved a hand in invitation. "By all means, continue."

This girl was full to bursting with surprises. He couldn't wait to hear what she came out with next.

"We smelled perfume," she went on. "It was a distinctive scent. I know I'd recognize it if I smelled it again."

"Considering that ladies don't wear such scents while paying calls or attending church, that seems unlikely."

"I agree. But now we come to the most important clue. The garter."

"It's a garter. It can't give you much to go on."

"You must have little experience with garters, then."

"I wouldn't say that. But I do not wear them, I admit."

She smiled. "To begin, it was scarlet red. Not only a sensual color, but an impractical one. The ribbon was silk, which is expensive. That indicates the lovers weren't servants. At least, not both of them. If a maid were involved with a gentleman, it could have been a gift. The garter was also slightly large when I tried it on myself. That tells me something about the woman's shape and form."

"Does it," Piers said absently.

He was momentarily lost in the image of Charlotte lifting her skirt and wrapping a scarlet ribbon about her smooth, pale thigh.

"All that, and we haven't even discussed the best part. The garter was embroidered with the letter C." With another glance around her, she withdrew a paper from her pocket and unfolded it. "I've drawn up a list of everyone in Parkhurst Manor that night. Family, guests, servants."

"How did you manage that? From memory?"

"Not entirely. The servants and family I could name on my own, of course. For the guests, I stole into Lady Parkhurst's parlor early this morning and copied her list of invitations. Then I scanned it for women with the initial C in their names or titles. Excluding myself, of course."

He cocked his head and looked at her.

"Please don't give me that disapproving look. I know it was wrong, but I'm trying to be helpful. Our futures are at stake."

It wasn't a disapproving look. Piers was impressed. He knew she was clever, but he wouldn't have expected her skills of deduction to be quite this keen.

She continued, "Once I've narrowed the suspects, identifying the female lover ought to be simple. From there, it's only a question of following the woman to find the man. With any luck, I should learn the names of the mystery lovers within a matter of days."

"How do you know they were mystery lovers?"

She paused. "What do you mean?"

"To use the word 'lovers' suggests a degree of sentiment. There's lovemaking, and then there's . . ." He sifted through the possibilities before opting for the least shocking of the vulgar terms. "Tupping."

"What's the difference?"

What, indeed. "An unprincipled man might take that as an invitation to demonstrate."

"Fortunately, you're as principled as they come."

She couldn't have been more wrong on that point. "Suffice it to say, the tryst we overheard fell into the tupping category. It lacked a certain . . . finesse."

"Perhaps *you* merely lack imagination."

Piers shook his head, amused. He did not lack for imagination.

At that very moment, he was entertaining a vivid fantasy of pressing her against the mirrored wall. Watching the shafts of light gild her eyelashes and play across her lips. Kissing her slowly, easing her into a fog of passion. Then—only when she was pleading for more—lifting her muslin skirts, sinking to his knees, and tasting her sweetness. Taking his time about it. Giving her pleasure again and again.

And then again.

That, he would tell her, was how lovemaking worked.

He gave himself a mental shake. Enough. That idea would keep until after the wedding. There happened to be a mirror or two—or hundreds—at his estate.

And his estate was exactly where she needed to be. Once he had her wedded and bedded and tucked away in the country, he could get a firm grip on himself.

"You may call them what you wish," she said. "I choose to believe they were lovers. And I'm going to find them."

"You can't traipse about Nottinghamshire playing at solving mysteries. It's not only improper, it's too late. We have an understanding."

"We may have an understanding, but it is *not* too late. Not too late to find the lovers, and not too late for us." Her blue eyes deepened with sincerity. "I want to marry for love. And I think highly enough of you to want that for you, too. You're a decent, honorable man."

Sweet, innocent girl. She had no idea. Her powers of deduction might be keen, but he must never allow her to deduce the truth about him. Decent? Honorable? Not even close. *Try ruthless, darling. Deceitful, cold-blooded, heartless, and worse.*

"Charlotte, I—"

"You don't want love, I know. You think it will make you weak somehow, but you're wrong. So wrong. Love with the right person makes people stronger. Better than they ever could have been apart. I know it. I've *seen* it. That's why I'm going to solve this mystery. We both deserve better than a patched-up affair based on half-truths."

"We are not marrying based on half-truths," he said. "We are marrying based on the fact that I pulled you into a clandestine embrace in the window seat. That alone was improper enough."

"Only in the strictest definition of the word."

"Strict definitions are the ones that matter."

He didn't like the idea of Charlotte running about the neighborhood, sniffing ladies' perfume and sizing up their thighs. But then, there might be a benefit: If she was occupied quizzing the local populace about their garters, she wouldn't be asking probing questions of him.

Nevertheless, it was an imprudent plan—one that could go wrong in any number of ways.

"I can't support this scheme of yours," he told her. "I certainly won't aid you."

"I never expected to have your help." She tipped a coquettish glance at him through her lashes. "I daresay it's your loss, however. I think you could use a bit of intrigue in your life."

Oh, Charlotte. You have no idea.

"Answer me this," he said. "When you fail to find—"

She shot him a wounded look.

He revised. "*If* you fail to find these mystery tuppers by the end of the fortnight, what then? Do you intend to refuse me and embrace ruin?"

She looked into the distance. "I'm not stupid."

No, he thought. She wasn't stupid. Far from it, in fact. She was clever, stubborn, and—as he was coming to appreciate—dangerously perceptive.

That was precisely what had him concerned.

Shortly after luncheon, Charlotte received a summons from her mother. She put off answering it for an hour, then two. At last she reasoned she might as well have done with it.

On her way to Mama's room, however, Frances Parkhurst stopped her in the corridor. "A word, Miss Highwood?"

Charlotte couldn't find any reason to refuse.

Frances spoke in a low voice. "I want you to know I care very deeply about my sister."

"I care about Delia, too. She's become my closest friend."

Frances eyed her with suspicion. "Truly? Because you seemed to be making close friends with Lord Granville earlier today. In the music room."

"You spied on us?"

"I didn't need to spy. The door was open."

"In that case, you should know that we were merely talking."

We were merely talking.

How many times had she uttered that phrase in recent days? Charlotte was growing weary—not only of saying it, but of no one believing her.

"He would never have you," Frances said. "You will only embarrass the marquess and yourself if you persist in chasing him."

The nerve of her. At her side, Charlotte's hand curled into a fist.

She thinks she's protecting Delia, she reminded herself. *You can't blame her for it. She only knows you from the scandal sheets.*

"I'm not chasing Lord Granville," she said.

"Oh, please. Do you think I don't know how you and your grasping mother think? I tell you, your hopes for an advantageous match are laughable. You are without accomplishment. Your bloodlines are nothing to boast about. Atop it all, you are utterly shameless. Once the rest of London grew wise to your true nature, you cozied up to my sister."

"Did you stop me in the corridor just to insult me?" Charlotte said frostily. "Because charming as this is, I have other things to do."

"I stopped you to tell you one thing. I will not

allow you to take advantage of Delia's kind nature and desperation."

"Desperation?" Now Charlotte was growing truly angry. "Delia's not desperate for anything. Except, perhaps, for some distance from you."

"She is vulnerable and much too trusting."

"She's a grown woman, perfectly capable of choosing her own friends. And I hope she never knows how little you think of her intelligence."

Frances's dark eyes narrowed. "If you hurt my sister, I promise you this. I will ruin you, and not only in London. Every good family in England will know exactly what you are."

With that, she turned on her heel and walked away, leaving Charlotte fuming.

Nothing could say more about Frances Parkhurst than this: After just a few minutes with the woman, Charlotte found herself positively eager to visit her mother.

She knocked on the door. "You asked to see me, Mama?"

"Yes. Do come sit down beside me."

Mama's tone was uncharacteristically gentle. Charlotte was mystified, but she wasn't going to complain. She could use a bit of comfort just now.

She went to sit with her mother on the bed.

"Charlotte, dear. It's time we had a discussion about the meaning of marriage."

"We have discussed the meaning of marriage, Mama. I can't recall a day since I turned thirteen on which you failed to underscore the importance of the institution."

"Then this day will be no different." She raised a silver brow. "A good marriage is the most important goal in a woman's life. Her choice of husband will dictate her future happiness."

Charlotte held her tongue. She didn't believe that making a good marriage was the most important goal of *every* woman's life. Certainly some women could be perfectly fulfilled without marrying at all. And among those who did marry, happiness was a many-faceted jewel. Marriage could bring joy to one's life, but so could friendship, adventure, intellectual pursuits.

Her mother had married at seventeen and been widowed at four-and-twenty, having never experienced anything of the world. All the security and warmth of their home died with Father, and Mama had grown anxious and scattered as a result. Now she was an object of ridicule.

Charlotte was resolved to never be the same. No matter what Mama's exhortations on marriage, she would not settle down before she was ready, and she would only follow her heart.

"A husband and wife must be well matched," her mother went on.

"Mama, I am convinced on that point. You may save your breath to cool your porridge, and then use the rest to complain that it is cold."

"I'm not speaking in abstractions, girl. I'm speaking of marriage, and what it means in its essentials. A union, of not only hearts and minds but . . ." Her mother's mouth twisted. "Bodies."

"Oh."

Oh, dear. So this was to be *that* kind of discussion. And she'd thought there couldn't have been anything worse than Frances's harangue.

"You might have observed," her mother said, looking everywhere but at Charlotte, "that within the animal kingdom, the male and female sexes are distinguished by differences in their breeding organs."

No, no, no.

This could not be happening. Charlotte looked frantically about the room for escape. "Mama, we needn't have this talk."

"It's my duty as your mother."

"Yes, but we needn't have it now."

"There may not be a better time."

"I've read books. I have married sisters. I already know about inter—"

"Charlotte." Her mother flashed an open palm. "Just hold your tongue and let's be done with it."

Defeated, Charlotte folded her hands in her lap and waited for it to be over.

"You see, a man's . . . ahem . . . is shaped differently from a woman's . . ." Mama fluttered her hand. ". . . whatsit. And in the marital bed, he will wish to place his . . ." More hand fluttering. ". . . inside yours."

"His ahem goes in my whatsit."

"In so many words. Yes. And then—"

"And then marital duty, just a pinch, lie back and think of England. I think I have it. Thank you, Mama."

She tried to rise from the bed and flee, but her mother pushed her back. "Do be still."

Charlotte was still. Miserable, but still.

"I thought this might be difficult to discuss. That's why I gathered some common objects to serve as illustrations." Mama reached for a basket covered with a linen napkin. "Now, you might have noticed on occasion, whilst taking a bath, that there is a cleft of sorts between your legs."

Charlotte held her tongue.

Really? She *might* have noticed her own body, at some point in her twenty years of existing?

She supposed there could be, somewhere, a young woman who had never taken stock of her own anatomy below the navel. But whoever that poor soul might be, Charlotte would not have known how to be friends with her.

"It's rather like this." Her mother drew a roundish object from the basket.

Charlotte peered at it. "Is that a peach?"

"Yes. The lady's intimate parts are represented by this peach."

"Why a peach? Why not an orchid blossom, or a rose, or some other flower?"

Mama grew strangely defensive. "The peach has a cleft. It's the right color. It's . . . downy."

"But it's not terribly accurate, is it? I mean, I suppose it's not as poetic, but even a halved cabbage would at least have the proper—"

"Charlotte, please. Allow me to continue."

Allowing her mother to continue was what Charlotte least wanted. In the world. She would, without a doubt, choose a whipping in the village stocks over finishing this conversation.

She might choose death.

She braced herself as Mama reached back into the basket.

"Now, as for the gentleman. It's important that when the time comes you should not be alarmed. In a state of repose, a man's . . ."

"Ahem," Charlotte supplied.

". . . is an unremarkable sight," her mother continued. "However, when aroused, he will look something like this."

From beneath the square of linen, her mother withdrew a vegetable. A slender, curved vegetable covered in taut, gleaming, deep purple skin.

Charlotte gawped in horror.

No. It could not be.

It was.

"An *aubergine*?"

"A cucumber would have served better, but the kitchen was out of them."

"I see," she said numbly.

"Good." Mama laid her illustrations on the coverlet. "You may now ask your questions."

Questions? She was supposed to supply questions? Only one question came to mind:

What on earth did I do to deserve this, and is it too late to repent?

Charlotte buried her face in her hands. She felt as though she were trapped in a nightmare. Or a very bad play. *The Peach and the Eggplant*, a tragic comedy in one endless act.

Fortunately, she had amassed enough friends, novels, and good sense to round out her understanding of sexual intercourse years ago. Because if she'd been forced to go on nothing but this . . .

She came to a bargain with herself. If Mama was going to subject her to this, Mama was going to pay for it. And there was only one way to exact revenge for this farce of a lesson.

To take it seriously.

She lifted her head and composed her expression into one of solemn, wide-eyed innocence. Reaching forward, she laid a single finger on the aubergine. "Is this the actual size?"

"Not every gentleman's is quite that size. Some are smaller. Some may, in fact, be larger."

"But most are not *quite* so purple, I hope." She picked up the two items and pushed them against one another, frowning with confusion. "How does the aubergine fit inside the peach?"

Her mother's face contorted. "The peach produces a sort of nectar to ease the way."

"A nectar? How fascinating."

"If the gentleman is skilled with his aubergine, it will not be so very painful."

"What about the lady's skill? Shouldn't the bride to know how to please the aubergine?"

Her mother was quiet for a moment. "He might . . . That is, some gentlemen might wish to be . . . er . . . stroked."

"Stroked. How does one stroke an aubergine? Is it like stroking a kitten?" Charlotte laid the egg-plant fruit across her palm and brushed it gently with a fingertip. "Or like strokes of a hairbrush?" She increased the vigor of her motions.

Mama gave a sort of strangled squawk.

"Here," Charlotte said, thrusting the vegetable into her mother's grip. "Why don't you demonstrate?"

At the sight of Mama's panicked, near-purple face,

Charlotte lost her battle with laughter. She collapsed into giggles. Then she dove for cover, to avoid being beaten about the head with an eggplant.

"Charlotte!" Mama hurled the peach at her as she reached the door. "Whatever will I do with you?"

"Never, ever speak of aubergines or peaches again."

Chapter Six

*A*fter checking his reflection in the mirror, Piers rinsed his blade in the basin and wiped the remaining shaving soap from his jaw.

If he requested it, Ridley would come in to help him dress for dinner. "Valet" was, after all, his nominal post, and perhaps Piers ought to have used him more in that capacity—if only for the sake of appearances. However, he'd begun the habit of shaving himself in his early years of service. He hadn't liked trusting anyone to hold a blade to his throat.

Even now that he was a seasoned agent, he still preferred to shave himself. It wasn't that he didn't trust Ridley with his life. He simply didn't trust him to get his shave satisfactorily close.

As he pulled on his shirt and began to button his

cuffs, something caught his eye. He paused, staring into the looking glass.

There was something outside his window.

Or some*one* outside his window.

Probably just the branch of a tree, he told himself. Perhaps an evening songbird or an early-rising bat.

Just in case, he was careful not to reveal any outward sign of alarm. He merely kept his eye slanted toward the reflection as he steadily buttoned his cuff.

Then he heard a noise.

A scraping noise.

He inhaled steadily. In the time it took to draw that one breath, he'd assessed all the potential weapons in the room. The straight razor, where it lay on the washstand, still glistening with water. The fire iron would make a formidable club. In a pinch, his readied cravat could make a decent garrote. He'd learned *that* the hard way one sultry night in Rome.

But he didn't need to get creative tonight. Not with a loaded pistol waiting in the top drawer of the washstand. Unimaginative, perhaps—but effective.

The scraping noise became a scratching. Then a rattle. The intruder was easing the window open.

Piers kept his pulse calm, willing the blood in his veins to be cold as a stream in February. He slid open the drawer, moved aside a stack of folded handkerchiefs, and lifted the small brass pistol.

Then he waited. If he turned too soon, he would frighten his attacker away and expose himself to a second attempt.

Patience. Not yet.

A cool breeze wafted across the small hairs of his neck.

Now.

He spun on his heels, cocking the pistol as he turned, and leveled the weapon at his intruder.

She flung up a hand. "Don't be alarmed. It's only me."

"Charlotte?"

He lowered the pistol at once, pushing the hammer forward.

A slim, stockinged leg eased through the open window, and then the rest of her tumbled through, landing on his floor with a dull thump. A heap of grass-stained muslin, muddy half boots, and disheveled golden hair.

"What the devil are you doing?" He held out a hand to her, tugging her up from the floor. "Where did you come from?"

"Sorry to interrupt," she said, her gaze ranging from his gaping collar to the untucked hem of his shirt.

The sight of her, looking breathless and flushed and smiling, took his blood from ice-floe cold to the temperature of erupting lava.

He was relieved. He was angry. He was, against all odds, amused.

Anything but cool and detached.

"You need to be in your room."

"I'd love nothing more, but I can't just now." Her gaze dropped. "Ooh. Is that a Finch pistol?"

She reached for the pistol still dangling, unfired, in his right hand. He let her take it, and she turned it over in her hands before pointing it toward the open window, shutting one eye to take aim.

He had to admit, she had a damn good firing stance.

"How did you recognize a Finch pistol?"

She lowered the weapon, turning it over in her hands to examine it. "Sir Lewis Finch's daughter is a close friend. I spent years in Spindle Cove."

Spindle Cove.

He thought back to Ridley's abbreviated report on the place.

Mondays are country walks, Tuesdays sea bathing. They spend Wednesdays in the garden, and Thursdays . . .

"Thursdays you shoot," he said.

"So you've heard of it." She smiled at him. "I've been in Sir Lewis's own gun room, and I've never seen an example this fine. It's rather light and slender, isn't it?"

"Special issue," he told her. "Only a few dozen exist."

"Remarkable." She handed the pistol back to him. "How did you happen to get one?"

"I believe I'll ask the questions right now." Piers replaced the pistol in his drawer, then turned to her. "Explain yourself. What on earth are you doing, climbing through my window?"

"Right. That. You see, this afternoon Mr. Fairchild . . . that's the vicar, if you recall."

"I recall."

"He came to call on Lady Parkhurst. Something about the parish holiday program. The music selection or such. It seemed as though it would take them hours to negotiate, so I knew it was my chance."

"Your chance to what?"

"To call on Miss Caroline Fairchild. She's on my list of suspects. You do remember my plan from the other morning?"

He lifted a hand to his temple. "I recall it, yes."

"Well, once I scanned for the C's, I was left with five suspects. I have to start eliminating them somehow. If Caroline Fairchild was engaging in a secret love affair, and she knew her father would be absent for hours, that would be the perfect time for her to plan an assignation. Would it not?"

Piers didn't know how to argue with that reasoning. Irritatingly enough.

"So I claimed that I'd fallen ill with a migraine and went to my room. I told the maids I was not to be disturbed. Then I locked the door and slipped out the window."

"Your window is nearly twenty feet above the ground. For that matter, so is mine."

"Yes, of course. But there's a convenient little ledge that runs beneath all the windows, and from the northwest corner of the manor it's a short leap to the plane tree."

He set his jaw and tried to dismiss the image of her making a "short leap" from a second-floor window to the branch of a tree. "Do go on."

"And then I cut across the meadows and walked into the village." She sat down on a bench at the foot of his bed and began to work loose the laces of her boots, the soles of which bore clear evidence of her walk across pastures and down muddy country lanes. "I went to the vicarage and asked for Miss Fairchild. And she was there. Alone."

"Not in the arms of a seducer."

"No. In fact, she seemed lonely and only too glad for the visit. A sweet girl, but I don't get the impression that she's ever tasted adventure. She certainly hasn't read any good novels."

She kicked off her boots, then drew her feet up under her skirts, sitting cross-legged on the bench.

Piers decided he might as well be seated, too. He dropped into an armchair.

"I think it's safe to cross Miss Fairchild off my list of suspects," she said.

"What do you plan to do when someone asks

how you were simultaneously in your bedchamber incapacitated with migraine, and down in the village calling on Miss Fairchild?"

She waved her hand. "Oh, no one will question it. The days all run together during a country visit. It's impossible to recall whether one went picking apples on Monday or Tuesday, and was it Wednesday we had the morning rainstorm? It will be assumed to be a matter of innocent confusion if it's ever brought up. Which it likely won't be. You know how it is."

Piers did know how it was. Not only did he know, he made use of it. The habit of paying attention to detail when no one else around you did . . . it gave one a distinct advantage.

But if Charlotte Highwood was paying attention, that was one less advantage he had over her.

That worried him.

"Anyway, I planned to climb back up the tree and slip into my room. I'd left the window propped open. But when I came back, it had slid shut."

"So you came down the ledge to my window instead."

"Well, what else could I do? Enter by the front door? Confess that I'd lied about being ill and escaped out the window?"

What else, indeed.

Piers braced his elbows on his knees and rubbed his face with both hands.

She continued, "Later tonight, well after the house is asleep, I'll sneak down to the housekeeper's office, borrow her chatelaine, and let myself back into the room. Or"—she lifted a single finger—"we could stage a fire."

"You are not starting a *fire*."

"Not a real fire. Just a false alarm to get everyone out of bed and give me a chance to slip back in." She rose from the bench and rounded his bed, sitting down on the edge of it. "We'll decide later. I could use a nap while you go down for dinner. I don't suppose you could stash a sandwich in your pocket and bring it up for me? I'm famished."

She reclined onto her elbow. Atop his bed. Partially dressed. And according to her "plan," she proposed to stay there for the better part of the night.

No. This would not do.

He rose to his feet and began rolling his uncuffed sleeves to his elbows. "I will open the door to your room."

"I told you, it's locked from the inside."

"Leave that to me."

He opened the door a crack and peered into the corridor. After waiting and listening for a few moments to ensure no one was coming, he turned to give her the signal to follow.

"You have a bit of shaving soap." Her fingertips grazed a patch of skin tucked under his jaw. "There."

The softness of her touch lingered.

She cocked her head to the side and gazed at him, making a thoughtful noise. "I'm just realizing I've never seen you without a coat. You're built rather more solidly than one would suspect."

Her flattened palm skimmed from his shoulder to his elbow, idly tracing the contours of his arm muscles. Despite his better judgment, he flexed.

She noticed.

A surge of raw male pride set his blood pumping. *Who's all wrong for you now, darling?*

"Let's be going," he said. "Follow me. And stay close."

Charlotte sent up a brief, silent prayer and followed him into the corridor, carrying her boots in one hand. He held her other hand firmly tucked under his arm. In relative terms, it was a short journey to the door of her bedchamber, but it felt like a mile.

He gave the latch an experimental rattle, having put his ear to the door.

"You said you left the key in the door?"

She nodded.

"It's not there anymore."

"That's odd."

Charlotte suddenly realized he'd known which door was hers without asking. She wondered if there was anything to make of that, but other concerns quickly took precedence.

Such as the sound of distant footsteps coming from the bottom of the servant stairs.

"Someone's coming," she whispered. "We should go back to your chamber."

He didn't react. "It's a moment's work."

Working in quick movements, he removed an onyx stickpin from his pocket, bit the pointed end to give it a crook, and inserted it in the keyhole with a firm push. He worked the bent stickpin like a lever, testing it at different angles to work the lock.

As she watched breathlessly, Charlotte wondered if gold and onyx had ever been employed in such a venial occupation. To say nothing of the Marquess of Granville's aristocratic hands.

The footsteps on the servant stairs had grown louder. At any moment, one of the housemaids would appear at the end of the corridor. Charlotte could hear her humming a tune.

"Hurry," she whispered.

He didn't acknowledge her plea.

His lack of urgency was maddening. They couldn't be caught like this. There was no way to explain how Charlotte had gone from nursing a headache in her room to standing breathless and disheveled in the corridor, outside her own locked door. Worst of all, in the company of Lord Granville.

She would never be able to escape marrying him, in that event.

Oh, no.

A horrid thought struck her. Perhaps that was what he *wanted*. Perhaps he wasn't even trying. Perhaps this entire stickpin nonsense was a mere charade.

The footsteps reached the landing of the stairs. Charlotte caught a glimpse of black linsey-woolsey skirt rounding the far end of the corridor.

She wanted to bolt, hide. But where? This corridor suffered from an unforgivable lack of alcoves, potted plants, and marble statuary.

Her heart was in her throat.

"There," he murmured.

With a soft click, the lock opened.

In a single motion, he drew her into the room, shutting the door behind them—and leaving nothing but her startled gasp on the other side.

He flattened her against the closed door, pinning her with his body weight.

They remained still and silent until the maid's humming passed Charlotte's room and continued down the corridor.

"I told you I'd have it in time," he said.

"Yes. You did. All that and your hair isn't even mussed. What does your valet put in it?"

"Nothing. No one touches my hair."

"No one?" She tilted her head, regarding his thick, dark hair. "What a shame."

His heart still thumped against hers, but his expression—difficult as it was to read—didn't appear to be concern.

It looked like amusement.

Could it be that while skulking about corridors and picking locks with his stickpin, the proper, restrained Marquess of Granville was actually having *fun*?

How interesting. Perhaps there was something about the hint of danger that made him come alive in new ways.

Charlotte felt it, too. Not only the lingering excitement of their near escape, but the closeness they shared now.

His strong, sinewy forearms braced on either side of her body promised to protect her.

But the dark intensity in his eyes was perilous.

"You should go." She slid out from between his arms. "You'll want to finish dressing for dinner."

"Wait." His hand closed on her arm, holding her in place. "I'll check your rooms first. Someone's been in here while you were away."

"Really? How can you tell?"

"Aside from the key being dislodged?" He looked under the bed and inside the closet. "Obviously it's been ransacked."

She looked about the room. "No, it hasn't. It's exactly as I left it."

"You left it like *this*." He picked up a shawl from the floor, holding it by one bit of fringe, and as he lifted it into the air, it pulled with it a tangle of stockings and the stray bootlace.

"I'm not the tidiest of ladies," she said defensively.

With a chastening arch of one dark eyebrow, he turned away and went about checking behind the closet door.

For Charlotte's part, she crossed to the window. "But someone *has* been in here. This window's not only shut, it's latched. How strange. I suppose it must have been the maid."

"The *maid*?" He emerged from her closet, plucking stray yellow feathers from his shoulder and wearing an irritated expression. "Believe me, no maid has been in this room."

"It couldn't have been my mother. She would have raised an alarm the whole house could hear. But if not a servant or Mama, then who?"

"Perhaps someone knows you're up to something," he said. "And that someone wants you to stop."

"One of the mystery lovers, you mean?"

"Listen to me, Charlotte. You don't know what kind of secret you could be poking at, or what the mystery *tuppers* might do to protect it. It's time to let this go."

Let it go?

She couldn't let it go. Giving up on the search would mean giving up on the rest of her life.

"Well, while we're giving one another advice, my lord . . . I think *you* ought to give more consideration to love. You might be good at it."

"I can't imagine what makes you say that."

She shrugged. "You seem to be good at everything else. But then, perhaps you became good at everything else *because* you worry you're not good at love. Do you lack for confidence?"

In answer, he straightened to his full, impressive stature and glowered at her.

"Not that I think you should. I just can't help but notice that although you've proposed to two ladies, they were both women who'd be compelled to accept you. The first by family arrangement, and me by the threat of scandal."

He stalked to her chest of drawers. "Save your inquiries for the vicar's daughter. My history has nothing to do with any of this."

"Perhaps it doesn't. But you're a most intriguing mystery on your own. I can't puzzle you out." She moved to the bedpost and leaned one shoulder against it. "You don't seem the sort of man to fear commitment. You committed to me on the thinnest of reasons. Why wouldn't you set your sights on a lady you liked and woo her?"

Ignoring her question, he slid open a drawer. "This is empty. What were you keeping in here?"

"Nothing. I hadn't used it yet."

He cast a meaningful look at the heaps of unmentionables on the floor. "You *do* understand the purpose of a drawer?"

"Not everyone keeps their handkerchiefs organized by day of the week." She crossed her arms. "I've told you, I'm all wrong to be your wife. Consider this yet more evidence that we're mismatched. I'm too young for you, too indecorous, a poor housekeeper. You don't even like me. I'm merely some impertinent girl who cornered you in the library. You needn't settle for that."

"Settle," he echoed, replacing the drawer in the chest. "You think I'll be settling by wedding you."

"Everyone will think it."

"You," he said, "are the most unsettling creature I have ever met in my life. I have not felt settled since the moment we met."

Charlotte smiled to herself. "I shall take that as a point of pride."

"You really shouldn't." He advanced on her, closing the distance between them. "Has it not occurred to you that I might have a very real, very pressing reason for wanting to wed you?"

The darkness in his gaze left no ambiguity as to what reason he meant.

"But you could get *that* from any woman," she said.

"I only want it from you."

She swallowed, suddenly nervous. "You really should be going. Dinner will be called soon."

"I'm the guest of honor in this house." He pushed aside a fallen lock of her hair, and the slight friction teased her neck. "They'll wait."

"If my mother knew you were in here . . ."

"She'd be thrilled."

Too true, too true. "I could cry out."

"And ensure we're caught alone together, in even more compromising circumstances than the last time? Go right ahead."

She sighed. He truly did have her cornered.

There was only one way she could think of to shake him up, change the rules of his game.

No one touches my hair, he'd said.

Until now.

She stretched one hand forward, sliding her fingers through his dark, thick hair. Lightly, playfully— teasing it to wild peaks. Until the clipped locks stood on end, in amusing contrast to his piercing gaze and serious expression.

He seemed to have no idea how to respond.

Oh, dear. This man needed unsettling in the worst way.

Was he so unfamiliar with affection? Perhaps just

very out of practice. He'd been restraining himself for so long. That propriety was an overstarched cravat, stifling all the emotion that must be lurking deep inside. Was it any wonder he didn't see the reason to wait for a love match? In all his years of being perfect . . . he'd forgotten the untidy, unruly bliss that human closeness could be.

If he'd ever known true closeness at all.

Bosh, she told her heart. *Stop twisting and aching. He's a wealthy, powerful marquess, not a lost whelp in the rain.*

She added her other hand to the first, toying more freely now. Biting back a mischievous smile, she teased her fingers through his hair, creating tufts that stood out at crazed angles—like the fur of an angry bear. Then she pushed all his hair to the center, giving him the look of a Mohican.

"Are you enjoying yourself?" he asked dryly.

"More than you could know."

His Adam's apple bobbed in his throat. But he didn't tell her to stop.

She took a bit of pity on him, flattening his teased hair with her palms, then raking her fingernails over his scalp from front to back.

He closed his eyes and exhaled roughly.

"That's it," she whispered, toying with the soft, close-shorn hair at the nape of his neck. "It's only a bit of tenderness. There's no shame in surrender."

She knew she was playing a dangerous game. With each caress, she edged closer to the border between teasing a response from him and putting her emotions and virtue at risk. It couldn't hurt to allow him a few minor liberties, could it? Show him a bit of affection. Just enough to awaken him to what *could* be, if only he'd open his heart to the possibility of love.

At some point, she'd stopped playing with his hair. Which would not have been a problem, if she'd remembered to withdraw her hands—but she hadn't. Her fingers remained tangled in his thick, dark, tousled locks. His hands had settled on her waist.

She was just holding him now. And he was holding her.

His gaze trained on her lips.

She knew he would kiss her.

She knew she would let him.

It all seemed entirely inevitable, wholly predictable—and yet nothing had ever thrilled her more.

Breathe, she told herself. *Breathe now, and deeply. In a moment, it will be too late.*

Piers held on tight. By necessity, not choice. She'd dismantled him. All his disguises and defenses were crumbling to dust at his feet.

What was it about her? Her fingers couldn't be so different from other women's. She was pretty, but not the most beautiful creature he'd ever beheld. As she kept reminding him, she was young and unpolished and impertinent, and nothing a man like him ought to want.

And yet he did.

She teased him. She touched his hair. She believed he deserved this and more.

He couldn't let her guess her effect on him. He couldn't let anyone see. He needed to claim her, possess her, and stash her somewhere where she couldn't wreak so much havoc on his self-control.

But seducing her wasn't even what he wanted most right now. He wanted to lay his head in her lap and let her stroke his hair all night long.

"What are you doing to me?" he murmured.

He allowed every part of their bodies to meet— the bony prominences of hips, the softness of bellies, the resistance of breast against muscle. The pounding of hearts and the mingling of breath.

He pressed the full length of his body to hers— every lean, hard, red-blooded, masculine inch of him. Wanting her to feel him, to know the size and shape and strength of his body. To be awed by what she did to him, and what he meant to do to her. He wanted to hear her gasp, make her tremble.

God help him, he wanted her a little bit afraid.

Because he was shaken to his core.

He pressed his brow to hers, and he tightened his grip on her waist.

Pull back, he told himself. *You can't allow this to happen.*

Then their lips met, filling that last bit of space between them. As though no matter how far their lives stood apart, if they could agree on this one thing only—it was the answer, the reason of it all.

Her mouth softened for him like a gift, unwrapped. He kissed her deeply, with increasing urgency, and she matched him stroke for stroke. Her grip tightened around his neck, causing parts of his body to tighten in response.

He slid a hand upward, palming the globe of her breast. She gasped against his mouth and broke the kiss, still holding him close. Her breathing grew ragged as he lifted and kneaded her softness. The point of her hardened nipple pressed against his palm.

He squeezed his eyes shut and searched himself for composure. He had to stop. If he didn't release her now, he wouldn't release her until she lay bare beneath him, clasped in his arms.

Tearing away from her was like so many things he'd done in his life—cold, ruthless. Necessary.

"Dinner," he said. "I'm expected downstairs."

She nodded.

He touched her cheek with the backs of his fingers. Her skin was flushed and smooth. Then he slipped from the room without looking back.

Eventually, she would glimpse him for what he truly was. That glossy veneer of honor that had her fooled would eventually wear away, revealing the darkness beneath.

But he wasn't ready. Not yet. He rather liked the sweet, pitying way she looked at him, even though he knew he didn't deserve it. Could never deserve it.

I've come to save you, she'd said.

She was a sweet, darling girl. But she was half a lifetime too late.

Chapter Seven

"And then," Charlotte said, indignant, "she beat me about the head with the aubergine!"

"Oh, dear." Delia laughed.

"It's not amusing."

"It is tremendously amusing," Delia countered, smiling. "And you know it."

Yes, Charlotte did. Circumstance might have thrown her and Delia together, but honesty and wicked humor had made them friends.

"I only wish I could have been there. I would have loved to see your—" Delia winced, slowing in the middle of the wooded path.

Charlotte winced a little, too. "Shall we rest for a moment?" She ventured a few steps off the path, into a small, sunny clearing. "I see a few blackberries left over here."

"Well, don't eat them." Delia rested against a tree.

Charlotte plucked the dark berries from the bush, gathering them in her palm. "Why not?"

"You know what they say. You can't eat blackberries after Michaelmas. They've been spoiled by the Devil."

"Spoiled how?"

"He spits on them."

"Spits on them?" Charlotte pulled a face. "What a loathsome bit of folklore. Dutch children have Saint Nicholas going from house to house, placing treats in their shoes. We English decide the Devil spends Michaelmas spitting on blackberries."

"It probably has a practical root. Some goodwife in the Dark Ages had a stomachache after eating blackberries, and they decided the Devil caused it."

Charlotte wasn't so certain. "More likely some bad husband drank too much ale and blamed his sickness the next day on blackberries."

"I suppose it doesn't matter who it was. They've ruined it for the rest of us."

"Only if we let them." Charlotte selected a berry from her cupped hand. "Do you dare me to eat one?"

Delia just shook her head.

"Really, I'll do it. Devil's spittle and everything." She tilted her head back and dangled the berry above her mouth. "Last chance to stop me."

"I would never attempt to stop you," said Delia. "Trying to stop you is the surest way to encourage you."

Quite true. Delia knew her all too well.

Charlotte popped the berry into her mouth and gave it a thoughtful chew. "It is rather mealy," she said, swallowing and throwing the rest to the ground. "Perhaps the goodwives were on to something after all."

"We should be going."

"Wait." Charlotte pressed a hand to her stomach and doubled over. "I . . . I suddenly feel so strange."

"Are you well?" Delia asked.

"It hurts. Like something's burning me from the inside. I taste sulfur." She clutched at her throat and made a gagging sound. "I . . . I think it's . . . Satan spit!"

Charlotte reeled in a circle and collapsed behind the bushes, limp and lifeless. She waited for Delia to laugh.

Instead of laughing, Delia whispered, "Charlotte, get up. Lord Granville is coming."

"No, he isn't," Charlotte said. Delia was just trying to repay her teasing.

"*Yes*," Delia hissed. "He *is*."

"Really, I'm not that easily fooled." Charlotte rose to her knees and peered through the bushes. "Oh, no."

Piers *was* approaching. Devouring the distance between them in long, purposeful strides.

She scrambled to her feet, brushing the grass from her skirts. "What could he want?"

"Whatever it is he wants," Delia murmured, "he looks quite determined to get it."

Yes. Yes, he did.

Heavens, he was so handsome. His handsomeness was not a new development, of course—but it had begun to affect her in new ways. She felt a strange sense of possessiveness welling in her breast. As if he—in all his strong, sensual desirability— belonged to her.

The sensation unnerved her. She attempted desperately to quash it.

Her attempts didn't succeed.

He bowed to them. "Miss Delia. Miss Highwood."

Charlotte and Delia curtsied in response. It was all very proper in appearances, despite all the improper thoughts simmering inside her.

"Are you on your way to the village, Lord Granville?" Delia asked.

"No, I came in search of you."

His gaze fell on Charlotte, dark and intent. Hungry. What with the wooded setting, she felt like Red Riding Hood confronting the wolf.

There'd been too much talk of folklore for one day.

"I do hope you're well this morning, Miss Highwood."

"I . . ." Could he sense her inner turmoil? Was it that obvious? "Why wouldn't I be?"

"Aside from flailing about, clutching your throat just now? You were ill last evening."

"Oh, yes. That."

At his mention of last evening, the breeze seemed to die. The air about her grew sluggish and warm.

"Come to mention it, you left the ball early the other night, too," Delia said.

"It's a concerning pattern," he said. "Have you consulted a physician about these episodes, Miss Highwood?"

"They aren't episodes." Charlotte spoke through a smile that was composed of gritted teeth. "And I don't need a doctor."

"I will brook no argument," he said. "If your condition recurs, causing you to miss even one more outing or dinner, I will send for my personal physician. He's remarkably skilled with leeches and purgatives."

Delia stifled a laugh. "How very good of you to offer, Lord Granville."

Oh, yes. How very good of him indeed. Compelling her to appear at the dinner table under threat of leeches.

If Piers thought he could inhibit her investigations, Charlotte would prove him wrong. It wasn't as though she *enjoyed* feigning illness, lying to Delia and her hosts. She was doing this for his own good, as well as hers.

"Shouldn't the gentlemen be shooting or coursing or something?" she asked. "I thought this was a sporting holiday."

"We had a bit of fishing early this morning, but now Sir Vernon is with his steward. I have business in town. It was suggested the ladies might like to visit the shops."

Charlotte would bet sovereigns to pennies that her mother had been the source of that suggestion. Mama was likely tying her bonnet strings and gathering her reticule as they spoke. She would invent any excuse to put Piers and Charlotte in the same place.

"You and Frances should go, Delia. I'll stay behind. There'll be too many of us otherwise, and we wouldn't want to make His Lordship's coach cramped."

"Have no worry on that score," he said. "My carriage is more than large enough to accommodate our group."

Indeed it was.

They emerged from the path onto the drive. In front of Parkhurst Manor sat the grandest, most elegant barouche-landau Charlotte had ever seen. A glossy, obsidian-black carriage emblazoned with a golden crest on the door. It was drawn by a team of four ebony-maned warmbloods—horses so perfectly matched they might have been struck from a mold.

Frances and Delia climbed in first, handed up by Lord Granville himself. Charlotte squeezed next to them on the front-facing bench.

Then it was Mama's turn. "Charlotte, you must move. You know very well I cannot sit facing backward."

"Actually, Mama, I can't recall you ever saying that before."

"It interferes with my digestion. Go on, then. Move to the other side."

She was so terribly, painfully obvious.

Rather than cause even more of a scene, Charlotte moved to the rear-facing seat. Which meant, of course, that Piers sat next to her.

As expected, Frances glowered at her. At least Delia had the kindness to send her a sympathetic smile. It was nice to have one friend who didn't believe her to be an audacious hussy.

Then again, perhaps she *was* an audacious hussy.

With Piers next to her, she couldn't help but remember the night before. How his hair had felt sliding through her fingers. How he'd leaned into her touch and murmured such entrancing, indecent words.

The coach bounced off a rut, and Charlotte went momentarily airborne.

Piers caught her, drawing her to his side. Her insides cartwheeled in response.

What to make of this man? He was proper. He was passionate. He had the public demeanor of an iceberg, but he kissed her as if she were his oasis in a vast, arid desert.

What are you doing to me? he'd whispered.

Charlotte had no idea.

But whatever it was, he was doing it back.

In the draper's shop, Mama went straight to a display of dreadful lace caps. "Come here, Charlotte. Tell me, which do you think is best?"

Charlotte grimaced. The fashion of married ladies wearing ugly lace caps composed at least one-third of her determination not to wed young. "None of them."

"Let's ask His Lordship."

"Mama, no." She lowered her voice to a whisper. "Remember? Silence."

"Pish. We're only discussing caps." Her mother raised her arm and waved, calling across the shop. "Lord Granville! Oh, Lord Granville! Do come to our aid. Over here, by the lace."

Piers lifted his head—slowly, as if hearing his name called from some far-off land of fantasy. Because surely, no one in this mortal realm would have the unspeakably bad manners to shout at a marquess as though she were hailing a hackney cab.

No one, that was, save Mama.

Charlotte wanted to hide behind the ostrich plumes, but it was useless. Oh, well. If Piers was truly considering marrying her, he ought to know what he was in for.

The dire truth seemed to be dawning on him as he approached.

"Now, Lord Granville," Mama said. "A certain newly betrothed young lady of my acquaintance is debating which style of caps to wear once she is married. Which would you choose?"

Piers regarded the array of lace caps before him. "I don't think any of them would suit me."

Mama laughed, a bit too enthusiastically to be credible. "Not for yourself, my lord. What would you choose for your bride?"

"I would still have no opinion."

Mama's impatience began to show. "Surely you would wish for the future Lady Granville to be admired."

"I fully expect she will be. However, I will have already entrusted her with the management of my households, the comfort of my guests, and the upbringing of my children. I would not presume to choose her caps."

Her mother persisted. "*Some* might say it is the husband's role to advise his wife on all matters."

"Some might say that," he replied evenly. "I would ignore them." With a slight bow, he turned away.

Mama was left alone with her fan and her flustered sensibilities.

Charlotte, on the other hand, wanted to cheer.

Well, Mama. Do you still want me to marry a marquess?

Piers Brandon was not a gentleman who could be nudged, persuaded, implored, or gainsaid. A man of his stature would be entirely out of her mother's depth to manage.

Out of Charlotte's depth, as well.

No doubt he had begun to realize the magnitude of the gulf between them. Even if he could stomach the notion of acquiring such a mother-in-law . . . Imagine, trusting *Charlotte* to manage five households—after he'd seen the state of her bedchamber. Madness.

Delia clasped Charlotte's hand. "Do let's go into the side room. They have spools and spools of ribbons."

"You go ahead," Charlotte said. "I'll be right there."

She wandered to the window and peered out into the street, looking down the row of shops. She didn't need lace, or ribbons, or gloves today.

She needed to find answers. Clues. Anything that could lead her to the mystery lovers.

Her gaze snagged on a small, dark shopfront with an engraved placard. The sign proclaimed, in print she had to squint to make out: "Finest French Perfumes."

Perfumes!

Yes.

Her pulse raced with excitement. She waited for a moment when no one was paying attention, and then she slipped out of the draper's shop and scurried down the street.

The perfume shop was empty, save for a shopkeeper with wispy hair and a brown cutaway coat that belonged in the previous century.

He looked at her over his spectacles. "Might I help you, miss?"

"Yes, if you please. I'm shopping for a new scent."

"Excellent." The shopkeeper rubbed his hands, then produced a tray from beneath the counter. The tray was lined with tiny vials, each fashioned from glass in a different color or shape.

"The ones in front are florals, mostly." The shopkeeper drew a touch down the vials in the first row. "Then the musks. As you move back, you will find the scents to be more earthy. Woodsy."

Charlotte hadn't the faintest clue what perfume she was looking for. Whether the scent could be described as floral or woodsy or musky or something different altogether. She could only hope she would know it when she smelled it.

"I want something unique," she said. "Luxurious. Not the usual orange-flower water or lavender sprigs."

"You've come to just the shop," the wizened man said proudly. "My cousin brings the latest wares from Paris. I've scents here you can't even find in London."

That sounded promising. "What can you recommend?"

"If you're after something truly special, I'd suggest you start here." The shopkeeper unstoppered a vial from the center of the tray and handed it to her.

Charlotte held it by the glass neck and gently waved it under her nose. Rich scent teased her senses, mysterious and exotic.

"Dab it on your wrist, m'dear. You can't tell the true scent of it from the vial." He took the vial and nodded at her gloved hand. "May I?"

She unbuttoned the cuff of her glove and extended her arm. The shopkeeper drew the glass stopper over her pulse, leaving the thinnest film of perfume cooling on her skin.

"Now," he said. "Try that."

Charlotte sniffed at her wrist. Once, and then again. He was right, the perfume opened in the heat of her skin, revealing layers and shades. It was the difference between sniffing a flower bud and a full-blown hothouse bloom.

"What's in it?" she asked.

"That's a rare blend, miss. Lilies and ambergris, with hints of cedar."

"Ambergris? What's ambergris?"

He looked shocked by her ignorance. "Only one of the most rare and valuable substances in the world of perfume. It's secreted in the bellies of whales."

"Whales?" Charlotte looked at her wrist and wrinkled her nose. "They cut open the bellies of whales to make this?"

"No, no. The whales vomit it out in a lump, you see. Then it bobs about the ocean for several years, curing." He made a wavy gesture with his hand, pantomiming the voyage. "Eventually it washes ashore as a chalky, grayish stone. Ambergris. A treasure worth its weight in gold."

"Fascinating," she said.

Nauseating, she thought.

She was wearing dried-up, sea-logged whale vomit on her wrist. And if she wanted to dab it on her wrists at home, she would pay—she discreetly checked the tag—one pound, eight shillings for the privilege.

Amazing.

"Perhaps you could show me something else? Something a touch less . . . marine."

"I have just the thing. This one's ideal for a younger lady of good taste." He plucked an elegant vial of blue glass from the tray and prompted Charlotte to extend her other wrist for dabbing. "There. See what you make of that one."

She lifted her wrist to her nose, more cautiously this time. As she inhaled, bright, sunny scents set her imagination at ease. "Oh, I do like this one."

"I thought you might. All the young ladies do. It's fresh and grassy, isn't it? Lemon verbena and gardenia blossoms. But the secret is in the fixative. A touch of castoreum is what makes the summery scents take hold, rather than fade."

"Castoreum. *That's* not from whales, is it?"

"Not at all." He chuckled.

Charlotte laughed, too. "Oh, good. What a relief."

"It's from beavers."

She stopped laughing. "Surely you didn't say—"

"Canadian beavers." His eyes grew wide with excitement again. "They produce the stuff in a special gland tucked just under their tails." He held up his hands, as if preparing for another vivid demonstration. "When the trappers gut the—"

The bell above the door rang, signaling the arrival of a new customer.

Charlotte had never been so thankful for an interruption.

With a smiled apology and Charlotte's enthusiastic blessing, the shopkeeper turned to help a pair of aging ladies replenish their supply of toilet water.

While he did so, she took the opportunity to sniff her way through the entire tray of samples. Heaven only knew what bestial secretions and netherglands might be represented therein, but she didn't have the stomach to ask.

Within a few minutes, she'd worked her way through the entire tray. No luck. None of them was the distinctive perfume she'd smelled in the library at Parkhurst Manor.

"Here you are. I've been searching for you."

The words, spoken in a smooth, deep—and familiar—voice, startled her. She wheeled about, nearly upsetting the entire tray of samples.

"Lord Granville. I didn't hear you come in."

"I didn't see you walk away."

"Everyone seemed occupied. I decided to duck in here for a bit of shopping."

"Looks more like a bit of snooping to me."

Charlotte decided to change the subject. "You wouldn't believe what goes in these things." She offered her perfumed wrists. "Here, tell me which scent you prefer. Lilies and whale vomit, or lemon balm and beaver's arse."

The corner of his mouth quirked. He took her right hand in his, lifted her wrist, bent his head, and inhaled deep.

Then he repeated the same with her left wrist.

All the while, his penetrating gaze never left hers. The exchange was intimate, sensual. Despite the nearby conversation of the elderly ladies and shopkeeper, it felt almost indecent.

"Well?" she prompted, her mouth suddenly dry.

He lowered her hands but did not release them. His gloved thumbs worked under the undone cuffs at her wrists, sliding back and forth across the exposed skin—leather sliding over her tender flesh. Her pulse quickened beneath his touch, pounded in her ears.

She went hot all over.

He stepped closer, closing the distance between them, and inclined his head until he hovered just inches from her neck. Then he inhaled.

Charlotte's breath sucked in, as well.

"I think," he murmured, "I prefer this one."

She swallowed hard. "I'm not wearing any scent there."

"Are you certain?" He lifted one hand to her hair, pushing the carefully arranged ringlets behind her ear and tilting her head to expose the slope of her neck. Then he breathed deeply again.

This time, a small sound rose in his throat.

A masculine sound.

A sensual sound.

A *satisfied* sound.

She nearly whimpered in response.

"Sun-dried linen," he murmured, "ironed smooth. A lavender and rose-petal pomander in the cabinet. Sips of chocolate at breakfast. Beneath it all, warm skin—washed with jasmine soap." He straightened. "Yes. That's the scent I favor."

The muscles of her inner thighs quivered.

How did he do this to her? His skin had barely brushed hers. Not six paces away, a pair of elderly women stood discussing the inflated prices of toilet water. And despite it all, Charlotte was . . .

Aflame. She worried her clothing would incinerate. Vanish into smoke, leaving her bare and trembling. Exposed to the world. No flirtation had ever affected her with one hundredth of this power.

She was being made love to, in plain view. That was how it felt. Illicit, exciting, dangerous.

Anything but proper.

"Did you decide, miss?"

Her eyes snapped open. She didn't even recall closing them.

How long had she been standing there, entranced? Piers had moved away. His back was to her as he inspected a row of colognes.

Devious man. She knew he didn't approve of

her investigation. He must have been deliberately trying to rattle her.

For a minute, he'd succeeded.

She cleared her throat and willed her vision to focus on the sample vials. "I'm afraid none of these are quite what I'm searching for. I was hoping to find a signature scent, if you will. One that few other women could have purchased. Are you sure you've nothing else?"

"I do have something new from Paris. I only received two bottles in, and I've already sold the other." He wandered briefly into a storeroom, returning with a bottle fashioned from dark, smoky glass with a gilded stopper.

Before she sniffed, Charlotte eyed it warily. "What's in this one?"

"In a word?" He lifted an eyebrow with dramatic flair. "Passion."

"But to put a finer point on it . . . ?" she prompted.

"Poppies, vanilla, and black amber."

"Black amber." Charlotte bit her lip. "Which is . . . ?"

"It's a resin, miss. A product of the rock rose bush."

"Oh," she said, relieved. "That doesn't sound so bad." At least no animal hindquarters were involved.

"It's the most remarkable process." The shopkeeper pantomimed once again. "Nomadic herdsmen in the Holy Land gather it by combing the beards and flanks of grazing goats."

"Really."

She paused, debating just how much she wanted to sniff Eau de Goat Flank, but there was no turning back now. This might be it—the clue that could lead her to the mystery lovers.

She lifted the bottle to her nose and inhaled.

Recognition hit her like a lightning bolt. She was transported there again, behind those velvet window drapes. The library, the whispers and rustling fabric. She could all but hear the squeaks and growling.

She could feel Piers's arms about her. Protective and strong.

"This is the one," she said, shaking off the memory. "Do you remember who purchased the other bottle? If it's going to be my signature scent, I'd like to know the other lady's name. We might move in the same social circles."

"Well, I suppose I could look in my . . ." The merchant's voice trailed off.

Piers had joined her at the counter. He made the slightest nod. One that the shopkeeper seemed to instantly know meant, *Wrap it up, and quickly. Cost is no concern.*

Piers didn't even need words to command immediate compliance.

The shopkeeper's tone became brisk as he reached for the money Piers laid on the counter. "I don't recall the lady's name, miss."

"Wait." Charlotte clapped a hand over the coins. "Can't you check your ledger?"

"She paid with ready money, not credit. Her name wouldn't be in the ledger."

She sighed, releasing the money. It was useless to insist. Thanks to Piers's quick payment, the shopkeeper was a blind alley. Even if he did recall the lady's name, he would never divulge it now—not when doing so could mean losing a guaranteed sale.

As the men concluded their transaction, she felt hope draining into her boots. She couldn't leave this shop without new information. That would mean she'd sniffed beaver glands and whale bile for nothing. Inconceivable.

"Do you recall *anything* about her?" she asked. "Was she older, younger? Tall or small-statured? Did she have a companion along?"

"Now, now. No need to interrogate the man, Miss Highwood." Piers collected the package, then put the other hand on Charlotte's back, steering her toward the door.

"I'm not interrogating him. I'm merely asking him questions."

"That's the definition of interrogating."

"You," she whispered, "are the definition of an interfering—"

"Dark hair," the shopkeeper called out, as a fishwife tossed a stray cat a bone. "She had dark hair, I think. Beyond that, I couldn't be certain of details."

Dark hair.

That was something. It wasn't much, but it was something.

"Thank you." She gave the merchant a smile. "Thank you so very much for your time."

"Are you going to thank me for the perfume?" Piers asked as they left the shop.

"I will thank you to stop thwarting my efforts to find the mystery lovers."

"Mystery tuppers," he corrected.

"You know, I'm certain he knew the other customer's name. He just didn't want to risk losing the sale once you and all your money showed up. And *then* you started chiding me for asking questions."

"I was concerned about the time."

"You were obstructing me. Don't think I missed your purpose with all that neck sniffing and wrist stroking. Trying to break my concentration."

"It seems only fair," he replied evenly. "You broke mine first."

She stopped in the lane and turned to him. "Could you—just for a moment—cease being so maddeningly perfect? For a minute or two, try to look beyond that allegiance to honor and propriety. Perhaps then you'll appreciate that I am trying to save you."

"You can't save me."

"Yes, I can. Save us both—from decades of exactly this frustration and bickering. Even you, with your stinting beliefs about love, cannot view this as any sort of ideal—"

She stopped in the lane. "Where is your carriage?" She turned in place, pausing to peer through the draper's window. "Where are Delia and Frances and my mother?"

"Gone." His gaze met hers, cool and grave. "That's the reason I came searching for you. There's been an incident."

Chapter Eight

An incident? What can you mean, an incident?"

As Piers watched, the pink flush of anger drained from her face. He offered his arm, and for once she didn't fight him.

"I'll explain everything," he said.

He steered her across the lane and into the square. There, in calm terms, he related the events of the past half hour. Mrs. Highwood, at some point after realizing her daughter had separated from the group, had suffered a sudden attack of light-headedness in the draper's shop—one which no amount of fanning or solicitous comfort could assuage.

"Your mother," he said, "suggested that the Parkhurst sisters had better return her to the manor at once, and then send the carriage to return for us."

Charlotte shook her head. "Of course. Of course she suggested that."

"You don't seem overly concerned for her health."

"That's because there's no reason to be concerned. If there were any true cause for worry, you would have interrupted me at the shop and let me know at once."

She *was* rather quick with these things.

Piers had been impressed with her questioning technique in the perfume shop. She lacked subtlety, but she had keen instincts.

When she'd first revealed her little plan, he wasn't in favor of it—but he'd told himself it couldn't hurt.

Then she'd burst through his window last night, and now he was reconsidering. Perhaps it could hurt, after all.

In fact, if he wasn't careful, someone could be gravely hurt indeed.

She balled her hand into a fist. "Now we'll be unchaperoned together for at least another hour. Frances will be salivating over the gossip." She moved away from him and sat on a park bench. "We cannot have any appearance of a courting couple."

He sat beside her on the bench. "Well, I cannot leave you alone. Not unaccompanied in a strange town."

"Just don't sit too near to me." She slid to the farthest end of the bench. "Or look at me. And most especially do not sniff me."

"Might I—"

"No." She drummed her fingers on the arm of the bench. "An attack of nerves, my eye. Really, my mother is shameless. Worse than shameless."

"It seems to me that she is anxious to secure your future."

Charlotte shook her head. "She belongs in an institution. She's addled."

"No, she isn't."

"I'm telling you, she's mad. Barking mad."

"No," he repeated, more forcefully. "She isn't."

"I should know. She's *my* mother."

"Yes, but she's nothing like *my* mother, who did go insane. So, in point of fact, this is a matter where I am well equipped to judge."

"Oh, Piers." She slid back toward the center of the bench. "That's horrible."

"It's in the past. It was ages ago now."

"It's still horrible."

"Others have it worse."

She gave him a look. "It's *still* horrible. No matter who you are, or how long it's been. Don't pretend you're impervious. You wouldn't have mentioned it if it didn't cause you pain. What happened?"

He kept to the simplest facts. "She was ill from as early as I can remember. Violent swings of passion, followed by weeks of melancholy. After years of suffering, she died in her sleep."

Charlotte tucked her arm through the crook

of his elbow and made a quiet, crooning noise.

"As deaths go, it was a peaceful one," he said.

A peaceful death, perhaps—but only after years of torment. Her words haunted him to this day.

I can't. I can't bear it.

"It must have been a terrible shock."

His jaw tightened. "Not for everyone. My brother was too young to understand, and . . . families like ours don't talk about such things. I'm not certain why I'm speaking of it now."

He'd never spoken of this at all. Not to anyone.

"I know why. You meant to chasten me, and it's worked. Here I've been complaining on and on about Mama, utterly heedless of your feelings. As if it's the worst burden in the world to have a mother who cares about me. You must think me so heartless." She squeezed his arm. "I'm sorry."

"You could not have known."

"But now I do, and I'm sorry. Truly."

And she *was*. He heard it in her voice. She was sorry for his loss, and sorry for her own unintended offense. Not in a way that made excuses, and not with any maudlin, melodramatic excesses, either.

He wondered if she knew how rare that was—the talent for earnest, unqualified apology. It was a diplomatic technique he'd never quite mastered himself.

She was so open about everything—and he'd known enough deception to last several lifetimes.

Add in those pink-petal lips and her sunny hair . . .

He'd never known temptation this acute.

As they sat in silence, her fingers lightly stroked his sleeve, fraying what little remained of his self-control. Each idle caress came closer to the core of him. The contact felt more and more raw.

There was nothing to distract him from the soft rise and fall of her breath. The pulse that pounded subtly against his arm. Her warmth. Her scent.

He tapped the toe of his boot on the gravel path. How long would it take the coach to return from the manor? An hour at the least, if not two.

Piers could withstand torture of several forms, but an hour of this would break him.

At any moment, he could lose himself. Right here on this bench, he would take her in his arms, draw her close. Weave his hands in that spun sunshine of her hair, tangling them in a feverish grip—the better to hold on.

Hold on tight, and not let go.

Good God. What was happening to him? He was falling apart.

Pull yourself together, man.

He cleared his throat. "We're meant to be shopping. What shall I buy you? A bonnet or bauble of some sort?"

"Luncheon, if you would. I'm famished."

* * *

Charlotte gladly followed him to a coaching inn, where they shared a steak-and-kidney pie. Ale for Piers, lemonade for her. For a time, they made an unspoken agreement to substitute eating for conversation.

Once the edge of hunger was dulled, Charlotte reached into her pocket and pulled out her list of suspects. After that painful conversation about his mother, he would no doubt be grateful for a change of subject. And she was more convinced than ever that despite his protestations, Piers needed love in his life.

She'd begun with five names, then whittled them down by process of elimination. Now it was only a matter of matching one of the remaining possibilities to the profile.

- Present the night of the ball.
- The initial C.
- An ample figure.

Now she added to her list:

- Dark hair.

She stared at the paper. "Oh, drat."

"Still more than one left?"

"Worse. None of them fit. Lady Canby is thin as

a rail. Cathy had no opportunity, and I've already ruled out Caroline Fairchild. Cross—that's the lady's maid—and Mrs. Charlesbridge are the only two left. Neither of them have dark hair." She massaged the bridge of her nose. "Perhaps the perfume merchant told us wrong."

"More likely you left someone—or several someones—off your original list."

"Perhaps."

Charlotte was dejected. But not defeated.

"I'll have to think on it more. The answer will come to me." She dug her fork into a lemon tart. "For now, why don't you tell me about your dog."

"I don't have a dog."

"Well, I know you don't have one here. But you must have one somewhere. Every gentleman does."

"A bulldog, called Ellingworth. I acquired him as a pup at university. During my years abroad, he lived with my father or brother. By the time I returned from Vienna, he was positively ancient—but he knew me still. We had a good run of it, but he died last year."

There was a guarded quality in his gaze, but something told her not to prod it.

He cleared his throat. "Your turn."

"Me? I've never had a dog."

"Tell me about your family, then."

"There's not much to tell. You've met my mother." She jabbed at the crust of the tart. "I've no memory of my father at all. He died when I was little more than an infant. The estate passed to a cousin. My mother married young, and was widowed young. With three daughters to support and see settled, I suppose the worrying took its toll."

"Why don't your brothers-in-law intercede for you? At least offer to take her in for a while."

"Colin and Aaron?" She shrugged. "I adore them, but they're both new fathers living in connubial bliss. I don't want to inflict my mother on their marriages."

"Do they know how you've been treated this season?"

"You mean the 'Desperate Debutante' nonsense?" She shook her head. "I don't think so."

"And you didn't tell them."

"I don't want them to feel responsible."

"But they *are* responsible for you. They're your brothers by marriage."

"That's not the kind of responsibility I meant." She bit her lip, hesitating. "I don't want them to feel *responsible*. For my humiliation."

"Ah. Because their own marriages happened under unconventional circumstances."

"Minerva is an odd duck. Bookish, awkward. She

was the last woman anyone expected to elope with a charming rake. There's always been gossip about their match. And Aaron's the best sort of man, but he is a blacksmith. He knew it would affect my prospects when he married Diana. That's why he asked my permission first."

"He asked your permission? When you were what, fifteen?"

"Sixteen, I think."

"And you gave it."

"Of course I did, and gladly. I'm so happy for him and Diana. I'm happy for Colin and Minerva, too."

"But *their* happiness has made it more difficult for you to seek your own."

She leaned one elbow on the table, then propped her chin on her hand. "To the contrary, seeing them marry for love is the best thing that could have happened. It taught me to believe I can find love, too. And if the circumstances of their marriages present a hurdle to prospective suitors . . . that's doing me a favor, as well. I needn't waste my time with gentlemen who are easily discouraged."

He regarded her intently.

There was something new in his eyes, behind the dispassionate appraisal. A hint of ruthlessness.

"What is it?" she said.

"I'm trying to decide whether you truly believe that little speech you just gave. Or if it's merely a thought that comforts you when you're watching yet another quadrille from behind the potted palms."

She was taken aback. Yes, in a few weak moments, she had stood forlorn in a crowd, indulging in the worst sort of self-pity. Much to her shame.

"When you're a marchioness"—he lifted his ale to take a casual sip—"you'll have your revenge. You'll show them all."

This must be his secret. How he bent kings and despots to his will. By seeing inside them and using their own broken dreams as leverage. The most dangerous weapon is the one that strikes closest to the heart.

"You're wrong," she said.

He lowered his glass. "Hm?"

"There's a flaw in your plan, my lord. Becoming a marchioness would only convince the *ton* that I am everything they believe me to be. A shameless schemer, willing to debase myself to catch a wealthy, well-placed husband. Unless . . ."

"Unless?"

"Unless the marquess in question fell madly, irretrievably, publicly in love with me."

He seemed to choke on his ale.

Charlotte lifted an eyebrow. She could be ruthless, too.

She didn't need to be rescued by her family, or Piers. Once she'd learned the identity of the mystery lovers, she would convince her mother and Sir

Vernon that Piers had no responsibility toward her. By next season, she would be exploring the Continent with Delia, and London would find a new laughingstock. When she returned, having broadened her experience and her mind, she would be free to marry—or wait—as she chose.

Thump.

The most enormous hand she'd ever seen clapped on Piers's shoulder, startling her in her skin.

The enormous hand was connected to an enormous man. One with broad shoulders and dark, wavy hair. "Piers. I thought it was you."

Piers pushed back from the table and rose to his feet. "Rafe."

The two men shook hands warmly before turning to offer Charlotte introductions.

As if she would need introductions. All England knew this man by name and reputation.

"Miss Charlotte Highwood, allow me to present Lord Rafe Brandon. My brother."

"You left out 'Heavyweight Champion of Britain' and 'Proprietor of England's Finest Brewery,' " Charlotte teased. To Lord Rafe, she said, "What an unexpected pleasure, my lord."

She extended her hand, and the broad-shouldered giant bowed over it before pulling up a chair to join them.

His manner was as easy and informal as Piers's was proper and restrained. Charlotte liked him at once.

"I hope that's Champion Ale." Rafe nodded at his brother's glass.

"Always." Piers sounded offended to have his loyalty questioned. "Are you in the area collecting new accounts?"

"I'm scouting locations for a regional brewery. Clio's keen to expand operations northward." He motioned to a serving girl for a fresh round of drinks.

"She's well, I hope."

"Oh, yes. Though she works herself harder than I'd like."

Charlotte was surprised at how easily the two men discussed her, considering that Lord Rafe had married Piers's former betrothed. Piers didn't appear to bear them any ill will.

"What a coincidence to find you here." Lord Rafe leaned back in his chair. "Funny isn't it, how often business puts us in the same place."

"Oh, Lord Granville isn't here on business," Charlotte said.

Lord Rafe looked from her to Piers, amused. "So it's pleasure, then."

Her face warmed. "I didn't mean to imply that, either. We're both guests of Sir Vernon Parkhurst for the fortnight. Lord Granville was kind enough to bring the ladies into town for some shopping, but there was an incident and we had to separate into two groups for the return trip."

"An incident, you say." Rafe accepted his drink and downed half of it in one swallow. "I know how often 'incidents' happen around my brother."

"Whatever frequency that may be," Charlotte said, "they occur doubly often around my mother. Lord Granville can attest to the fact."

Piers shrugged. "Mrs. Highwood believes her daughter deserves the admiration of highly placed gentlemen. As well she should."

She put her fork down and smiled. "Now, really. Why are you taking her side?"

"I beg your pardon. I believed I was taking yours."

Charlotte blushed a little, and had to look away.

Lord Rafe cleared his throat. "Well."

"Come back with us for dinner," Piers said. "Sir Vernon would be glad to meet you, and he has a son who could do with some distraction."

Charlotte doubted the invitation was for Sir Vernon or Edmund's benefit. Piers might be restrained, but even he couldn't conceal true brotherly affection. She was comforted to know that he had this much love in his life, at least. After losing his parents, his betrothed, and even his dog—he needed it.

"Afraid I can't," Rafe said. "I've promised to start back this afternoon."

The brothers chatted for a few minutes longer, exchanging news about their homes and business dealings. Piers excused himself to settle the bill.

When they were alone, Rafe turned to Charlotte and lowered his voice in confidence. "Forgive me for leaving so quickly, but it's not only my brewery that's expanding. My wife's doing a bit of enlarging, too. To put it delicately."

"How wonderful. Please relay my congratulations."

"You'll have a chance to offer them in person soon, I hope."

"Oh, I doubt I'll have that pleasure."

He chuckled into his porter. "I don't."

Oh, dear. This was an unforeseen complication. Charlotte had been hoping to put a swift end to the lover mystery and nip any gossip in the bud. The last thing she needed was Piers's own brother spreading tales of an impending engagement.

"Did Piers . . ." *Drat.* "Did Lord Granville say something to you? Surely he didn't give you any indication that—"

"Other than the fact that he just *happens* to be having luncheon alone with you, in a coaching inn in Nottingham, on very same day I *happen* to be traveling through? He must have wished for the two of us to become acquainted."

Feeling frantic, she whispered, "Lord Rafe, please. Don't misunderstand. There was—"

"An incident."

"Yes. This is all mere coincidence."

"If you know my brother, and it seems you do, you understand this much." He raised an eyebrow. "With Piers, there's no such thing as coincidence."

"I don't know what you mean."

"I saw the way he looked at you. For God's sake, he *teased* you. Piers doesn't tease."

Strange that he would say that, since Piers had been teasing her since their first meeting. And what did he mean, no such thing as coincidence?

"He likes you," Lord Rafe said.

"No, he doesn't."

"So it's love, then?"

"*No.*"

Charlotte didn't have time to argue further. Piers returned from settling the bill.

He didn't take his seat but instead offered Charlotte assistance in standing. "Miss Highwood, I suspect the carriage will have returned for us by now."

"And my stagecoach will be leaving, too." Lord Rafe gave his brother a clap on the shoulder and slid Charlotte a look. "Bring her around to the castle when your schedule allows. We'll ready a room."

Chapter Nine

As he bid his brother farewell and they left the inn, Piers hoped Charlotte had lost interest in pelting him with questions.

"Let's have it," she said. "What's your big secret?"

He scowled at the pavement to disguise the hitch in his step. "Secret? What makes you believe there's any secret?"

"Meeting Lord Rafe just now."

He silently cursed. Rafe was one of only a few people who knew Piers's true role with the Foreign Office—and even so, they avoided discussing detail. If his brother had given something away . . .

"Did Rafe say something to you?"

"Nothing specific, if that's your concern. It was all in the way he treated me. As if I'd be the latest member in an exclusive club of people who comprehend the real Piers Brandon. So what's the secret handshake? What is it you're not telling me?"

Good Lord. What had he done, becoming involved with this woman? Everything was a puzzle to her. A knot that needed untangling. Meanwhile, whenever he was near her, his own powers of discernment and dissembling went promptly to hell. He blurted out old family secrets. He let her stroke his hair. He dragged her behind window seat curtains and held her close.

If she were an enemy agent, this problem would have been so much easier to solve. He wouldn't have needed to marry her. He could have had her captured, or killed, or exiled to Corsica. Come to think of it, perhaps that last was still an option.

If only Nottinghamshire weren't landlocked.

"It must have something to do with that time you spent overseas," she mused.

"I worked as a diplomat for the Foreign Office. You know that already."

"And I've been wondering about it ever since. I knew there was something more to you. What kind of diplomat picks locks and kisses like a rake?"

"This diplomat, apparently."

She gave a theatrical sigh. "If you won't tell me, I'll be forced to guess."

He gave her a firm silence. Which she interpreted as an invitation. Because of course she did.

"Let's see. You ran an illicit gaming hell in the glittering Vienna underground. Half the Habsbergs owe you their fortunes."

"I've no interest in collecting fortunes. I have my own."

"Burglary, then."

He recoiled at the suggestion. "I've even less interest in petty theft."

"It wouldn't have to be petty theft. It could be significant theft, performed for a good reason. Let's see . . . You liberated priceless works of art from the homes of French aristocrats, saving them from certain destruction at the hands of revolutionaries."

"Wrong again."

"If not art, then . . . secrets? Ah, I have it. You were an international spy, completing dashing missions and foiling assassination plots under the guise of a diplomacy career."

"Don't be absurd."

She stopped dead in the lane. "Oh my goodness. Oh my word. That's it."

"That's—"

"That *is* it. That's the truth. You were a spy." Her eyebrows soared, and she clapped both hands over her mouth, squealing into them.

Damn it.

He took her by the elbow, steering her out of the lane and pulling her into a dark, narrow alleyway.

"I tell you, I am not—"

"Don't bother lying to me. I've learned how to tell when you do." She raised her hand to his face. "Your left eyebrow. It wrinkles every time."

"I," he said, ignoring her touch by sheer force of will, "am not a former international spy. There, did it wrinkle?"

"No," she said, disappointed.

Piers relaxed. "Well, then."

"So you're not a former spy." After a brief pause, she gasped. "You're an active spy."

Jesus Christ.

She gave him a light punch on the shoulder. "Oh, well done, you. And you have the world believing you're just a boring, stuffy, proper lord? No wonder your brother looked like a cat who'd swallowed the goldfish. This is tremendous, Piers."

Tremendous?

This was decidedly not tremendous. This was a grave problem. And, quite possibly, the end of his career.

He'd been good at this once. Hadn't he?

She had some naïve, fanciful idea of espionage that involved downing stiff drinks and swanning through gaming hells. If she knew the cold, brutal reality, she would regret having ever guessed.

He took her by the shoulders and gave her a little shake. "You must let go of this silly notion. The truth of it is, I *am* a boring, stuffy, proper lord. There are no dashing missions, nor thrilling escapades. And I am most emphatically not a sp—*Down*."

He pushed Charlotte to the side.

A footpad lunged from the shadows, reaching for her reticule strings with one hand and brandishing a grimy knife with the other.

Years of training took control.

With his left hand, Piers grabbed the cutpurse's wrist, immobilizing his knife hand. Then he lowered his right elbow in a vicious strike—not quite hard enough to break the rogue's arm, though he would have deserved it.

Once the knife went clattering into the shadows, he dealt the scum a swift kick to the stomach and flung him into the gutter.

It was over in less than five seconds.

As the criminal lay doubled up and groaning, Piers straightened his gloves.

Charlotte's eyes widened. She looked at the cutpurse, then back at Piers. "You were saying?"

Charlotte ought to have guessed how well Piers would take it when she unraveled his secret.

Which was to say, not well at all.

He abandoned any further discussion, hustling her with purpose to the corner where his coach stood waiting, and all but shoved her into it.

"It's all right," she assured him, once the carriage was in motion and they were alone. "I promise, I won't tell anyone."

He looked straight ahead. "There's nothing to tell."

"I really can't believe I didn't guess earlier. I should have known from your special Finch pistol. Or the stickpin that opens locks."

"Any pin would have opened that lock."

"Do you have other spy tools?" She began to look around the carriage compartment. "False mirrors? Bullet-deflecting doors? Oh, I'll wager there's a hidden compartment under this seat."

"*Every* carriage has a compartment under the seat."

"Secret codes tucked in your hatband, perhaps? Ooh, what about this walking stick?" She reached for a cane he kept on the back of the seat. "A man in his prime of life doesn't need a walking stick. I bet it's really a sword or a rifle, if one knows the trick of opening it." She turned it this way and that, swishing it experimentally through the air.

He wrested it from her and set it aside. "It's a walking stick. Nothing more."

"But you're an agent of the Crown. You must have *some* kind of exciting, lethal weapon on your person."

"Since you mention it . . ." He caught her by the waist, dragging her onto his lap. He said in a seductive growl, "That's not a pistol in my pocket."

She laughed. Where had he been hiding this wicked, dangerous charm?

The irony was rich. She should not have been so keen to uncover his secrets. This revelation made him desperately attractive. She might start to like him even more. Not only in flashes and rare moments, but at regular intervals.

From there, it was only a short jaunt to friendship. Then a mere hop to affection . . . or worse.

Oh, drat. Why had she been so curious?

But there was no undoing it now.

She hadn't nearly puzzled him out yet—but she'd gathered enough pieces to understand this: The entire picture of Piers Brandon was wider and more complex than she'd ever dreamed it could be. He wasn't maddeningly perfect.

He was perfectly thrilling.

"Are you on a mission here in Nottinghamshire? Is that why you hid in the library?" She slapped a palm to her brow. "Of course. It all makes so much sense now. You couldn't leave your assignment. That's why you insisted on proposing. No one's *that* honorable, and I knew it couldn't simply be that you'd taken a fancy to me."

"Listen to me." He caught her chin in his hand, forbidding her to look away. "You are dead wrong about me in almost every particular, but you are right about that last. I hadn't simply taken a fancy to you."

"No?"

He shook his head slowly. His thumb traced the shape of her lips. "Fancy doesn't begin to describe it. This is closer to . . . an obsession. An enchantment, or perhaps a curse. You're like a little fair-haired witch who cast a spell on me, and I can't concentrate. I can't sleep. I can't think of anything but hearing you laugh and holding you close and imagining what you'll look like naked in my bed. Do you understand that, Charlotte?"

She nodded, breathless. His left eyebrow hadn't moved once.

The longer he stared at her, the more excited she grew. This was a game they'd been playing all day . . . his hand on her waist at the coaching inn, his breath on her ear at the perfume shop.

"What's your plan, Agent Brandon?" she whispered. "Do you mean to kiss me so long and so hard that I'll forget your identity?"

"No." His hand slid to the back of her head, tangling in her hair—so tightly she gasped. "I mean to kiss you so long and so hard that you'll forget yours."

His lips fell on hers, and this time he offered her no light, patient kisses as a preliminary. He claimed her mouth, thrusting his tongue deep to toy with hers.

She clung to his neck, trying her best to keep pace.

He bent to kiss her neck, her ear, her cheek. She loved the urgency in his kiss, how much he seemed to want her.

Perhaps even *need* her.

Arousal pounded through her body, made her swell and tighten and yearn. It was as if the more boldly he tried to possess her, the more independent she felt.

He gave her power, and she wanted to use it. She wanted to choose passion over propriety, knowledge over innocence.

He stroked her breasts through the fabric of her frock and spencer, driving her mad with need. It wasn't enough. She needed more. His hands on her bare skin. His fingers pinching, pulling. Anything to ease the ripe, coiling tension in her nipples. The need was so intense, so urgent, it made her wonder how she'd lived this long without his touch.

Her shame was gone, and yet she didn't know how to ask for such things.

"Please," she whispered, arching her spine to thrust her breast into the cupped palm of his hand and hoping it would be enough. "Please."

Please touch me. You know what I need.

As they kissed, his fingers went to the buttons of her spencer, sliding them free one by one. At the same time, his other hand slid up her spine to find the hooks closing the back of her frock. She was being undone from both sides at once. This man had a great many skills indeed.

Her body sang with joy and anticipation of what was to come. Once he had the edges of her jacket parted, he slid his hand inside. His fingertips found the low, bosom-skimming border of her frock's neckline. Pushing aside the gauzy fichu she wore for modesty, he pushed two fingers under the neck-line and skimmed up to her shoulder, cleaving the loosened bodice from her body and then easing the sleeve down her shoulder, revealing her breast.

He broke the kiss, staring down at her bared breast. A twinge of modesty shivered through her, but it was lost in the rapid pounding of her pulse.

Upon contact with the crisp late-afternoon air, her nipple tightened. She felt as if a whole body's worth of yearning had gathered in that single, aching point.

Please.

Please, please, please.

The first pass of his thumb was so light, so teas-ing. Almost like the brush of a feather. She could have believed she'd imagined it. He drew madden-ing circles around her ruched areola, tilting his head to examine her from a slightly different angle. As if she were a bit of clockwork and he was curious to see how she worked.

And then—finally—he covered her nipple with

his thumb and pressed down. The jolt of pleasure zinged through her. She gasped. It was better; it was worse. It was wonderful.

He kissed her again, and as his tongue taught hers some new, sensual dance, he rolled and pinched the puckered nub between his thumb and forefinger.

She clung to him, digging her fingernails into the back of his neck. A low, throbbing pulse began to beat between her thighs. She shifted on his lap, pressing her thighs together in an attempt to ease it. And in the process, she rubbed against the solid, growing ridge of his erection.

He groaned softly into their kiss.

The taste and sound and feel of that guttural confession . . . it did something wild to her. It was honest, that moan. Elemental. Raw. There was an undeniable thrill to know she had such power over a powerful man.

She sat taller on his lap, teasing him with another slow drag of her hip against his hardness. She slid her hands into his hair, sifting her fingers through the dark, heavy locks and teasing them to wild angles. She caught his bottom lip between her teeth and gave it a playful, puppyish tug.

They stared at each other, breathing hard.

"I haven't forgotten your identity," she whispered, still teasing her fingers through his hair. "Nor mine."

He swallowed hard. His hands settled on her hips.

"You're Piers Brandon, the Marquess of Granville, diplomat and secret agent in the Crown's service." She ran a fingertip down the noble slope of his nose. "And I'm Char—"

Her words were lost in a gasp.

With the speed and strength of a whip, he had her turned on her back, sprawled beneath him on the tufted carriage seat.

"You will be Lady Charlotte Brandon, the Marchioness of Granville, diplomat's wife and mother of my heir."

She started to argue back. Then his mouth closed over her nipple, and Charlotte lost all power of speech, all semblance of thought.

Along with them went any urge to resist.

"You'll be mine," he murmured. "I swear it, Charlotte. I will make you mine."

Mine.

Mine, mine, mine.

The word tumbled in endless circles through his mind.

Piers licked a circle around her taut, dusky pink nipple.

She moved and sighed beneath him. All arguments and questions forgotten. He reveled in the sound.

He meant to show her just who was in control. Just whose secrets were bared.

He tugged at her clothing, desperate to reveal more of her body to his touch, and to his mouth. As he wrenched at her frock, he heard a slight rip of fabric. He froze, thinking the sound might frighten her, or at least bring her back to awareness.

Instead, she rolled onto her side to help him.

She *helped* him.

And once her frock was pushed down, revealing her sheer, simple undergarments, she welcomed him into her embrace, wrapping his shoulders in her soft, fragrant arms and arching her back to offer her breasts to him.

Her lips touched his bared neck.

When had his cravat come loose?

Good God. Good God.

He prided himself on control. Restraint. Careful management of both internal emotions and outward reactions. Lives had depended on it, and Piers had never let them down.

And then along came Miss Charlotte Highwood. Announcing her own entrance into his life with the most absurd of declarations.

I'm here to save you.

Impossible. She was the most dangerous person

he'd ever encountered. His equilibrium was in constant turmoil whenever she was near.

She'd decoded the secret language of his left eyebrow.

If he wasn't careful, he could lose himself with her.

In her.

God, the mere thought of being in her. Sinking into all that warm, willing softness . . .

The mental image had his cock hard as Italian marble, throbbing in vain against his buttoned trouser falls.

Piers forced himself to slow down, pushing aside the fragile muslin of her shift and exploring every inch of her bared, luscious breasts with his lips and tongue. Occasionally adding a light graze of teeth.

No matter how much he took, she only offered him more. He couldn't for the life of him understand why.

He slid one hand to her waist and wedged his hips between her thighs, thrusting against the soft rustle of her bunched petticoats.

Soon, he promised himself. Not today. He wasn't going to deflower Charlotte in a moving coach. That wasn't the way he'd treat any woman, and most certainly not a woman he meant to marry. He hadn't lost *all* semblance of restraint.

Besides, the journey back to Parkhurst Manor wasn't long enough.

When he bedded her for the first time, he meant to take hours pleasuring her properly. Thoroughly. Until she sobbed his name and begged for more.

"We're almost there."

She gave him a sleepy, drugged look. "How do you know?"

"The road beneath us changed from mud to gravel."

"Always so attentive to detail." She smiled, with that adorably smug pride he'd come to recognize, and he knew he'd given himself away. Yet again.

There was a moment of tenderness between them, and for a moment he experienced the most rare, ridiculous emotion—hope.

Was it possible?

She'd seen him dismantle that cutpurse in the alleyway. She knew he'd deceived not only her, but everyone. She hadn't run screaming or turned from him in disgust.

Perhaps . . . Perhaps he could make her happy.

Not with the Granville money or his social cachet, but just by being the man he was, at his core. Sometimes, when he looked deep into those blue eyes, it felt like anything was possible.

But there was still so much she didn't know, about

what he was and what he'd done. There was true darkness in him, and if she found her way past all his defenses, ventured into the cold, black center of his being . . . he doubted she would smile into the face of it.

Besides, she wanted love in return. Not mere tenderness or affection, but a public love affair to convince even the most skeptical gossip. That was the one thing Piers couldn't offer her. Not even if he wanted to.

It was useless to think of winning Charlotte's heart.

He must stick to his first plan: securing her hand and completing his assignment here, by whatever means required.

He kissed her brow one last time, then righted himself and helped her to a sitting position. "Come, then. I'll help you with your buttons."

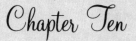

Chapter Ten

It was well past time for Piers to settle down to his work.

When Ridley came in that evening, ostensibly to prepare him for bed, Piers decided it was time to confer on the investigation thus far.

"So," Piers said, unknotting his cravat. "What have you learned from the servants?"

"Nothing of use." Ridley lounged in a chair. "They have nothing bad to say about the man. Nor Lady Parkhurst, for that matter. Sir Vernon is only in residence a few months a year, and when he's here, he's mostly out-of-doors, living the sportsman's life. He pays wages on time; gives annual rises to all, and sets aside pensions for the most devoted. According to the steward, he doesn't meddle overmuch in routine management, but he demands regular reports and questions any discrepancies."

"No rumors of gaming? Mistresses? Children in the neighborhood with a striking resemblance?"

"Not that I've heard. If he has any such secrets, he's hiding them well from the staff."

"That's unusual."

Typically servants knew everything that went on in a house like this. They brought in the post. They swept out the grates. They gathered the laundry. Nothing escaped their notice.

"I'll keep eyes and ears open belowstairs, of course. I've worked my way into the footmen's twice-weekly card game, and I think the house-keeper has taken a fancy to me. Anything else you'd like me to do?"

"Nothing."

Piers couldn't fault Ridley's attention to detail. He was the one who'd been shirking his part. He was meant to be gaining Sir Vernon's confidence. This was exactly the sort of work the Office needed a man like Piers to accomplish. There weren't many aristocrats in the service of the Crown, and even fewer who could elicit an invitation to an autumn hunting party, just by expressing a passing interest over brandy in the club.

His rank and standing were key to gaining access and trust. In nearly a decade of service, he'd never once compromised his upstanding reputation. Then, within one night of arriving here, he'd given his host reason to believe he defiled virgins on desktops, and the heir to the manor was convinced he had murder on his mind.

Worst of all, Charlotte had stumbled onto the truth.

"On second thought, Ridley, there is something you can do. Come and stand in front of me."

Ridley obliged him at once. "Here?"

"A bit closer. No, not like that. Face me. Just so."

They eyed one another.

"I am going to tell you a series of falsehoods. And as I do, I want you to keep close watch on my left eyebrow. Tell me if it moves in the slightest."

If Ridley was bewildered by this request, he did not show it. "Yes, my lord."

"The sky," Piers said carefully, "is pink. I breakfasted on kippers and toast. I'm wearing a fashionable waistcoat." He paused. "Well? Any movement?"

"No movement."

"Not a wrinkle. You're certain."

"Nothing."

With a curse, Piers turned aside, whiffing the air with a strike of an imaginary cricket bat. This couldn't be happening to him. He'd perfected the art of deceit in his childhood. How the devil was it possible that Charlotte Highwood could read him, when the rest of the world could not?

After a pause, Ridley asked, "What's wrong with the waistcoat?"

"Nothing. But there's nothing especially right with it, either."

"The tailors told me it's all the rage this season, that color. Called it curry."

Piers shrugged.

The younger man gave a sigh of lament. "Were you ever going to tell me? Here I'm meant to be a marquess's valet, and you've been letting me dress you in an unflattering waistcoat."

"Enough about the waistcoat."

Somehow he had to regain control of this situation. Put his head back on straight. Rein his eyebrow into submission. Do his bloody duty.

He couldn't risk losing his career. He wouldn't know who he was anymore.

The very next day, whatever sport Sir Vernon proposed, Piers would find an excuse to leave their outing early. He would return to the manor alone, head to the library, open that locked drawer, and retrieve the information he'd been sent to gather.

From there, everything would fall into place.

He would announce his engagement to Charlotte before departing Nottinghamshire. His solicitors and Mrs. Highwood would no doubt require a few months to settle the marriage contracts and make wedding arrangements. They would have a

Christmas wedding. Then winter at Oakhaven to work on starting an heir. By the time he was due back in London for the new session of Parliament, he would leave Charlotte pregnant and preoccupied at his estate—where she would be well out of sight of his left eyebrow and unable to disrupt his concentration.

There. He had a plan.

Now to execute it.

"Has there been any mention of the sport for tomorrow?" he asked Ridley. "Angling? Coursing? Shooting?"

"I heard something from the gamekeeper about plans for a proper foxhunt. But I doubt there'll be any sport for two or three days. Maybe four."

"Damn." He could not spend two to four *days*, confined to this house with the entire party underfoot, and Charlotte provoking him to all manner of disastrous mistakes. "Why?"

Thunder rumbled in the distance.

Ridley raised a brow. "That's why."

Piers was a bit peeved. "Where *did* you acquire that irritating talent for perfectly timed foreshadowing?"

"Perhaps you missed that day of training, my lord."

"Yes, well. At least I'm not rubbish with waistcoats."

Piers sent Ridley to the servants' quarters and

waited an hour or so before gathering a candle and quietly leaving his room. If it was going to rain, he wouldn't be able to do any searching during the day. That left him the nights—less than ideal. If he was caught poking around private rooms in the dark, explanations became much more difficult. But his stay was almost halfway over, and the damn British weather wasn't leaving him much choice.

Moving in smooth, silent steps, Piers entered the corridor and turned toward the main stairs.

He hadn't made but a few feet of progress before he froze and tightened his grip on the candle.

A still, shadowy figure hunched in the middle of the carpet, some ten paces ahead.

Piers took a few steps forward and lifted the candle to illuminate the space. He squinted and peered into the gloom. It took a few moments, but eventually he was able to make out . . .

Edmund.

The boy sat cross-legged at the head of the staircase, a quilt wrapped around his shoulders. He held a wooden sword gripped in one hand. Gesturing with the other, he laid a finger to the side of his eye, then pointed it at Piers.

"I have my eye on you," he whispered in an unnerving high-pitched rasp. "I know what you did."

Right. Piers passed a hand over his face. So much for searching the house tonight.

He reached for a book on a nearby side table, lifting it and waving it for Edmund's view, as though it were his entire reason for emerging from his bedchamber. Then he turned on his heel and went back the way he came.

After closing the door, he angled his taper to read the spine of the book he'd picked up.

The Collected Sermons of Rev. Calvin Marsters.

Well. That should put him to sleep.

He flung the book aside, irritated at having been thwarted by a child standing sentry, and sat on the bench to remove his boots. He might as well go to bed.

Then something in the darkness outside caught his eye. He moved closer to the window, extinguishing his own candle to better make it out.

A tiny, warm light flickered in the walled garden below. Darting this way and that. If he were a fanciful man, he would have thought it a fairy. But Piers had no such illusions.

Someone was moving about the garden in a strange, directionless fashion, bearing a small lamp or a single candle in hand.

The sight was odd. Suspicious. He needed to investigate.

But with Edmund standing—sitting, rather—sentry in the corridor, he couldn't go that way. It would have to be out the window. What was it

Charlotte had said? Down the ledge to the northwest corner, and from there a short leap to the plane
tree.

He threw on a black coat, then opened the
window as far as he could. His shoulders made for
a much tighter squeeze than Charlotte had likely
encountered. After a few twists and contortions, he
managed to pull himself out and attain solid foot-
ing on the ledge.

What with the approaching rain, the night was
windy. He had to take care. Facing outward and
stretching his arms to either side, he edged his way
along the lip of stone. When he felt a window with
his leading hand, he first twisted his neck to check
for any signs of someone stirring within. After he
made sure no one was watching, he slunk across.

Before long, he had a rhythm established and was
making swift progress. He reached the northwest
corner with little difficulty and located the plane
tree. As Charlotte had mentioned, a thick, leafy
branch stretched most of the way toward the ledge,
like a beckoning arm.

He sized up the distance and made a mental calculation. But just as he prepared to make the jump, a
gust of wind kicked up and pushed him off-balance.

Too late to the abort the leap. He had to lean into
it and pray for the best. The jump was ungainly and
too short by half. He only just barely managed to

grab the limb with one hand. He dangled there a moment, heart pounding, then reached up to grab the knotty surface with the other.

By using his body weight as a pendulum, he managed to sway back and forth until he could hook one boot over the branch. From there, he swung himself upright and straddled the limb.

And found himself looking straight into the housekeeper's window. He knew it was the housekeeper's window, because the housekeeper was staring right back at him.

Brilliant.

Just bloody brilliant.

Allowing Sir Vernon to believe he defiled virgins on desktops was bad enough. Now he'd be caught peeping in at gray-haired housekeepers in their nightgowns? He was going to leave Parkhurst Manor with a reputation for sheer depravity.

Piers froze every muscle in his body and held his breath. The squinting housekeeper slowly raised a pair of spectacles to her face.

Before those spectacles could reach the bridge of her hooked nose, Piers dropped. His fall was broken by one branch; then another, until he collided with the ground with a muffled groan. He flattened himself at the base of the tree—hoping the housekeeper would blame it all on a trick of her eyes and the wind.

Also because he was hurting everywhere.

After a few minutes had passed and no alarm had gone up, Piers decided he was in the clear. He rose to his feet, brushed the dirt from his coat and trousers, and tried not to think about the magnificent bruises he'd be sporting the next day.

Instead, he rounded the corner of the house and headed for the enclosed garden.

Because of the high walls, he couldn't even see the flickering light from this vantage. In fact, it was probably only visible from a few rooms of the manor other than his own.

Was the light bearer waiting on a midnight assignation? Hiding or burying something in the garden?

Piers found the iron gate slightly ajar, and as he pushed it inward, the hinges creaked.

The small, yellow light bobbing in the darkened garden stilled.

And then, a female whisper: "Who's there?"

Piers exhaled in a rush. "Charlotte?"

"Piers."

They walked toward one another, until they stood on opposite sides of the lamp she held. She wore her night rail and a dark cape, hastily tied. One look at her face told him something was gravely wrong.

"What are you doing down here at this hour?"

She sniffed, and her voice caught. "I . . ."

"You've been weeping." He put his hand on her

shoulder. She trembled under his touch. "Charlotte, what is it? What's wrong?"

"I've lost it. It's gone. I've searched everywhere in the house I could think of, and then I remembered I'd been here earlier. But I've been looking for an hour now, under every bench and bush. It's not here, either. It's gone."

She pressed her lips together and turned her head, as though to keep herself from crying. Her chin quivered.

"Come here." He took the lamp from her hand and hung it from a nearby trellis. Then he guided her to sit on a bench. "Let me help you. Tell me what it is you're searching for."

"It will sound so silly. You'll laugh at me."

"Never."

Over the past week, the girl had been accused of loose virtue, accosted by a cutpurse, and held briefly at gunpoint—and she'd taken it all in relative good humor.

He'd never seen her like this.

Whatever she'd misplaced, it must mean the world to her.

"It's small." She formed a rectangular shape with her fingers. "Just a scrap of flannel with ribbon edging and a bit of stitching on it. I use it to mark the place in my books. I know how inconsequential it must sound, but it's important to me."

Piers knew better than most that even small, humble-looking items could be of great importance. "You're certain it isn't in your bedchamber?"

He hated to sound like a scold, but considering the state of her other possessions . . .

She shook her head. "This isn't like stockings or shawls. I'm untidy, but I'm never careless about this. It's either in my book or under my pillow at all times. But this evening, when I settled down with my novel it wasn't there. I searched everywhere. My chamber, the drawing room. Then I'd recalled I'd been out here reading this afternoon."

"Where did you sit?"

"Over there." She indicated a stump tucked under a bit of ivy.

"Then it's likely still in the garden. Or perhaps you lost it somewhere along your path back into the house."

"Oh, Lord." Her hand fluttered in her lap. "If the wind took it . . ."

"Charlotte. Don't fret so." He put an arm around her and drew her to his chest, holding her close. Both to soothe her and to calm himself. His heart ached to see her so distraught. He pressed a kiss to the top of her head. "We'll find it."

"But I've searched everywhere."

"We'll find it."

"You can't promise that."

He tilted her chin so that she faced him. "I can, and I will. It's probably still in this garden. If not, it's somewhere on this estate. But if it's that important to you, I'd search Nottinghamshire, the whole of England—even the world—if that's what it took. You'll have it returned to you. Do you believe me?"

She nodded.

"Here's what we're going to do," he said. "We'll begin at the gate and move clockwise about the garden together. One of us will search while the other holds the lamp. If we haven't found it by the time we return to the gate, then we'll widen our search. Agreed?"

He held out his hand, and she took it.

"Agreed."

They searched for hours. Piers tried to keep up a reassuring patter and maintain a steady pace, so that she didn't become upset or anxious. He'd never appreciated how many plants, shrubs, and flowering vines could be in one garden. Together they checked beneath every bush and branch in one section before moving on to the next.

They'd reached eight on their makeshift "clock" of the garden, and it was likely closing in on five o'clock in the actual morning. The sky began to turn from black to gray. The bit of light made searching easier, but the wind had picked up and the occasional sprinkle of raindrops made itself felt. Piers just hoped they could locate this thing before the rain started in earnest.

He turned to scan a wall covered in thick ivy, parting each cluster of vines and leaves to peer within. He began at the base of the wall and worked his way upward.

"I don't think it could possibly be up there," she said as he stretched his arms to push through a clump of ivy overhead. "No gust of wind would have blown it that high."

"Wind isn't the only force at play in nature."

"No, you're right. There's rain as well. We should move on to the path, perhaps. Or it will end up washed away and buried in mud."

"Give me a moment."

Piers had a hunch, and he wasn't ready to abandon it quite yet. Patience rewarded thoroughness.

At last, in the corner where wall met wall at nine o'clock, he parted a thick patch of greenery to find what he'd been searching for.

A bird's nest, hidden within the branches just at shoulder height. Some clever wren had crafted a deep, hollow bowl of branches and bits.

"Did you find something?" Charlotte approached.

"Perhaps." He reached into the nest gently, reluctant to disturb any eggs or feathery occupants therein. His fingertips skimmed over a variety of textures. Wrens would line their nests with any soft material they found. Downy feathers, moss . . .

Yes.

"Aha." He grasped the corner of flannel and pulled, turning to offer it for Charlotte's examination. "Is this it?"

She stared at the meager scrap of ribbon and fabric for a moment. Then she clapped a hand to her mouth and sobbed into it, leaning forward to bury her face in his chest.

He'd take that as a yes.

He wrapped his arms around her and stroked her back and hair. The night of sleepless searching had caught up with her all at once. It wasn't surprising she'd be overwhelmed.

However, his own emotions were a puzzle to him. He'd ached for her when the thing was missing, but he could not share her relief. Quite the reverse. He felt as if her small fist had reached inside his chest, gripped his heart, and wrung it. He should have felt triumphant to have found her treasure.

Instead, *he* felt lost.

After a moment, she'd collected herself enough to draw away and wipe her eyes. "I don't know how to thank you."

"Perhaps you can tell me what it is we've found."

She smoothed the rectangle of ivory flannel.

"I've had this all my life. It began as a blanket in my cradle. When we left our home, it came with us. From as far back as I can remember, I wouldn't be parted from it. Once I'd turned . . . oh, seven or eight? . . . Mama threatened to burn the thing, it was so dirty and threadbare. I cried, she complained. We compromised. She helped me cut it down and bind the edges with ribbon. I used it to practice my first stitching. See?"

She showed him a few misshapen figures embroidered on the flannel. A slanting house, a lopsided Tudor rose.

"Is that a dog?" he asked.

"A cow, I think?" She gave him a rueful look. "I'd like to say my needlework has improved since, but it really hasn't."

"What can I say? I look forward to tablecloths and handkerchiefs embroidered with scanty blossoms and three-legged cows."

She smiled, and the sweet curve of her lips unknotted the tightness in his chest.

"I told you I don't have any memory of my father." She ran her thumb over the flannel, stroking in an idle rhythm that must have been ingrained habit. "But when I hold this I can recall his presence, at least. The comfort of knowing myself to be safe, and surrounded by love." She looked at him. "Does that make sense? Do you know what I mean?"

"I don't know that I do."

He couldn't even imagine it. For as long as he could recall, his home had been a place filled with tension and fear.

Charlotte carried a scrap of flannel. He carried lies, shame, and a haunting echo of despair.

I can't, she'd wept. *I can't bear it.*

"Then you'll have to take my word for it," she said. "I just know that feeling exists, and not only in the past. I need to believe it can be my future, too. All my life, I've been trying to get back to a home I can't even remember."

Drops of water spattered his shoulders and the slate garden path beneath their feet.

"It's raining," he said.

Her gaze didn't waver. "You could have that, Piers. With the right person. One you love. That's why I've been trying so hard to untangle this misunderstanding we've landed in. It's why I won't give up on solving it now. It's not only for me anymore. The more I come to know you, the more I believe you deserve love, too."

God. She was killing him.

"We should go inside." He rubbed his hands up and down her arms to warm her. "The house will be waking soon."

She nodded.

"Go on ahead," he told her. "I'll follow in a few

minutes. I know you don't want to be seen together. Not like this."

"Yes, but I didn't think *you* cared."

He shrugged. "I'm too fatigued to invent excuses this morning."

She kissed his cheek before leaving. "Thank you again."

After she was gone, Piers paced the garden alone, letting the rain pelt his back as he turned three simple facts over and over in his mind.

Charlotte wanted love.

He wanted her to have it.

He couldn't offer it himself.

An honorable, decent gentleman would find another way out of this. A way to let Charlotte follow her heart.

But here was the fourth fact that made all the rest ring hollow.

Piers wasn't that kind of man.

Chapter Eleven

It rained for two days straight.

On the second night, Charlotte lay awake in bed, listening to the patter of raindrops and staring at the well-creased paper on which she'd written her list of suspects.

Cathy, the scullery maid—eliminated at once for lack of opportunity. She would have been hard at work preparing the supper, and she wasn't at all likely to be wearing expensive scent. It would have drawn notice.

Lady Canby—too thin. The garter would have slipped straight off her leg, like a barrel rim placed over a lamppost.

Miss Caroline Fairchild, the vicar's daughter—highly unlikely, given her dearth of romantic imagination.

That had left only two: Mrs. Charlesbridge, the doctor's wife; and Cross, the lady's maid. Both of whom had been ruled out by the perfume merchant. Neither had dark hair.

Charlotte sighed. There were only two possible reasons for this stalemate. Either her deductions had gone wrong somewhere, or she'd overlooked a suspect.

Perhaps there was another female guest at the party . . . Someone with a C that she'd missed. Maybe one of the ladies had a maiden or Christian name that hadn't appeared on Lady Parkhurst's list of invitations.

It seemed a stretch, but at least it gave her another avenue to investigate. To follow that path of inquiry, she needed a book. The one book her mother actually urged her to read, and the one Charlotte had stubbornly refused to ever peruse.

Debrett's Peerage, Baronetage, Knightage, and Companionage.

The list of everyone who was anyone in Britain.

Once the idea had seized her, there was no chance she'd be able to sleep. She rose from bed and wrapped herself in a dressing gown before gathering a candle. Then she quietly ventured out into the corridor.

At the bottom of the stairs, she paused. The library was to the right, but she felt certain she'd seen a copy of *Debrett's* in the drawing room. It was the sort of book certain families liked to have close at hand. How else would Frances keep all those venomous rumors straight?

She turned left—then paused.

The doors to the drawing room were open, and a faint wash of yellow lamplight spilled out into the corridor. From within, she heard a light rustle of paper and the scratch of a quill.

Perhaps she ought to retreat and save this errand for the morning.

However, even Charlotte—poor investigator that she'd proved to be thus far—could deduce that there was only one soul in this house who would still be awake and working at this hour.

A peek around the doorjamb confirmed it.

Of course it was Piers.

He sat at the escritoire, his back to her. And what a fine back it was—his strong shoulders defined by a crisp linen shirt, and a buttoned waistcoat tapering his torso to a trim waist. His sleeves were rolled to the elbow, and a tower of half-opened correspondence loomed on the corner on the writing desk. As he sliced open a sealed envelope, his physicality was palpable. He might have been a stonemason, settling down to build an empire with bricks of paper and mortar made from ink.

First, she'd slipped in through his window. Then,

he'd surprised her in the garden a few nights ago. It was her turn again.

Charlotte set the candle aside. Then she walked on tiptoe, crossing the carpet as though the embroidered medallions were steppingstones across lava, holding her breath and coming to stand just behind his tufted leather chair.

She placed her fingers lightly over his eyes, like a blindfold. "Guess who?"

Except that it came out more like "Geh—ack!"

In a swift motion, he shoved his chair back from the table and grabbed her by the forearms. She found herself inverted, pulled directly over Piers's shoulder. She landed in his lap, both her arms pinned with one of his, breathless.

And with every racing heartbeat, a cool, metallic point throbbed against her pulse.

He had the letter opener held to her throat.

"Charlotte." He cast the impromptu weapon aside, releasing her. As she started to breathe again, he rubbed his face with his hand. "Jesus."

She was dizzy, still a bit breathless from her somersault. Her shift had tangled about her legs, and her hair was everywhere. She laughed a little, as was her habit in moments of awkwardness.

"It's not amusing," he said.

"I know."

"I could have hurt you. I could have . . ."

Killed you.

She realized for the first time what should have been obvious since he'd dismantled the cutpurse in that alleyway.

In all likelihood, given his chosen duty, Piers had taken lives.

It was a sobering thought. But on reflection, it didn't make him any different from most men of his generation, thanks to England's endless wars on multiple continents. She doubted he'd found any pleasure in it. So few of them had.

He ran his hands down her arms, scanning her body for injuries. Now that the clamor of her own pulse had quieted, she could feel the rapid thump of his heart. The tension coiled in his arms and shoulders.

"I'm not hurt," she said. "And I'm not frightened. I'm fine."

"You must stop creeping up on me like that."

"But it's the only way you'll let me close."

He smelled of brandy and warm linen and the musk of his skin. The collar of his shirt hung open, and she could see the muscles of his neck, the dark hair on his chest.

She slid her fingers under his shirt, gliding an exploratory touch along the ridge of his collarbone. "What are you doing up so late?"

"Just going over correspondence."

"Correspondence?" She raised an eyebrow. "And

what kind of correspondence would that be? Diplomatic affairs? Parliamentary business? Or encoded spy letters, written in invisible ink?"

He flipped open a leather folio and fanned the contents with one hand. "See for yourself."

Charlotte looked at the papers splayed across the desk blotter.

They were architectural plans and decorative schemes. Diagrams of a building, floor by floor. Interiors painted in washes of color with samples of fabric attached. All of it tasteful and surely expensive. She sifted through the sketches until she located a view of the exterior: a grand façade with Grecian-inspired columns and large, modern windows. The cost of glazing those windows alone . . .

"Is this Oakhaven?" Despite herself, she was a bit dazzled by the idea of being mistress of such a place.

"No, no. That's the dower house."

"Dower house?"

"It's a mile or so down the lane. Close enough for visiting, but well out of earshot. Surely you didn't think I'd permit your mother to live with us? God, no."

He chuckled. Could it be that after the better part of a week, this was the first time she'd heard him laugh?

He had a lovely laugh, too. Deep and warm. He really ought to use it more often. She would have to work on that.

He plucked a paper from beneath the others and drew it to the top. "That's Oakhaven."

She looked at the drawing, alarmed. "Goodness. It's enormous. Whatever do you do with it?"

"Not much of anything, lately. It's rather a lonesome place for one."

As he sorted through the drawings and diagrams with one hand, his other hand caressed her back. His fingers traced up and down her spine, treasuring her vertebrae as though they were pearls on a string.

"The furnishings are in good condition, of course, but you'll likely find them outdated in style. You'll see potential for a great many modernizations and improvements, I hope."

I hope.

Her heartbeat caught on those two little words. Did he hope, truly? Could he want a lifetime with her—even see her companionship as a way to make his vast, grand, important life a bit less cold and empty?

The idea touched her.

And so she touched him, more boldly this time, easing his shirt aside and adjusting her position on his lap until she straddled his hips.

The searing heat of his mouth met hers, and she melted into it, giving herself over to the mastery of his kiss and the warmth of his embrace.

Oh, this man. He'd built a wintry fortress around himself—whether out of desire, necessity, or both, she didn't yet know—but inside it, he was anything but cold.

He broke the kiss. His eyes were lit with blue flames. Possessive, desirous.

Even his gaze could arouse her, all on its own.

"Go to bed, Charlotte," he said.

She poised herself to remind him that commanding her to do one thing was the surest way to make her do the opposite, and really—he ought to know her better by now.

But then it struck her.

He wasn't a fool. He did know her better by now.

He must understand that commanding her to go was tantamount to daring her to stay, and he intended to provoke precisely that rebellious response.

He *wanted* her here. With him.

She wanted the same.

She lifted his hand and cupped it over her breast. His thumb brushed her nipple through the fabric of her shift, sending ripples of pleasure through her.

Bending her head, she kissed his throat. The underside of his jaw was deliciously rough with whiskers. She shifted in his lap and nestled closer still.

The swelling ridge of his arousal pressed against her thigh.

She teased it, dragging her knee a few inches up . . . then down.

The motion was like dropping a spark on dry tinder. In an instant, his hands were on her, all over her, possessive and claiming. Gripping and twisting the linen of her night rail, cupping her backside and bringing her hips flush with his.

He kissed her deeply, moaning into her mouth as he guided her hips up and down, rocking her against the hard, thick ridge of his erection. The rhythmic pressure sent bliss swirling through her.

"It's good?"

She nodded, breathless. "Yes."

"When we're wed," he said huskily, sliding his hand under her shift, "it will be even better. I'll be inside you. Here."

His fingertips slid up the quivering slope of her thigh, until they found the center of her. His touch teased up and down her sex until she thought she would go mad. She could not have brought herself to ask for what she needed, but her body knew. And so did he.

She ached to be filled.

At last, he slid one fingertip inside her. She whimpered with relief, wrapping her arms about his neck and clinging tight.

"Like this," he whispered against her ear, moving his hand in a firm rhythm. "Deep. And hard. Over and over."

"Please . . ." She gasped. "Don't stop."

"Never. I'll never stop until you come." His thumb circled the swollen bud at the crest of her sex. "You do understand what that means? You've touched yourself here?"

Charlotte nodded, breathless. "Innocent, not ignorant."

"Good."

His approval emboldened her. She began to move with him, seeking more of the exquisite pleasure he gave. She did understand the paroxysm of pleasure a woman's body was created to feel, and she had learned how to bring it about herself. But it had never, ever been like this.

Her body was aflame, alive with need. It seemed unfair, his ability to drive her to distraction while remaining so cool, controlled . . .

Relentless.

She bit her lip.

"That's it. I need to feel you come for me."

All the rebellion had been sapped from her, washed away in the encroaching tide of desire. She rode his hand, shameless, climbing to a peak so devastating she was certain to cry out.

He captured her mouth in a kiss, and she sobbed into it, grateful, clutching his neck tight while the climax dissolved her to jelly from the navel down.

When the waves of pleasure subsided, he gathered her in his arms, drawing soothing circles on her back as her breath calmed and her pulse slowed.

As she returned to herself, a small sense of mortification whispered at her from the shadows of her upbringing. His fingers had been inside her, slick with the moisture her body had created. She held fistfuls of his shirt in her hands, and perspiration had broken out on her brow.

It was all very unladylike. But she wasn't supposed to be a lady in times like these, just a woman.

She wanted to see Piers like that. Stripped down to a man—raw, elemental, animal. Panting and damp with sweat. She wanted to see him lose himself. She wanted to break through his defenses like a blazing meteorite and leave nothing but a smoking ruin.

She wanted *him*. More than she'd ever wanted anything.

Her heart swelled with a sudden, bewildering tide of affection.

"Piers?"

He must have heard the confusion in her voice.

"Hush." He stroked her back in that same, calm rhythm, ignoring his unsatisfied arousal. Denying his own needs while tending hers. "It's natural to feel a rush of sentiment afterward. Women often do. It will pass."

Would it pass?

Or would it deepen, like a hole widening in the earth? One misstep, and she would tumble and fall in love with him forever?

She wasn't feeling terribly bold or clever any longer. She felt small and fragile and very confused.

"I don't suppose this is why you came downstairs." He brushed the hair from her brow.

"No."

"Was there something you needed?"

She nodded, willing her muddled thoughts to clear. "A book. The *Peerage*. I need to check again for C's."

"Charlotte." He tipped her face to his. "You don't *need* to do anything of the sort."

The meaning in his gaze was clear. He'd just spread on this desktop, in black and white, the proof that he intended to provide handsomely for her, and for her family, as well. He'd given her both searing pleasure and tender protection. He'd whispered those intriguing words: *I hope.*

And maybe—just maybe—he'd made her start hoping, too.

Charlotte could all but hear her mother's voice: *Foolish girl, what more could you want?*

Love.

Love was what she wanted. What she'd always wanted. More than fine houses or the title of marchioness. Even more than breathless orgasms, lovely as those were.

Could she come to feel love for Piers? Could he ever feel the same toward her? He kept his heart so closed off, so walled away. If he'd courted her purposely, that might have given her a foundation to build dreams upon, but there could be no assurances in a forced match.

She could *hope* all she wished, but before surrendering her life to a man, Charlotte needed to *know*.

"I . . ." She pushed herself off his lap, arranging her shift and dressing gown as she stumbled to the side table and gathered the book. "I just want to be sure. That I haven't missed anything. Good night."

She clutched the book to her chest and hurried from the room.

She needed this book. She needed to find the mystery lovers.

She needed certainty, now more than ever before.

Chapter Twelve

Charlotte was going cross-eyed.

Debrett's Peerage was a book of nearly nine hundred pages, all of them printed in minuscule type. Despite the free time afforded by another rainy day, she still had more than two hundred of them to search.

The ladies had assembled in the drawing room, just as they had for the past two days of foul weather. Mama was nibbling squares of shortbread and leafing through a ladies' periodical. Delia sketched, Frances worked at a bit of embroidery, and Lady Parkhurst played solitaire at the card table.

Charlotte sat alone by the rain-streaked window.

"I'm so glad you are finally taking an interest in that book," Mama remarked.

"Is this a recent development?" Frances asked. "I

would have wagered you had your own copy memorized. If not annotated."

Charlotte ignored the baiting comment. Frances would not distract her from the task at hand.

It would have been much easier if she knew the C corresponded to a surname or title. But it was just as likely to correspond to a Christian name, which necessitated scanning each page and, when she located a C, flipping back to the peer with whom she was associated and checking the location to see if the lady might reside anywhere nearby.

And of course, if the woman in the library was not somehow related to a peer, baronet, or knight, the entire exercise would have been a waste of time.

Weaver, Lady Catherine . . . Lincolnshire.

Westwood, Hon. Cora . . . Devon.

And then . . .

Then!

White, Hon. Cornelia . . . Nottinghamshire.

The name White was familiar to her. She thought she remembered seeing it on Lady Parkhurst's guests—but then it was such a common name, she might be imagining it.

"Lady Parkhurst, was there a Mrs. White at the ball last week?"

"Nellie White?" Lady Parkhurst looked up from her cards. "Oh, yes."

Nellie. Short for Cornelia. She must be the one.

Charlotte tried to rein in her excitement. It might come to nothing, after all.

But all the signs were there. Mrs. Cornelia White had been at Parkhurst Manor. She had the right initial. Did she have dark hair?

"I'm trying to picture her in my mind. Was she the one with the . . ." Charlotte gestured toward her head.

"Dreadful yellow turban?" Lady Parkhurst sighed. "Yes. I have tried to talk the dear thing out of it, but she won't be moved."

Drat.

Though Charlotte was encouraged by the indication that the lady preferred bright colors.

"I don't suppose we could pay her a call," she said to Delia.

Delia made a face. "Why we would do that?"

"Well . . . we had a brief discussion of books. She mentioned a novel that sounded so interesting, but I've forgotten the title. I'd like to ask her."

"She lives all the way over toward Yorkshire," Delia said. "Much too far away for a morning call, I'm afraid. Perhaps you could write to her."

Oh, yes. Charlotte could write to the woman she'd never actually met, inquire after a book that didn't exist, and ask her to kindly enclose a lock of her hair with the reply. *That* would be well received.

"No need to write." Lady Parkhurst turned over a card. "You may ask her at the hunt."

"The hunt?"

"Father hosts a foxhunt every autumn and invites all the gentlemen from the area," Delia explained.

"It will take place the morning after next, if the weather clears," Frances said. "The ladies don't ride to hounds, of course. We ride up to Robin Hood's Hill and observe the spectacle."

Delia shuddered. "The bloody, violent spectacle. I despise hunting."

"Perhaps you could take your watercolors and paint the countryside," Charlotte suggested.

"I've painted the view from that hill a hundred times, in every light and every season. I'd much rather stay home."

In any other situation, Charlotte would have gladly stayed home with her. But this could be her only chance to see Mrs. White again.

"What about you, Miss Highwood?" Lady Parkhurst asked. "Will you stay back, too?"

Charlotte gave Delia an apologetic look. "I . . . I think I would like to go. I've never seen a hunt before, and I'd love to walk in the footsteps of Robin Hood. Only, I don't have my own horse."

"We'll loan you one," Frances said. "Do you prefer a gelding, stallion, or mare?"

Oh, dear. Charlotte could count the number of times she'd been horseback riding on one hand. It wasn't an activity they'd had the money to finance in her youth. Gelding, stallion, mare? She wasn't even certain she knew the difference.

"Oh," she said, "whichever horse you think would suit me."

Frances's slow, smug smile was rather alarming.

The next morning, Charlotte understood why.

They'd barely set out from the stables when the dappled gray horse beneath her whinnied and danced sideways.

Charlotte tightened her gloved hands on the pommel.

Frances called to her. "Lady isn't too much for you, I hope?"

"Not at all," Charlotte called back, trying to sound breezy and confident. "I enjoy a horse with spirit."

Unfortunately, the particular spirit possessing this mare seemed to be an ill-tempered, malevolent demon fed on soured milk. Charlotte wished she'd thought to bring apples or sugar lumps. Or holy water.

Frances nudged her horse into a canter, and Lady followed suit.

Charlotte felt her teeth rattle and her tailbone bounce. Under her breath, she muttered a curse.

She managed to hang on across several fields and over a narrow bridge. Fortunately, as they neared the prominence, the horses were forced to slow to a walk.

When they reached their picnicking spot atop the hill, Charlotte slid gratefully from the saddle and gave Lady's neck a loving pat. "Good girl. I'll save you a sandwich."

In return, the mare snapped at her, nearly removing two of her fingers.

Perhaps she'd walk home instead.

Charlotte left the sulking mare and turned her attention to the reason she'd come here.

Stealing a close look at Mrs. White and her hair.

"Oh, Nellie," Lady Parkhurst called. "Would you be a dear and help with arranging the baskets?"

Charlotte watched closely as a lady stepped forward to answer the call.

The good news was, Mrs. White wasn't wearing a dreadful yellow turban today. However, she *was* wearing a bonnet. An enormous bonnet that not only covered all of her hair, but shielded most of her face and was secured under her chin with a firmly knotted blue ribbon.

Drat.

In this business of solving mysteries, one encountered the most vexing and mundane obstacles. Thwarted by a bonnet, of all things.

The distant blare of bugles sounded.

"Oh, look! They're off."

Charlotte turned to watch, shielding her eyes with her hand.

The hounds appeared first. Scores of them, racing out from the wooded valley in a yapping, churning pack. Then came the men, riding swiftly behind. There were more than a dozen of them, all told— local squires and even some of the more prominent farmers had been invited to join.

She could make a few out even at this distance, however. Sir Vernon's portly figure and hunter-green coat were distinguishable at the head of the pack.

And then, trailing a polite distance behind his host, came Piers.

He wore a black coat, indistinguishable from those of several other gentlemen, but Charlotte knew him at once. She would have recognized his figure anywhere. He guided his mount over the hedges and stiles with ease. So smooth and power-ful, moving as one with his bay gelding.

Or was it a stallion?

She tore her gaze from the spectacle.

Mrs. White had wandered away from the ladies arranging the picnic baskets. Her enormous, con-founding bonnet bobbed toward the other side of the hill.

Charlotte hurried to catch up with her. "Oh, Mrs. White."

The woman slowed.

"Mrs. White, do you remember me from the other evening? I'm Miss Highwood."

"Oh." The widow looked her up and down. "Yes, of course."

Charlotte curtsied. "Isn't it a fine morning for a hunt?"

"I suppose it is."

Mrs. White looked a bit baffled at Charlotte's friendly overtures.

Perhaps she was shy.

Or . . . perhaps she was riddled with guilt over her torrid, illicit *affaire* in Sir Vernon Parkhurst's library.

"I think I'll remove my hat," Charlotte said, unpinning her pert riding hat and making a show of basking in the sun. "Oh, the sunshine feels divine. Wouldn't you like to remove your bonnet?"

Mrs. White smiled. "I freckle most dreadfully."

"Just tip it back for a moment," Charlotte urged. "Truly, the sun feels so delicious. You won't freckle that quickly."

The widow seemed to consider it, tilting her head skyward.

The sun promptly moved behind a cloud.

"Perhaps later," she said.

Charlotte sighed. She began hoping for a strong

gust of wind to catch that bonnet like a sail and pull it back. Even a stiff breeze would suffice, if it could tug loose a small wisp of hair. She wasn't asking for much.

"Do let's take a turn about the hill." Charlotte linked arms with the woman. "I'd be so grateful if you could point out the local landmarks."

The widow didn't seem especially eager, but Charlotte hadn't left her any polite way to refuse.

"I wish we'd had more opportunity to talk the other night," Charlotte forged on, once they'd left the earshot of the others. "I could tell at once we'd have so much in common."

"Truly?"

Mrs. White sounded skeptical, and Charlotte couldn't blame her. The woman was at least ten years her senior, and, it was becoming increasingly apparent, not terribly vivacious. It was difficult to imagine what they would have in common.

It was also difficult to imagine Mrs. White wearing a scarlet garter, dousing herself in rich perfume, and shrieking her carnal pleasure atop a desk.

But it had to have been her. Charlotte's deductions left no other option.

"Appearances," Charlotte said, taking another approach, "can frequently be deceiving. Don't you agree? The heart has so many secrets."

The widow pointed. "There's Oxton, over there. And to the north, all that green is Sherwood Forest."

They'd completed their circle of the hill. Soon they'd be heading back to join the others.

She looked askance at her companion. She'd yet to spy even a stray lock at her nape or temple. What sort of hair preparation did the woman use? Plaster of Paris?

She had to do something. Something rash. She might not have another chance.

She gave a dramatic gasp. "Mrs. White, do be still. There's a spider."

"A spider?"

"A large spider. On your bonnet. Don't startle, or you'll tip it down your neck." Charlotte moved close and slowly reached for the ribbons tied beneath the woman's chin. "I'll just unlace this very cautiously and then I'll shake it out on the grass."

"There's no need."

"But there is! Believe me, Mrs. White, this is a very nasty spider. It's . . . it's hairy. And fanged."

Mrs. White put her hands over Charlotte's, stopping her. "My dear girl, let us do away with pretense."

"Pretense?"

"There's no spider, and I know it."

Charlotte's shoulders sank. "You do?"

Mrs. White smiled. "My dear, you were correct. We do have something in common. I, too, know what it is to be young and confused. Wondering if you'll ever meet a soul who understands the desires in your heart."

"Really?"

Charlotte held her breath. Never mind the bonnet or the hair. Perhaps the woman was going to confess. This was going better than she'd dared to hope.

"There are many like us," Mrs. White continued. "So many more than you'd think. You needn't feel alone. I can't say it will be easy, but there are ways to follow your heart."

"What ways?"

"You could follow my example, marry an older man. Just a few years of submitting to his"—she cleared her throat—"attentions gave me a lifetime of security and freedom. My darling Emmeline, on the other hand . . . Well, the dear thing couldn't countenance the prospect of marriage. She went straight into service. We took different paths, but somehow we found each other."

Charlotte frowned in confusion. "But Mrs. White—"

"Oh, we can't attend balls and picnics together. But in our own home, no one troubles us. We're happy. You will find that happiness, too." The widow pressed a fingertip over Charlotte's lips. "You are a lovely young lady. So pretty and lively. There will come a day when you needn't resort to imaginary spiders. Save your kisses for someone else."

Save her kisses?

Her *kisses*.

"Oh, dear." She forced a little laugh. "Mrs. White, I do beg your pardon. I think I've been misunderstood."

"It's all right. I'm rather flattered, truly. And I'd never dream of telling a soul."

With a genuine, sympathetic smile, Nellie White turned and walked back toward the picnic gathering.

Well.

Charlotte was left to stand there, blinking at the Nottinghamshire landscape and absorbing the enormity of her foolishness.

She still hadn't learned the color of Mrs. White's hair, but apparently it didn't matter. The widow wasn't interested in the company of men.

Her investigation had reached another blind end.

Had she missed someone else on the list of guests? Had the perfume shopkeeper lied about the dark hair? Her deductions must have gone wrong somewhere.

So unspeakably frustrating.

Everything hung in the balance. Her reputation, the Grand Tour with Delia . . . the entirety of her future. And yet, Charlotte was most disappointed simply because she'd gotten it wrong.

Her talents didn't make for impressive exhibitions. She wasn't an artist like Delia, or a scientific scholar like her sister Minerva. Foolish as she imagined it would sound to others—in particular, to Piers—solving this mystery had taken on deeper meaning for her. It was her chance to claim an accomplishment. With each suspect she'd crossed off her list, she'd felt herself closer to the moment where she could stand back and say, "I did that."

And now, it seemed, she hadn't done anything. Except waste a great deal of effort and time, and further damage a treasured friendship. Her entire visit in Nottinghamshire had been one mistake heaped on another.

For the first time all fortnight, a sense of true despair came over her. Tears pricked at the corners of her eyes.

In a week's time, all her foolish errors would be exposed to the world. She had only a few days remaining.

What was she even doing here? She should return to spend the afternoon with Delia, before Delia stopped speaking with her at all.

Chapter Thirteen

After completing what seemed like an hour-long, painfully audible stream of urination, Sir Vernon buttoned his falls and stepped out from behind the tree, tugging on his tweed waistcoat.

"Nothing like a good ride to hounds to get the bodily humours flowing. Eh, Granville?"

Piers completed his unnecessary inspection of his gelding's girth and saddle. "Pity the hunt was for naught."

"Oh, it's never for naught. No, no. It's not the fox we're after. It's the chase. The thrill. We sportsmen can't live without it, can we? Feeds one appetite as surely as it works up another." He gave Piers an elbow in the ribs. "Now let's turn our sights to prettier quarry, shall we? The ladies will be waiting for us on the hill. There's a vixen there you should be chasing. I understand Miss Highwood made the ride out, even though Delia wouldn't. She must want to share a picnic with a certain gentleman."

Piers thought about Charlotte waiting with the ladies on the hill. Her golden hair coming loose, her cheeks pink from exercise, and her eyes the same bright, clear blue as the sky. He thought about sitting next to her, accepting morsels of cheese and meat from her fingertips, and watching her suck the juice from a ripe, red berry.

He thought about pushing her back on that picnic blanket to taste those berry-stained lips.

And then he thought better of the entire plan.

Even though Sir Vernon saw him as a fellow gentleman of leisure, Piers had a task to complete. He couldn't let pass the opportunity to have Parkhurst Manor to himself for a period of some hours. At last, he could get to opening those locked drawers in the library.

In the grand scheme of his career, this was an insignificant assignment. But to Piers, it had become vital. He needed to prove to himself that he could still carry out his role. Because if he couldn't . . . ? All the shame and guilt he'd been outrunning for the past twenty years would catch up to him.

He would die inside.

"Thank you," he said, "but I'll ride back to the

manor. I must see to some correspondence. If I mean to announce the engagement before the end of my visit, the betrothal contracts need to be settled."

Sir Vernon gave a deep belly laugh. "I never met the female mind what was wooed by contracts. You need to pass some time with the girl, Granville. Our fox might have run to ground today, but you can't have Miss Highwood doing the same."

Piers began to reply, but the older man interrupted.

"Now, now," he said, in a manner of confidentiality. "You're a man of tremendous achievement. No one can dispute that. But if Miss Highwood changed her mind about the wedding, we both know that wouldn't be without precedent. Your previous would-be bride slipped away."

Piers bristled at Sir Vernon's implication. Clio had not "slipped away." Piers had stayed away from *her*, and for good reason. Her safety had depended on Piers keeping his distance, and who could have known the war would drag on so long? In any event, their betrothal had been a friendly arrangement between families, not a love match. He didn't blame her for seizing happiness with Rafe.

To be sure, Piers hadn't rushed to find a bride that first season back in London. Nor the second. He'd been occupied. Much too busy for courtship, or even for casual *affaires*. If he had wished to marry, however, he would have had his choice.

"Miss Highwood," he said, "will not be slipping away."

"Good. Good. I hope you won't fault me for asking, Granville. Deserved or not, the girl has a bit of a reputation. You did an honorable thing in offering for her. I'd merely like to be assured that you'll have this settled by fortnight's end. I've my own daughters to think about, and I wouldn't want any hint of scandal landing on them."

This struck Piers as a strange concern, coming from a man who was, by all available evidence, embroiled in a scandal of his own making.

"I give you my word," Piers said tightly. "The engagement will be secured."

"Just don't neglect her. The ladies like a bit of chasing." Sir Vernon clapped him on the back. "That's a sport."

As he headed back to Parkhurst Manor, Piers was met by an arresting sight.

Charlotte, riding overland toward him on horseback. Just as he'd imagined her in his fantasy—her golden hair streaming behind her, her complexion bright, her blue eyes . . .

Closed?

As he got a better look, he noticed her desperate grip on the horse's mane. Her terrified expression. No doubt as to why.

The mare was headed directly for the stream. The

stream that was nearly a river this time of year, with high, mossy banks on either side.

It was a jump that would have challenged even a seasoned horseman, and nothing about Charlotte's white-knuckled, eyes-closed, breakneck approach to the obstacle said "seasoned."

It said "inexperienced" and "idiotic" and "dangerous as hell."

"Miss Highwood!" he called, nudging his own gelding into a trot—and then, as soon as possible, a full-speed gallop.

But it wasn't any use.

There simply wasn't enough ground between her and the stream.

He wouldn't reach her in time. He couldn't.

There was nothing he could do.

His heart thudded in his chest, drumming even louder than the hoofbeats pounding the mud.

"Charlotte!" Even his shout died in his throat, ineffectual.

It was rare that he experienced the sensation of true helplessness. In fact, he couldn't recall feeling it since he'd been a boy of seven years old.

He'd known even then, he didn't like it.

He'd resolved to never, ever feel that way again.

And here he was, watching Charlotte Highwood race toward disaster, powerless to do anything but watch.

The mare, it turned out, didn't want to make the jump any more than Charlotte did.

The horse skidded to a halt on the far bank. Charlotte, however, kept moving. The momentum catapulted her over the horse's head in a cartwheel of dark velvet and golden hair. She landed headfirst in the stream, making a prodigious splash.

Piers pulled his gelding to a halt. He held his breath, waiting for her to emerge onto the bank.

An eternity passed in every heartbeat. Emotions exploded inside him like buried grenades. Anger, confusion, fear, despair. Everything he'd sworn to never feel again.

His mind shattered into bleak fragments, and each one was edged in blood.

She's hit her head on a rock. She's broken her neck. She's drowned.

She's gone, she's gone.

You can't do anything.

She's gone.

A few moments ago, Charlotte would have said she'd rather be anywhere other than on the back of that dratted horse.

She would have been wrong.

Being on the dratted horse was better—marginally— than hurtling through the air like a cannonball.

And both those things were better—considerably—than being plunged headfirst into a swift, icy stream.

The water helped break her fall, and she was lucky enough to avoid striking her head—but she banged her shoulder hard against the rocky bank. The emerald-green velvet riding habit she'd been so enamored with in the London dressmaker's shop acted like a sponge, soaking up all the water in Nottinghamshire, it seemed.

Within the space of a moment, she was disoriented, chilled, swollen to twice her size, and generally feeling like a drunken whale.

Eventually she managed to get a foot under her, brace it against a stone, and flex her leg muscles enough to stand.

She drew a gasping breath.

Then the moss made her slip, and she lost all the ground she'd gained, finding herself submerged to her ears once again.

The rushing water carried her downstream, introducing her to a boulder with a helpful smack.

Ouch.

In retaliation, she clung to the rock with both hands, using it to catch her breath. She'd stopped drifting, but she wasn't gaining any ground, either. And the water was chilling her further by the second. Her fingers began to numb, and her legs felt heavy.

She would have to make her escape soon, or she'd end up floating all the way to the sea.

She braced her feet beneath her, flexed her arms, and made a lunge for the bank.

Her fingers scrabbled and slid over loose rocks and clumps of turf. The stream's current tugged at her skirts, tangling them into a knot about her legs. She kicked to little avail, struggling for the leverage to push herself out.

She dug her fingernails into the dirt.

Come on then, Charlotte.

A large, gloved hand gripped her wrist.

The hand's owner pulled her out.

She emerged from the water slowly. Not by choice, but by necessity. The sparkling green velvet had become a choking mat of seaweed. Her hair was plastered to her face in stringy clumps, obscuring her vision.

And it made perfect, tragic sense when she made her ungainly collapse on the grassy bank, parted the slimy curtains of her hair, and blinked away the remaining river water to take a look at her rescuer to find—

Piers.

"Of course," she muttered between labored breaths. "Of course it's you."

"You don't seem happy about it."

She looked down at herself. There was no fetching

mermaid or selkie to be found in this scene. No painted Ophelia, clasping her hands at her breast as the waters claimed her with poetic dignity. Charlotte looked as though she'd been tied to the keel of a ship, dredged up and down the Thames a few times, and then left to the eels and barnacles for a year or two.

And he was gorgeous, naturally. Not a knight in shining armor, but as close as a modern girl could find to it. He practically gleamed in his fitted black riding coat, buckskin breeches, polished Hessian boots, and a cravat of crisp white.

His hair was perfect.

It all made her suddenly, irrationally vexed.

"Are you injured at all?"

"I'm fine."

He offered a hand. "Let me help you stand."

"I don't need help. Just leave me be."

"I will not leave you be. You were thrown from a horse and nearly drowned. You're chilled, alone, possibly injured, and your mount is on the other side of the stream."

"Thank you, my lord, for recounting every facet of my mortification so efficiently."

She pushed herself to her feet, plucking clumps of moss from her riding habit.

His tone gentled, and he put a hand to her waist. "Charlotte. Allow me to—"

She bristled way from him. "I can't. It's what she expects, don't you see?"

"What who expects?"

"Frances. She hates me. She gave me that demonic horse."

Charlotte flung an arm in the direction of Lady. The dappled gray mare was currently chewing clover in a picture of rustic tranquillity.

"Well, she looks harmless now. But I tell you, she's possessed."

"Yes, I saw," he said.

"I know you did." She disentangled a dead leaf from her hair.

Charlotte knew she was being churlish, but she couldn't help it. Everything had gone all wrong. She'd abandoned Delia. She'd discovered a critical error in her investigating. She'd made unwanted romantic advances toward a local widow. Now she had little hope of ever finding the mystery lovers, and even if she could—it wouldn't matter how long she traveled the world. Women like Frances would never let her live down the Desperate Debutante. They would keep needling, keep whispering about her, even if—no, *especially* if—she appeared in London married to Piers. Charlotte told herself she shouldn't care about gossips, but it was all so demoralizing.

"Let's return to the manor. We can both ride on my gelding."

"I'll walk." She set about wringing the excess water from her skirt. "I can just imagine Frances's ire if she thinks I landed shrieking at your feet and forced you to come to my aid."

"No one forces me to do anything."

"They don't need to. You do it to yourself." She huffed a sigh, exasperated. "Piers, I'm not accomplished. My dowry is small. My connections are fathoms beneath yours. You've never needed to treat me like a respectable lady. Look around you. No one else does."

"You," he said, taking her by the shoulders, "will be a lady. My lady. I will treat you with the respect that title deserves. As will Miss Frances Parkhurst, her friends, the entirety of the *ton*, the Royal Court, and anyone else who wishes to avoid my extreme displeasure."

By the hint of barely concealed violence in his voice, Charlotte wondered if his "extreme displeasure" involved sharp edges or blunt objects.

"Why?" She searched his face. "And don't answer me with that nonsense about wanting and desire. At the moment, I must look about as desirable as pile of wet rags."

He glanced down at her body and raised a brow. "You'd be surprised."

She gave him a damp, ineffective thump in the shin and tried to wriggle away.

His grip tightened on her arms.

"Let me go," she insisted, almost shouting.

His reply was every bit as angry. "*I can't.*"

She looked up at him, breathing hard.

"I can't let you go, Charlotte. I couldn't that first night in the library. I most assuredly as hell won't let you walk away from me now."

His hands framed her face. Not tenderly, but with impatient force. She couldn't have turned away if she'd wanted to.

He searched her face with a penetrating gaze. "It wasn't enough for you to invade my thoughts, was it? Oh, no. You had to get under my skin, as well. Sometimes I think you've found a way into my blood."

The dark note of anger in his voice intrigued and aroused her. His gloved thumbs pressed against her cheeks.

"And now you have the temerity to demand I let you go. It's too late for that, darling. It's done." He released her face. "And I'm done discussing it."

Without another word, he plucked her off her feet—heavy, waterlogged velvet and all—and lifted her up on his horse. Then he mounted behind her, lashed one arm around her waist, and spurred his mount into a canter, carrying her off into the countryside. As if they were characters in some demented fairy tale.

The Prince and the Sea Monster.

Chapter Fourteen

Charlotte clung to him, resigned.

She had no warmth left in her body to fight it, no wits remaining to find a path out.

If Piers Brandon, the Marquess of Granville, in all his proud, decisive, muscular handsomeness, had made up his mind to be her champion . . . ?

Very well, then.

It would take a stronger woman than Charlotte to refuse.

She fell against him, sinking into the romance of the moment. It hit her all at once, the effort she'd expended resisting this sensation all along. Like a swimmer who'd spent hours thrashing against the current, only to surrender from fatigue.

She was, in every sense, swept away.

He held her in a tight, possessive embrace against

his chest as they set a course for the woods. His presence behind her was so strong, so warm, so safe.

And he smelled like a dream. The kind of dream that left a woman short of breath and damp between the thighs. Woodsy, spicy, entirely masculine.

She closed her eyes and pressed her cheek to his waistcoat, breathing him in.

He slowed as they entered the woods, guiding the horse to a secluded, sunny clearing.

There, they paused.

Piers dismounted, then took her by the waist and helped her down.

"Why are we stopping?"

"I want to see for myself that you're well and unharmed. I can't do this once we've returned to the manor."

He settled her on a freshly hewn tree stump. First, he divested himself of his coat and riding gloves, hanging them over a convenient branch. Then, working in brisk, businesslike motions, he unbuttoned the jacket of her riding habit before easing the sleeves down her arms. She shivered a little, hugging herself. Her white, thin chemisette was painted to her torso with river water and nearly translucent.

If Piers noticed, his gaze didn't linger. Having laid her jacket in a sunny patch of grass, he went on one knee before her. He took her right foot and propped it on his knee. After wrestling with the wet knots of her bootlaces for a few moments, he reached into his own boot for a knife and sliced them clean down the middle. Then he slipped the boot from her foot and set it beside the stump before reaching under her petticoats to untie her garter and peel the wet, clinging stocking from her leg. His hand passed from her ankle to her thigh, not groping or caressing—merely making an assessment. He satisfied himself that her toes still wiggled, and her ankle still bent in all the proper directions, and confirmed that she didn't yelp in pain when he pressed there, or there, or there . . . or there.

Then he set her foot gently in the grass, propped her left boot on his right knee, and began the same process anew.

As she watched him from her perch on the stump, Charlotte warmed inside. The afternoon sun had begun to dry her hair and revive her spirits. She didn't feel so monstrous anymore.

As Piers swept his touch from her ankle to her thigh, she bit her lip.

"Did that hurt?" he asked, looking grave.

"No. It only took me by surprise."

She looked at the ground, where he'd set her boot directly to the side of its mate and even folded her stockings into neat, matching bundles. So orderly. So very Piers. The same habit that would have irritated her a week ago now landed in an altogether different way. It struck her as endearing. Sweet.

Possibly the best thing anyone had ever done for her.

Good heavens. From the fount of tenderness welling in her heart, one would think those two bedraggled stockings had been baskets of flowers, or ropes of diamonds. They were lumps of useless, itchy wool. Not even her best pair. And yet, as she stared at them . . . She wanted to cry.

What was wrong with her? Something must be. The possibilities unspooled in her mind, each worse than the last.

She was nearing her monthly courses.

She'd incurred an injury to her skull.

She'd inherited Mama's nervous complaint, or perhaps . . .

Or perhaps she was falling in love.

Oh, no. Oh, Lord. That had to be it.

She was in *love*.

On instinct, she curled her fingers around the edges of the tree stump. As though if she didn't hold tight, she might slip off. Or float away.

Piers returned her foot to the ground and leaned forward.

She clutched the stump for dear life.

Oh God oh God oh God.

He was so close. So close and so handsome.

Well, he'd always been handsome, but now . . . looking at him hurt. That small, perfect cleft in his chin reached inside her somehow, and squeezed.

Her head spun. Her heart pounded so hard it would burst.

No one had warned her it would be like this. Love was supposed to feel good. Wasn't it? Not terrifying.

Perhaps this wasn't love after all, but malaria.

His hands encircled her waist. "Your ribs feel all of a piece."

Did they? A small miracle, considering how her heart was battering them from the inside.

He felt her crown for lumps and pushed her hair back from her face. "No headache?"

"No."

"Any trouble breathing?" he asked. "Do you feel faint or dizzy?"

"A little," she answered, honestly.

And who could fault her? She'd fallen in a stream. She'd fallen for this man. Headfirst, both times, with no warning.

It was all too much.

"When we're back at the manor, I'll call for the local physici—"

Charlotte kissed him.

She couldn't help it. She needed to touch him, desperately, and her hands weren't going to cooperate. Her fingers were so fused to the stump at this point, they might have grown roots.

She pressed her lips to his, haltingly. Once, and then again. Silently begging him to kiss her back.

Please.

For a horrible moment, she doubted. Not him, never him. Only herself.

Then he banished all doubt—every cold, lonely question—claiming her mouth in a passionate kiss.

Yes. *Yes.*

Here was the Piers she craved. The one that danger brought forth from the diplomat. The man who was possessive, impatient, more than a bit wild.

And not to be denied.

They kissed openmouthed, with tongues and lips and teeth. Struggling not to vanquish each other, but the space between them.

Kissing wasn't enough. Not this time. She wanted—no, needed—more.

She needed to touch him, hold him, be as close to him as two people could possibly be.

She worked her hands between them and pried at the stubborn, prudish buttons of her chemisette, then abandoned them for the equally maddening buttons of his waistcoat. They resisted her, too.

Frustrated, she finally tugged his shirt free from his breeches, then thrust her hands beneath it.

He sucked in his breath. The chill of her fingers against his abdomen seemed to shock him to awareness.

Undaunted, Charlotte stroked her hands over the tensed muscles of his torso. Caressing, soothing. Tempting him to touch her, too.

As his gaze wandered her face, a debate raged behind his cool, blue eyes. The proper gentleman inside him was putting up one last fight. She could sense him balanced on the razor-thin edge between duty and desire.

"I'm cold," she whispered.

And that was all it took.

I'm cold.

Those two quiet, simple words were all Piers needed to hear.

To her, they were a plea. Perhaps an invitation.

To him, they were a call to action.

She was cold. His blood was on fire.

The rest was logic.

He would bare her. Hold her, skin to skin. Warm her in every way, with every part of him God had fashioned for the purpose.

Not merely because he wanted it—and bloody hell, he wanted it. But because she was his to care for, now and always.

And she was cold.

He went into ruthless action, dispatching every button that had dared disobey her chilled fingers. The skirt and petticoats gave way easily enough. He peeled the wet chemisette from her body, stripping her down to her shift and stays, then reached behind her to untie the laces of her corset with one swift tug.

She gasped as the air rushed into her lungs.

The sound inflamed him.

He counted in his mind as he slipped the corset laces from their eyelets.

One, two, three . . .

Her sweet, pink lip folded under her teeth.

Four, five . . .

Still not too late. Turn back. Tell me to stop.

Six.

That was it. Persephone was his.

He took her by the arms and pulled her to him, kissing her deeply, without any reserve. As he'd never kissed any woman, holding nothing of himself back. Not his desire, not his yearning . . .

Not his heart.

His *heart*?

Damn. He couldn't grapple with that idea now. Not when his hands were full of Charlotte. Her tangled hair, her wet chemise, her chilled, trembling body beneath.

He lifted her off her feet, and she gave a startled laugh. The sound danced over his skin like a cascade of golden sparks, singeing and teasing him. Making him feel alive.

He made a bed of his coat for her, spreading it in a sunny patch of grass, and she reclined on her elbows, watching intently as he stripped off the unbuttoned waistcoat and moved to yank his shirt over his head.

"Wait," she said. "Go more slowly. I'd like to watch."

As she wished.

Gathering the hem in his crossed hands, he leisurely lifted the garment over his head and shook it down his arms.

He stood on his knees before her, torso bared to the full midday sun.

She stared at him, rapt. "I changed my mind. Be quick."

It was his turn to laugh. He removed his boots and breeches as quickly as he could manage, joining her in the grass before the wide-eyed curiosity on her face could transform to alarm.

She was a virgin, and he was exceedingly . . . ready. Hard, aching, and primed by a week's worth of frustrated lust. He wanted to make this good for her, but he didn't know if he could.

"Charlotte." He ran his hand from her breast to her hip. "I want you. I want you more than I've ever wanted anything. I am aching to get inside you. I don't wish to hurt you, but I suspect I will. I fear I must."

"Goodness, don't be so solemn." She stroked his brow. "I know it will be a little painful. I'm not afraid. You don't need to be afraid, either."

Afraid.

He wanted to shrug off the word in a show of manly bluster. But he couldn't—not convincingly. His breath was shaky, and his hand trembled as he drew a caress down her thigh. Unlike Charlotte, he couldn't blame it on the chill.

He needed to get her out of that shift. The linen was thin enough that it had already begun to dry— but he wanted her bare. He slipped a hand beneath the hem and drew the shift upward, peeling the milky gauze from her body and revealing everything she was beneath.

She didn't hide herself from his gaze. He drank it in—the sight of her body bathed in sunshine. So beautiful, it rendered him speechless. Judging by the shy smile gracing her lips, she intuited his admiration well enough, even without words.

Her fingernails teased the hair on his chest and raked over his flat nipples. He slid a palm over the smooth, silky planes of her back and nuzzled the softness of her breasts.

Nestled in the tickling grass, breathing the green and burnt-orange scents of autumn . . . They might have been the first man and woman in Creation, discovering one another in the Garden of Eden. Exploring all the parts that made them different. Sharing all the desires that made them the same.

He kissed his way down her body, worshipping

every inch of her. She bucked and gasped as he nudged her thighs apart and ran his tongue along her crease.

"Let me do this for you," he murmured, in between light passes of his tongue. "I'll make it better. I'll make it so good."

He framed her waist in his hands and reached toward her center with his thumbs, spreading her wide. After exploring every pink, secret petal of her sex, he centered his efforts on the swollen bud at the crest.

Her hand tangled in his hair, and all he heard was the shallow rasp of her breath. She began to writhe beneath him, twisting her hips to seek more contact, more pleasure.

He held her in place, never ceasing the gentle flicks of his tongue. Once she'd resigned herself to the pleasure, he moved a hand between her thighs and pushed two fingers inside her, thrusting them in and out as he kept up his kisses and tender suckling.

"Piers," she gasped.

He didn't pause for even a moment to reply, only settled in to his task with renewed dedication.

He felt the quiver of her thigh against his cheek, and it encouraged him to work his fingers deeper, faster. Her body tensed.

Yes. That's it. Surrender to it. Let it happen.

He would have licked and kissed her all day if she'd needed him to do so, but she broke apart beneath him in stunning fashion, gasping and arching off the ground.

He pulled her down to the earth with gentle nuzzling and caresses until her breathing slowed.

He kissed his way back up her belly, crawling on hands and knees as he moved atop her. He guarded her body between his arms, offering himself as a shelter. But what she gave him in return was so much more. Comfort. Succor. A soft place to lay his heavy heart.

Her thighs parted, making a cradle for his legs. The hard, eager curve of his cock wedged tight between their bellies, straining toward her navel.

He raised himself up on straightened arms. Then he rocked his hips, so that the head of his cock parted her and fitted just where it wanted to be.

She looked up at him with clear eyes and absolutely no misgivings. She was so damn trusting it made his chest ache. He fought the impulse to claim her fast and hard. Make her his own before she could change her mind.

"If we do this," he said, "you must marry me. You do understand that?"

She nodded, but it wasn't enough. He needed words.

"Once we're joined, you'll be bound to me. Irrevocably. Always. Tell me you understand that. Tell me you *want* it. I need to hear it from your lips, Charlotte. Say you . . ." The breath rushed out of him. "Say you'll be my wife."

Charlotte gazed up at him, her heart wrenching with emotion. It seemed she had finally heard a true proposal. Or as close to it as she was likely to get.

"Yes, Piers. I'll marry you."

I will marry you, and I will love you. And somehow, some way I will make you love me back.

She was resolved on one thing. She was *not* going to be one of those virgins who whimpered and cried upon her deflowering. She could take a bit of pain. Anyway, his fingers had already been inside her. How much bigger could this part of him be?

Much bigger, she discovered, as the tip of him nudged at her entrance. Bigger, thicker, harder, hotter.

Just . . . *more*. In every way.

Nevertheless, she thought she was dealing with it all rather admirably.

And then he pushed inside.

Oh Lord oh Lord oh Lord.

She couldn't help it. All her resolutions were abandoned. She cried out and tensed, digging her fingernails into his shoulders like claws.

He cursed. "Sorry."

It's all right, she wanted to tell him. *It's fine, truly. Plow on ahead. No need to worry about me.*

But it wasn't all right, and she wasn't fine, and if he plowed on ahead just now, she would likely serve him an involuntary punch in the eye.

"I'll go as slow as you need me to. I won't move again until you tell me you're ready. I swear it."

Charlotte nodded. She breathed in and out, willing her body to relax.

When the pain finally began to ebb, she released her tight grip on his shoulders. He slid in a bit farther, and a bit farther still, and—miracle of miracles—it didn't make her want to scream.

"Better now?" he asked.

"Yes."

He cared about her comfort. He was working so hard to make this not only bearable, but wonderful. And that made everything better.

His every careful, inching thrust went easier than the last. Her body stretched and ached, but in a tolerable way. Perhaps even a pleasant way.

When he was finally fully seated inside her, he gave a low moan. The last bit of tension in her arms and neck melted.

And then she did the most ridiculous thing:

She lay back and thought of England.

It came to her all at once: house parties and foxhunts, partridge shooting and prizefighting. Lovers meeting in libraries and carriages and autumn dales.

All those strange, silly, so very English quirks of manners and mystery that had formed their characters and forced them together.

He noticed her smile. "What's so amusing?"

"Only everything."

He bent to kiss her. "I rather adore that about you."

I rather adore that about you.

Her heart gave a bittersweet twinge.

Don't be greedy, she told herself. With a bit of strategic memory, the redaction of a word or two, she could remember that as *I adore you*—or close enough to it.

He took her in slow, gentle strokes at first. Then his thrusts became rougher, more urgent. It hurt, but this was what she'd been waiting for. She wanted to watch him, see his face contorted with raw pleasure and unfettered need. But at the last moment, he withdrew and turned aside, spending himself into the folds of his discarded shirt.

Preventing conception was a considerate gesture, she told herself—even if she was left feeling hollow and a bit disappointed. Even in that last moment of abandon, he'd managed to keep his restraint.

Afterward, he stroked her naked body in the sunlight, touching and exploring and looking where he pleased.

"You are like a boy with a new plaything," she said.

"I'm not a boy, Charlotte. I'm a man. A man who's been trusted with royal secrets, battle plans, and international treaties. And now . . . I'm seized by the notion that you're the most precious thing I've ever held." His eyes burned into hers. "You're mine now."

Part of her wanted to rebel at his possessive tone, but part of her found it thrilling, too. There seemed no point in denying it, anyhow. He had her heart. He had her body.

She was his.

The sooner she accepted that, the sooner the true challenge would begin.

Making him *hers*.

Chapter Fifteen

Charlotte dreamed of being on a boat, rocking to and fro. Then the sea grew violent, tossing her this way and that. Where was Piers? He would make this stop. The waves themselves would not dare disobey him.

"Charlotte. Charlotte."

Her eyes fluttered open. "Piers?"

She looked at his hand curled tight on her arm. He wasn't her safe port in the storm. He was the one shaking her.

"What is it?" she asked. The words came out in a sleepy slur: *Whaeesit.*

Cool grass tangled with her toes. The hunt. The stream. The meadow. Their joining.

She struggled up on her elbow, pushing away a lock of hair crusted to her cheek.

Oh, Lord—had she been drooling? Had he seen?

As her vision came into to focus, she could see that his expression was grave.

Now she snapped awake.

She clutched his shoulder. "Is something wrong?"

He shook his head. "No."

"Then what's the matter?"

"Nothing." He turned to pull on his breeches.

"Are you certain?" She hugged his waist and propped her chin on his shoulder. Beads of cold sweat had risen on his hairline, and his heart was pounding in his chest. She could feel it through his ribs and hers. "Piers. What is it?"

"It was difficult to wake you, that's all."

She pressed her forehead to his back. "So sorry. I sleep like the dead. Everyone in my family knows it—and the servants, besides. But I hadn't thought to warn you."

The sun was sinking lower, and shadow cloaked the meadow.

"Goodness." Charlotte sat up and began reaching for her chemise, jerking it over her head and pushing her arms through the sleeves. "They'll be wondering about us by now. I don't suppose it will have escaped notice that the two of us disappeared together." She reached for one of her stockings and jammed her toe into it, then paused, remembering something worse. "Oh, no. That demon horse. She's probably halfway to Scotland by now."

"She knows where she's fed and watered. She'll have returned to the stables."

"I hope you're right. Otherwise, I don't know how I'll explain it to—"

"Charlotte," he interrupted. "If there are any explanations required, I'll make them." He tilted her face to his, then gave her cheek a light caress. "I will take care of everything. From this moment forward. Do you understand that?"

"I . . . Yes, I suppose I do."

I'll take care of everything.

It was a promise she'd been waiting to hear since she was a girl, but she wasn't a girl anymore. Especially not now, after what had just happened in this meadow.

All the questions she'd submerged an hour or two ago . . . they bubbled to the surface of her conscience now.

How was this going to work? Not only now, but for the rest of their lives? He'd sworn to look after her. Would he ever allow her to look after him? Trust her with his fears and secrets? Would he ever let her come anywhere near that fiercely guarded heart?

Desire and pleasure were all well and good, but they wouldn't be enough to sustain a lifetime.

Only one thing was clear to Charlotte as they left the meadow. From this point forward, there was no going back. Never mind the lovers in the library. Now she had an even greater mystery to solve—and it was Piers.

"I can't wait any longer. We must do it now." Delia inched closer to Charlotte on the drawing room divan.

Charlotte looked up from her book. "Do what?"

"Ask them," Delia whispered. "The Continent? The Grand Tour? Our escape from stifling parents and English society . . . ? Is any of this sounding familiar?"

"Oh, of course."

Charlotte felt a stab of guilt. She hadn't been thinking of Delia and their plans when she made love to Piers.

She hadn't been thinking of anything. Just feeling.

Feeling glorious and adored and impetuous and in love.

But apparently, she ought to add selfish and heedless to the list. All the while, Delia had been counting on her as a friend.

"Of course it does, all of it. But we can't ask them now."

"There won't be a better time. Papa is pleased

with the stag he shot this afternoon, and he's had at least two glasses of port. Mama was proud of that dinner, and she has Lord Granville's farewell ball to plan. They're in a charitable mood. We won't have a more advantageous moment than this."

"But . . ."

"But what?"

But your father still believes me to be a shameless, fortune-hunting hussy, your brother believes I'm a murder target, and your sister has threatened to ruin my life.

"Is it your mother?"

"Yes," Charlotte said hastily. "Yes, the problem is my mother."

That was one good thing she could say for Mama. She made such a convenient excuse for everything. At the moment, she had her feet propped up on a footstool as she leafed through the pages of a ladies' magazine.

"She'd never agree," Charlotte said. "Not now."

"You don't think she's still trying to match you with Lord Granville?" Delia asked.

"It's likely."

Highly, definitely, certainly likely.

"But you've made it clear how much you dislike the man," Delia murmured to her sketchbook. "And for the past few days, he's taken no notice of you whatsoever."

"I know he hasn't," Charlotte said, more dispiritedly than she ought to have allowed herself to sound.

Somehow she and Piers had managed to avoid notice after returning from their tryst in the meadow. Everyone had been resting or preparing for dinner, and they'd all assumed Charlotte was already upstairs in her room. Piers hadn't needed to offer any explanations.

And now, for two days, he'd scarcely spoken at all.

He was avoiding her, belatedly—just as she'd begged him to do when they first met. Now, however, she wanted nothing more than to see him, speak with him. Be held by him and breathe in the scent of his skin.

At the very least, take a stroll around the garden one afternoon.

She couldn't understand why he'd become so suddenly aloof. Unless . . .

Unless everything *she* was feeling had simply left him cold.

"You do still want to go, don't you?" Delia's voice grew small, hesitant. "I wouldn't blame you if you'd changed your mind. I know I won't make the most convenient traveling partner. I walk slowly, and I—"

"Never think it. I couldn't imagine a better companion."

"Oh, good." Her friend looked relieved. "Because

if I have to spend another season sitting in the corners of ballrooms—"

"We're going to break free, the two of us." She reached out and squeezed Delia's hand. "This time next year, you'll be painting views of the Mediterranean. I promise."

Somehow, Charlotte would make it happen.

She looked across the room, at Piers. *He* could make it happen. They needn't marry straightaway. He would likely even pay for the journey, arrange for them to stay with his diplomatic acquaintances overseas. A chance for their daughters to socialize with princesses and archdukes? Sir Vernon and Lady Parkhurst—and Mama—couldn't refuse that, no matter how protective they were.

Charlotte dared to believe she could convince him. He was a man who understood loyalty. He knew the importance of keeping a promise.

But she would need to speak with him first, and for the past half hour he'd stubbornly kept his nose in a newspaper.

Look up, she willed. *Look at me.*

He turned a page of *The Times* instead. It must have been a particularly riveting issue.

Delia set aside her sketchbook. "Do let's ask them now. If they refuse, so be it. I just can't bear any further suspense."

Charlotte put out her hand. "No, wait."

"Vegetables." Lady Parkhurst laid aside her pince-nez and looked up from her lists of recipes. "I can't decide on vegetables for our supper at the ball."

Hallelujah. Saved by vegetables. All lessons on nourishment aside, Charlotte had never expected to think those words.

"I was hoping for something in the French style," Lady Parkhurst went on, "and my egg-plant in the conservatory has produced some lovely aubergines."

"Aubergines?" Sir Vernon asked. "What the deuce are those?"

Charlotte gripped Delia's arm, hard. She couldn't dare look at her. If she did, they would both burst out laughing.

"If you ever took an interest in my plants, you would know. It's the latest variety from the Continent. Produces a long, purplish fruit like so." She drew the shape with her hands. "Why, some of them must be seven or eight inches long."

Charlotte stared hard at the carpet and breathed through her nose. Beside her, Delia began to quietly wheeze.

"A purple vegetable?" Sir Vernon snorted. "What do you do with the things?"

"Well, that's the question, isn't it? I haven't any recipes. Though I hear the French do wondrous things with their aubergines."

Piers looked up from his paper, casting a worried glance in Charlotte's direction. Evidently he'd been paying some attention to her after all. He was probably wondering if he needed to call a doctor to diagnose her convulsions.

"Lord Granville, you've spent time on the Continent," Lady Parkhurst said earnestly. "How do you like your aubergine?"

There was no holding it back then. A shriek of laughter escaped Delia, and Charlotte tried—with only modest success—to covers hers with a coughing fit.

Mama closed her magazine. "Girls, really. Whatever is so amusing?"

"Nothing, Mama. I was just showing Delia a humorous passage in my novel."

"What sort of novel?" Frances asked, setting aside her needlework.

Delia tried her best to help with the subterfuge, pointing at the book. "You see, there's a girl, and she meets with a . . . a . . ."

"A pigeon," Charlotte supplied.

"A pigeon?" Frances asked.

A pigeon? Delia mouthed.

Charlotte gave her friend a yes-I-know-but-I-panicked look. "It wasn't an ordinary pigeon. It was a malicious, bloodthirsty pigeon," she went on. "A whole flock of them."

Frances blinked. "I've never heard anything so absurd."

"Precisely!" Delia declared. "So you can see why we found it so hilarious."

Charlotte had finally managed to contain her laughter. Then she made the mistake of looking at Delia, and they giggled all over again.

"I sometimes wonder if the two of you aren't spending too much time together." Sir Vernon studied them over his glass of port. "I won't have it said that I raised a foolish daughter."

Once everyone had settled back into reading or needlework, Delia whispered, "I suppose this isn't the time to ask about our Grand Tour after all."

"No," Charlotte agreed, and though she would never say it aloud, she mentally added: *Thank heaven.* "We may as well go up to our beds."

There was one other confession from this evening that she would not only keep to herself, but take to her grave:

Mama's "marital duties" lesson had come in useful after all.

Chapter Sixteen

When Piers opened the door of his bed-chamber later that evening, he'd scarcely shaken his arms free of his topcoat before he noticed a small, folded paper had been pushed under the door.

He hung his coat on a peg with one hand, unfolded the paper with the other, and read the single line of script:

I need to speak with you.

It wasn't signed, but he knew it could only be Charlotte. And if she'd risked this method of communication, the matter must be urgent.

Seeing that the corridor was empty, he wasted no time. He knocked lightly on the door of her chamber.

No answer.

He rapped again. "Charlotte."

Nothing.

He tried the door latch.

Locked.

He freed his stickpin from his cravat and inserted the sharp end in the lock. He was typically able to keep impatience and frustration at bay, but this time they slipped past his defenses. His fingers fumbled with the stickpin, and the damn thing clattered to the floor, rolling into a darkened crack between the floorboards. Curse it.

Piers stood back from the door. He wasn't about to get down on hands and knees to search for the pin, and he wasn't going to head off in search of another one, either. She ought to have heard him and opened the door by now, unless . . .

Unless there was something wrong.

He shifted his weight to his left leg and delivered a swift kick with his right, breaking the door latch and sending the door swinging inward on its hinges. Not the most surreptitious way of breaking into a room, but undeniably effective.

As usual, her chamber looked to have been ransacked. His mind told him the reason for the shambles was untidiness rather than life-and-death struggle—but his heart wasn't so easily convinced. His pulse accelerated as he searched the room.

"Charlotte?"

The carpet was littered with piles of discarded clothing. A pelisse and bonnet draped over a bedpost gave the look of a scarecrow. A hodgepodge of hairbrushes, ribbons, and tins of dusting powder covered the dressing table.

As he made his way to check the window, he tripped over a boot and went sprawling. Luckily, a heap of petticoats and chemises broke his fall. He struggled to regain his feet, a task which required disentangling himself from yards of sweetly scented linen. "Godforsaken son of a—"

"Piers?"

Charlotte stood in the doorway that led to her suite's small dressing room. She looked first at the broken door. Next, at the flouncy lace petticoat in his grasp.

And then, finally, her gaze met his.

"Piers, what on earth are you doing?"

Excellent question.

Going mad, perhaps. Losing the cool detachment and sharp instincts he'd amassed over the years, certainly.

He couldn't even enjoy the relief of seeing her in nothing but a thin, half-unbuttoned chemise, her unbound hair tumbling below her shoulders in thick waves.

"What am I doing?" He tossed aside the petticoat. "What the devil are you doing? You didn't answer the door."

"I didn't hear a knock." She nodded toward the attached dressing room. "The maids prepared me a bath."

"A bath."

"Yes. A bath. Water, soap, tub."

Well, that . . . was a perfectly reasonable explanation.

Damn it.

He pushed both hands through his hair, dislodging an errant stocking in the process. The garment slithered to the floor, and his last shred of dignity went with it.

Charlotte sealed her lips over a laugh.

"This isn't amusing," he said curtly.

"No," she said, with affected seriousness. "It isn't. To begin with, I don't know how I'm going to latch my door now."

He picked up her dressing table chair with one hand, carried it over to the door, and propped it under the broken latch. "Like so."

"Why were you rifling through my underthings?"

"I wasn't rifling through your underthings. I was being attacked by them."

She shrugged. "You know tidiness isn't one of my virtues."

"There's untidiness, and then there's . . ." He gestured at the room. ". . . a linen death trap."

"That's a bit melodramatic, don't you think?"

"No."

She pressed the heel of her hand to her mouth and smiled behind it.

For God's sake. This was all so amusing to her.

Piers tried to remind himself that she didn't understand. That he didn't want her to understand. If he was serious about his responsibilities, she—and anyone in his keeping—would never comprehend the vigilance that went into ensuring their safety.

If protection wasn't a thankless task, that meant he wasn't doing it right.

Nevertheless, he couldn't help lecturing her. "I like things in their places. That way, I'm ready to react. In a moment. In the dark. On any occasion. Especially an occasion when you declare that you need to speak with me."

"I didn't mean to alarm you. I hoped we could chat tomorrow. I had no idea you'd come straightaway."

"Of course I would come straightaway." He caught her gaze and held it. "If you tell me you need me, I would never delay."

"But you've been ignoring me for days. Ever since we . . ." She didn't complete the sentence. She didn't need to. "You've scarcely acknowledged my presence."

"Believe me. I've been aware of your presence."

Constantly, exquisitely, achingly aware.

He couldn't escape it. She'd begun recalibrating his senses the moment she came through that library door. His peripheral vision was now trained for flashes of golden hair; his ears, trained for her melodic laugh. He found himself following the drifting scent of her soap and dusting powder, like a dog panting after the butcher's wife.

He had years of experience and training. She'd unraveled them in a week, and he was left at loose ends. This distraction, this madness of desire and yearning—it was everything a man in his position needed to avoid.

On second thought, perhaps his senses hadn't been muddled. After all, they had been meticulously attuned to detect the slightest hint of peril.

This woman—this beautiful, unbiddable, all-too-perceptive woman—was his personal embodiment of danger. She could ruin him. Destroy everything he'd worked to become.

And she would do it all with a smile.

Charlotte didn't know what to make of the man standing in her bedchamber. He looked like Piers, and he spoke like Piers. But a darkness hovered about him. It was as though Piers's shadow had come to life, unstitched itself from the person of Lord Granville, and traveled down the corridor to pay her a call.

"May I ask you something?"

He spread his hands in invitation.

"Are you reconsidering the engagement?"

He paused, a bit too long for her comfort. "No."

"Then why have you ignored me so thoroughly?"

"You don't want a truthful answer to that question."

"Yes, I do. I really do."

She needed to know what was going on in his mind. Even if it hurt her pride.

He began to cross the room in slow, deliberate strides. "Because, Charlotte, it simply wouldn't do. Every time we share the same room, I think of nothing but touching you. Holding you. Tasting you."

He continued moving toward her.

Charlotte began to back away.

She wasn't intimidated. She was excited beyond measure, craved the hardness of his body pressed close to hers. Still, some instinct made her take steps in retreat.

When she saw the wild gleam in his eye, her body thrummed in response and she understood why. He wanted the chase. She wanted to be pursued.

"So I have to ignore you, you see," he continued in that low, devastating tone of aristocratic command. "If I were to look at you, I would want to strip you naked. If we conversed, I would need to hear you sigh and moan. That's not proper drawing room behavior."

He had her backed up against a wall now. Which was a fortunate thing, because her legs had gone weak.

"In fact, if I let myself come anywhere near you"—he caught her wrists and lifted them, pinning her arms to the wall—"I'd have your skirts tossed up to your ears and my cock buried inside you before the rest of them looked up from their tea."

Excitement pulsed through her veins. He had her at his mercy, but she didn't feel the slightest whisper of fear.

"And that," he said, staring hard at her mouth, "would be very bad manners."

"Well . . ." Charlotte wet her lips, daring to look up at him. "I've never been too concerned with etiquette."

His response was like lightning. In a flash, he'd pressed her against the wall with the full length of his body. Desire sparked along her nerve endings as he kissed her, making her tingle from crown to toes.

He overwhelmed her. All of her. His tongue explored her mouth. His chest rubbed against hers, drawing her nipples to tight, aching peaks. His arousal made firm demands against her belly.

He released her arms. His hands slid downward, to her hips. He grasped the frail linen of her shift in impatient handfuls, hiking it to her waist. Then he attacked the buttons of his trouser falls, loosing them one by one.

Charlotte reached between their bodies. She hadn't been brave enough to touch him there the other day, and she meant to make up for it now. She reached inside his trouser falls, freeing his hardening erection from the confining fabric.

Emboldened by his unsteady breath and the cloak of darkness, she took her time exploring. Stroking up and down the hot, steely thickness filling her hand, skimming her thumb over the broad, silky crown. A bead of moisture welled beneath her touch, and she spread it in widening circles.

With a muttered curse, he grasped her bared backside and lifted her straight off her feet.

Startled, she gave a little shriek of pleasure. Her spine met the damask silk-covered wall. She wrapped her legs over his hips. She wasn't certain if that was what he had in mind, but it seemed the thing to do.

He seemed to like it.

His erection swelled even larger in her grip, and he began to thrust against her. Slowly. Teasing.

Yes. Oh, yes.

She was reeling, stunned by the speed of her body's response. In a matter of mere moments, she'd grown desperate for him. She tangled her free hand in his hair, drawing his mouth to hers for a deep, openmouthed kiss.

He rocked his hips in a rhythm, rubbing the head

of his cock up and down the seam of her sex. Parting her with firm, insistent strokes. The smooth pressure teased her most sensitive places, driving her hard and fast up a steep mountain of bliss.

When he encountered the hot, wet evidence of her arousal, he groaned against her mouth.

She ached to be filled.

He broke their kiss, panting. "Now?"

The word skipped down her spine. "Now."

"Guide me in."

She tilted her hips and positioned his hard, eager length where it fit with her body. Where she needed it to be. Then she withdrew her hand from between them and clutched his shoulders.

He pushed into her in strong, incremental thrusts. "God," he moaned. "You're so tight."

She wasn't certain if he meant that as a good or a bad thing, but it was undeniably the truth. Despite her feverish arousal, her body was still painfully new to the act. Their joining was torturously, maddeningly slow, and then—when she began to vibrate with need, as though the tension would break her apart—blindingly fast.

He hadn't even seated his full length inside her when her crisis began to build. She couldn't wait any longer. She pushed her own hips forward, frantic for more of him, all of him. Deeper, harder, faster.

There.

When at last his pelvis met hers, the first brush of sweet friction flung her over the edge. She shook and cried out, clinging to his neck as he thrust unrelentingly, pushing her through crest after crest of pleasure.

He kissed her as she floated down from the peak. She locked her ankles together at the small of his back. They moved together in an easy rhythm.

She tugged his mussed cravat free of his neck, letting it fall to the floor before sliding her palms beneath the open collar of his shirt. She ran her hands over the taut, straining muscles of his shoulders and explored the sprinkling of dark hair on his chest. She kissed his neck, ran her tongue over his Adam's apple, nuzzled the light growth of whiskers on his jaw. Loving the taste of him, and all the masculine textures of muscle and scruff and sweat.

He froze, anchoring her to the wall, as deep inside her as he could possibly go. His chest was heaving.

Charlotte lifted her head, cupping his face in her hands so she could search out his gaze. "What is it?"

"I can't—"

She shifted her hips a fraction, and he groaned as he slid deeper still.

"I don't . . . I don't think I can . . ."

She wasn't sure how he meant to complete that sentence, but her answer would have been the same, regardless.

"Then don't," she told him.

His jaw tensed beneath her palm.

Then, with a firm flex of his arms, he shifted her weight. He bent his head, bracing his sweating brow against her shoulder and tugging her hips away from the wall. His thrusts doubled in speed and intensity, and his breath came in short, ragged gasps.

There was no finesse now, nothing remotely like tenderness. He wasn't patient or gentle any longer, just wanting. Taking. Using her body as roughly and crudely as he needed, relentless in pursuit of his own pleasure.

And she loved it.

She'd been desperate to see this side of him, raw and unrefined. The tendons of his neck and shoulders were rigid and taut. His thighs slapped against her bottom. He pulled at the sleeve of her chemise, ripping the neckline wide, and his teeth scraped against her bared shoulder.

His rhythm stuttered, then accelerated once again. He thrust faster, harder.

She would be sore tomorrow, perhaps even bruised. She couldn't have been more thrilled by the idea.

With a wrenching growl, he pulled free of her body. His seed spilled on her belly, gluing her body to his as they kissed and breathed and kissed again.

"That," he said, some moments later, "was tupping."

She hugged his neck and laughed a little, rocking him from side to side. He *had* promised her a demonstration, and he was a man of his word.

She slid down until her toes met the floor, then reached for his hand. "Come along, then. If we hurry, the bath will still be warm."

Chapter Seventeen

The tub was a tight fit, for two. They were forced to sit very close.

Piers had no complaint.

Charlotte nestled behind him, her slick breasts pressed against his back as she worked scented lather through his hair.

It felt glorious.

"It's just occurred to me that I completely forgot your note. You wanted to speak with me."

"Yes. I need to ask you a favor." Her fingertips massaged his scalp and temples, lulling him into a languid state of bliss. "It's rather a big favor, I'm afraid."

Anything. Everything. Just never stop touching me.

"Would you mind a long engagement?"

Anything but that.

"Yes, I'm afraid I would mind."

In part, because he'd had one long engagement, and it wasn't an experience he cared to repeat. Then there was the matter of starting on an heir. But mostly, he wanted to be with Charlotte. Have her all to himself, in his own home, as soon as possible and for a good many weeks thereafter. It wasn't a matter of tender emotion, just a straightforward calculation of benefits. Would he prefer a winter's worth of long, lonely nights spent at his desk? Or months of good, hard tups against the wall followed by sensual baths?

He would take the tupping and baths, please.

"I wouldn't ask if it was only for myself," she said. "I made a promise to Delia. We want to take a Grand Tour together next year. That's why I came for a visit. We were supposed to convince her parents to agree to the scheme."

He dashed the water from his face. "The two of you, traveling alone on the Continent? Her parents would never allow it. I wouldn't permit it, either."

"We'd hire a chaperone, of course."

"A doddering, useless one with cataracts, knowing you."

"Piers, you know I'm not stupid. I wouldn't take risks. Delia needs this. She's depending on me, and it would devastate us both if I let her down." She swabbed a sponge across his back. "She has a remarkable gift, and she deserves the chance to explore it. And as for me . . . I don't have a natural talent for art. Or music, or poetry, or mathematics, or anything, really. Certainly not housekeeping."

He smiled to himself.

"I thought mystery solving might be my chance to finally claim a true accomplishment. But that didn't work out, either. I need a chance to experience a bit more of the world before settling down. Expand my mind and see new horizons. I don't want to become a vapid, featherbrained woman like my mother."

He sighed. What she asked of him was impossible. Even if he'd wished to, he could not have agreed. Sir Vernon could be appointed to Australia by the end of the year. He wouldn't leave his daughter half a world behind.

"I can't deny there's another reason," she said. "It would dampen at least some of the gossip."

"You will be a marchioness. Why should you care what petty people say or think?"

"Perhaps I'm weak, I don't know. The past year of whispers has battered my pride. I'd like the gossips to know you didn't *have* to marry me." She was quiet for a moment. "I'd like to know that for myself, as well."

Good God. This was the woman who'd divined secrets Piers had never willingly divulged to anyone. She could read his left eyebrow as clear as a broadsheet. How could she still be questioning this?

She slid her arms around his waist, resting her chin on his shoulder. "You could plan the journey so we'd be safe. I know you could. You can arrange to be in a Nottinghamshire coaching inn on the exact day and hour in which your brother will pass through, just to check on him."

There it was. Another case in point. She was too perceptive by half.

"I don't know what you mean," he said.

"Yes, you do. I wouldn't be surprised if you arranged your entire holiday here for that luncheon. Rafe suspected it, as well." She dropped a kiss on his shoulder. "I only have sisters. Why men can't come out and say such things, I will never understand. But I hope *you* know that your brother understands how very much you love him."

His throat tightened.

He caressed her wrist, letting the touch speak where he could not.

He wouldn't know how to admit it, but her words came as a profound relief. He had always loved his brother, even when they hadn't been friends. And even though Rafe was a champion prizefighter—and the man who'd stolen his intended bride—Piers was fiercely protective of him.

His little brother was the only family he had left.

He slipped from her embrace and, through an ungainly process of twisting and rearranging limbs, eventually managed to face her.

He pulled her close, settling her so that she straddled his lap and rested against his bent legs. God, she was lovely. So clean, her skin could squeak. Her breasts bobbed just at the level of the soapy, cooling water. The steam had curled her fair hair in fetching ringlets. A bit of lather clung to her cheek.

He wiped it away with his thumb. "So. You can believe that I care for my brother."

"Oh, yes. Unquestionably."

"And yet you continue to doubt the sincerity of my offer to marry you."

"Well, that's different. We were forced into a betrothal. We scarcely knew each other. Propriety was the only reason for it."

He lifted an eyebrow. "Not the only reason."

"You know what I mean. Clearly we've always had a physical attraction, and you're undeniably an excellent catch."

"Yes, I seem to recall ranking in the top quartile."

She gave him a wicked look. "And I seem to recall that our bedsport would be tolerable."

"Touché."

"But all of that is beside the matter. You're not required by blood or history to care for me."

He propped his elbow on the edge of the tub and regarded her thoughtfully. "You're right, Charlotte. I'm not compelled to care for you at all."

Charlotte began to regret this turn of conversation.

The bathwater had begun to chill. She shivered and thought of reaching for a towel, but his blue gaze held her captive.

"Do you have any idea of how much influence I wield?" His fingertip tapped the edge of the tub. "How much money and manpower I have at my disposal?"

She shrugged. "I've formed some notion."

"You don't know a tenth of it."

He wasn't bragging, simply stating it as a fact.

She believed him.

"When we were discovered together, it was hardly a crisis. I could have dealt with that situation in any number of ways. I could have found you another willing suitor. Or a dozen of them, for you to take your choice. I could have quashed the entire scene, removed all possibility of scandal."

"You could have let me look like a desperate debutante and thrown me to the wolves."

"Or," he said evenly, "I could have hunted down the caricaturist at the *Prattler* who gave you that vile moniker . . . and made all trace of him disappear."

Charlotte started to laugh, and then she quickly realized he wasn't jesting.

No, his eyes were dead serious.

He was telling her something important, something close to the core of the man he believed himself to be. It was vital that she listen without laughter or judgment.

"But you didn't do any of those things," she said cautiously. "You took the honorable way."

"I took you." He reached for her, drawing her close and sending a wave of soapy water to the floor. "I took you, because I wanted you."

"In your bed."

"In my life."

She swallowed hard.

"There is little that's truly honorable in my line of work. You're going to be my wife. You deserve to know that much, although I pray you never fully understand it. Suffice it to say, I've spent the past ten years making cold decisions. And not looking back."

Her curiosity was intense, but she resisted the urge to press for details.

She had good friends who'd married officers who'd come home from battle. And that was what Piers was, at the heart of it—a man who'd shouldered terrible responsibility in a time of war. Men like him didn't need prying questions. They needed time—sometimes years of it—and warm baths and the closeness of skin on skin.

And friends. To listen, accept, understand.

She searched his face. Could it be that he'd reached out to her in his own emotionally stifled, autocratic way? That's what he seemed to be saying, if she read his expression correctly.

Yes, she thought. This must be the explanation.

A marquess could find any number of women eager to take his name or share his bed.

This marquess, however, had needed a friend.

Oh, Piers.

Her heart swelled with tenderness.

"Listen to me." His arms and legs wrapped around her. His heartbeat thumped against hers. "I chose you, Charlotte. And I'm not looking back."

He kissed her softly, letting his lips drift from the corner of her mouth, to her cheek, to her neck. And then lower, to her naked, slippery breasts. Beneath the water, his cock began to stir against her thigh.

She adjusted her hips, wedging his length tight against her cleft. The sudden contact drew a gasp from them both.

He flicked his tongue over her hardened nipple before drawing it into his mouth. As he suckled her, gooseflesh rippled over her neck and down her arms.

She rocked against the ridge of his arousal, dragging her body along his hardness, working that tight, pulsing bundle of nerves at the crest of her sex. He tangled and twisted one hand in her damp hair, arching her neck to cover it with kisses.

"You're lovely. So lovely."

He lifted her by the waist and nudged at her entrance, his brow furrowing with doubt. "You're not too tender?"

She shook her head.

He gritted his teeth as he sheathed himself in her depths. "You're certain?"

"Yes."

It was a harmless lie. She *was* tender—and raw, and vulnerable. Not only between her thighs, but in her heart.

If he hurt her, so be it.

She'd chosen this, too.

They moved together slowly, trying not to splash all the bathwater on the floor.

His brow pressed to hers. She could feel him swell even larger within her. His arms trapped her like a vise as he thrust.

With a groan, he lifted her off his cock and drew her hand between them, wrapping her fist around his thickness and closing his hand tight around her fist. He guided her hand in a swift flurry of strokes, pumping his release into her grip.

He slumped against her, and she caressed his shuddering back.

"Charlotte, darling?"

Darling. One more scrap of an endearment to add to her collection.

Her heart fluttered, stupidly. "Yes?"

"I think you've gravely miscounted your natural talents."

She pressed a smile to the crown of his head. Perhaps there was something unique to her after all. "Well, that's a comfort. I'd given up on being an accomplished woman, much less an exceptional one."

"You are anything but unexceptional."

"You needn't flatter me."

"I'm serious. How many hours have you spent humoring your mother? Or listening to your rock-mad sister, or staying indoors with the one who was ill? Think of all the years you lived in Spindle Cove when you would have rather been in London. Most would find that boring indeed. That's where you're exceptional. The art of people."

"You truly think so?"

"I know so. Because dealing with this particular person"—he pointed to himself—"requires a virtuoso."

She laughed.

"I'm not joking. I haven't met the woman who could do it yet."

"You're lucky I came and found you then."

His praise settled around her like bathwater,

soothing and warm. Quite different from the stiff, shiny fabric of compliments.

It wasn't as though she suddenly believed in herself because Piers pronounced her worthy. But he'd reasoned his case well, and she'd come to trust his powers of observation—especially when they agreed with her own.

He hadn't *made* her feel exceptional. They'd arrived at the conclusion together. And that was something altogether different.

It was, she decided, exactly what she'd been hoping for in a partner—what she couldn't have known how to put into words, but had been willing to wait years and years to find.

Which meant she was lucky to have found him, too.

Perhaps she was even fortunate to have a meddling, scheming mother.

No.

No, that was going too far.

Then an idea—a spectacular, perfect idea—blazed through her mind like a comet and struck a fire in her chest.

She sat back and looked at him. "Let me be your partner."

"I thought that much was already agreed."

"No, not only your wife. Your partner in"—she

gestured vaguely—"your work. We'd have so much fun together."

He scrubbed a hand over his face, then slicked back his wet hair. "No. Out of the question."

"I could make a brilliant spy. Think about it. I love a good puzzle. I can gain people's trust. I know my way around weaponry. I'm clever and daring. I . . . I can sneak through windows."

He chuckled a bit. "It's not like you're imagining. You'd find it dull. Espionage is mostly reading paperwork and writing reports and listening to mind-numbing conversations at parties. It's nine-tenths pure boredom."

"Everything worth doing is nine-tenths pure boredom. Think of your brother the prizefighter. I'd wager he spends weeks and months of preparation for just one hour in the ring. Or my sister the geologist. She'll sift through mountains of dirt to find one ugly little fossil. Even Delia makes dozens of sketches before she even begins to paint." She paused. "No pursuit ever called to me that way before. But this could be it. My true talent. My passion."

He only shook his head.

"Can't you see what ideal partners we'd make? We fill one another's shortcomings so perfectly." She reached for his hands and squeezed them. "Send me to the Continent with Delia. While she's sketching,

I can work on my languages. Practice my etiquette. I . . . I'll even learn to hang things on pegs."

"Charlotte . . . it would be much too dangerous."

"Hanging things on pegs?"

"Working with me."

"But you just told me it's all boring paperwork and parties."

"It is. Except for the times when it isn't." He stood up, stepped out of the tub and reached for a towel.

She took a moment to admire his hard, masculine body, glowing like bronze in the flickering candlelight. The lean muscles of his shoulders and back. The dark hair on his forearms and calves. His male organs, resting sated in their nest of shadow. He shook his hair, spraying droplets about the room, then scrubbed the towel over his face and dried the spots behind his ears.

The whole ritual was intimate and normal. Rather endearing, as well.

He was only a man, after all. A strong, powerful, complicated man—but human, just the same. Made of skin and bone and sinew and heart.

There was love in him somewhere, tightly bottled and waiting, like a rare vintage of wine. It might take her months or even years, but Charlotte was determined to search the man to the deepest, darkest cellars of his soul—and pull the cork.

He slung the towel over his shoulder and offered her his hand. "Take care. The floor is slick."

Once she was out, he snapped open another towel and wrapped it about her like a cabbage leaf, tucking in the ends securely. He was treating her like a swaddled babe.

"You don't believe I could do it," she said.

"I didn't say that."

You don't have to.

She was wounded by his lack of confidence, but she couldn't blame him for doubting. What did she have to recommend herself? A habit of laughing at inappropriate moments and a few not-quite-solved mysteries in her pocket?

"Please," she said, looking up at him through her wet eyelashes. "Give me a chance to prove myself. Just don't make any decisions tonight."

He exhaled heavily. "Too late. I've already made a decision."

"Oh?" She cringed. "What is it?"

"This."

He plucked her off her feet, slung her over his shoulder like a bundled sheaf of mowed wheat, and carried her to the bed.

Chapter Eighteen

Charlotte woke alone in her bed, sunlight streaming through the windows. It had to be mid-morning, at least.

She had no recollection of dressing herself in a night rail, much less being tucked securely beneath her coverlet. But then, she did always sleep like a stone. Piers must have been unwilling to disturb her.

Piers.

Piers, Piers, Piers.

Her bearings sorted, she fell back against her pillow and pressed both hands to her heart.

Last night hadn't been a mere moment of weakness in a meadow. It had been a revelation. She'd glimpsed new facets of Piers, and of herself, as well. A whole world of possibilities had opened.

This was real.

She was in love. She had a lover.

A good one.

Her body ached all over. She was tenderest between her legs, but there were other hurts, as well. Her nipples throbbed from being suckled. Her inner thighs were chafed just the slightest bit raw from his whiskers.

Little echoes of pleasure pulsed between her legs.

She squeezed her thighs together.

"Charlotte," she said aloud. "Whatever would your mother say?"

As she lay motionless, a wide grin spread from one cheek to the other. Unable to contain it, she rolled over onto her belly and buried her shriek of delight in the pillow, kicking her toes against the mattress.

Then she stopped abruptly as the door opened, going limp and playing asleep. Just in time, or so Charlotte hoped. She'd probably looked as though she were having a fit.

"Beggin' pardon, Miss Highwood. Your breakfast tray."

Charlotte muttered a sleepy-sounding thanks and peeked just long enough to see the maid leaving the room.

Then she threw back the bedclothes and reached for her dressing gown.

The smell of buttered toast and hot chocolate

was as irresistible as a certain man's kisses. She was famished.

Piers must have sent this up. Charlotte normally took breakfast downstairs with the Parkhurst ladies. But he would have known she'd be exhausted this morning, and hungry, as well.

Such caring. Such attention to detail.

As she slid one arm through her dressing gown, she noticed a sprig of green and violet laid across the corner of the tray.

A flower?

Perhaps the man had true romance in him after all.

Smiling to herself, she plucked the purple blossom from the tray and twirled it between her fingers. She peered at it. At first glance, she'd thought it to be one of the Michaelmas daisies cropping up everywhere this time of year. But it wasn't a common aster. Some sort of iris, or orchid perhaps? A gardener, Charlotte was not.

She set it aside with a shrug.

Whatever it was, it was pretty and most thoughtful. But the surest way to her heart was through her stomach, and the heap of perfectly browned toast on a plate might as well have been gold.

She tied her dressing gown sash in a knot, preparing to sit down and feast. But her fingers fumbled with the knot. How strange. Her right hand didn't want to work properly. A pins and needles feeling spread from her fingers to her wrist.

She shook it out, assuming she must have slept on her trapped arm.

But the shaking didn't help. Instead of fading, the tingling sensation increased. By now it had spread up her wrist to her elbow.

Stranger still, she couldn't feel her fingers at all.

Her heart began to pound in the queerest way. A flurry of rapid beats, then none at all. Then off it went galloping again.

How vexing. She had inherited Mama's flutterings, after all.

She ought to lie down, she supposed.

But as she turned toward the bed, her vision grayed and blurred at the edges. As if life were suddenly an engraved newspaper vignette.

This was more than a "fluttering." Something was wrong.

Piers would know what was wrong.

"Piers."

The word stuck on her drying lips. She tried again. "Piers?"

Not loud enough. Drat.

Her knees wavered. She grabbed the chair with her left hand, clinging to it. Her right arm was nothing but three feet of dead weight dangling from her shoulder.

She had to get out of this room.

Charlotte knew she was going to collapse, and she couldn't be alone when it happened.

Her heart thundered in her ears as she stumbled toward the door of her bedchamber. She watched her own left hand grappling with the broken door latch, as though it belonged to someone else.

Charlotte, concentrate.

At last, her fingers obeyed. They closed on the door latch and pulled the door inward a foot—two at most.

Just wide enough for Charlotte to collapse through it and faint into the corridor.

Thud.

At Sir Vernon's invitation, Piers settled down to tea and light refreshments in the library.

"I appreciate your time, Sir Vernon. This morning was most instructive."

They'd just completed a tour of the farmland under the guise of discussing irrigation methods. So far as Piers could see, nothing looked amiss. No signs that the man was economizing or selling off possessions, or making any outlandish purchases. Overall, Parkhurst Manor seemed to be an estate in remarkably good financial health—almost as thriving as his own.

In over a week, Sir Vernon hadn't suggested cards or dice, or anything more high-stakes than "poorest catch buys pints of cider at the pub." A gaming habit seemed unlikely.

So where was the money going?

To a long-ago mistress, or a bastard child. There were no plausible alternatives remaining.

But he needed access to the man's private correspondence and accounts to confirm the truth. What with all the distractions, he hadn't found another opportunity to search.

Be honest with yourself, Piers.

The truth was, he could have found opportunities to search. But he'd been making opportunities to spend time with Charlotte instead.

And then he'd made Charlotte his own.

"Don't you think?"

Piers raised his eyebrow and his teacup in a diplomatic, noncommittal gesture that would hopefully be taken as . . . whatever response he ought to have made, had he been paying attention.

He thought of Charlotte looking as he'd left her, sleeping in her own bed just as the first rays of dawn touched the horizon. Snoring faintly, in an adorably unabashed way.

Was it any wonder he couldn't concentrate this morning?

Every moment that crawled past was a moment

he wanted to be with her. Holding her. Inside her, pushing her toward another sweetly voiced crisis of pleasure. Talking and laughing with her afterward.

"Ahem." The butler appeared in the doorway. "Forgive the interruption, sir. Lady Parkhurst has a matter that requires your attention."

"Does she?" Sir Vernon shrugged. "You don't mind, do you, Granville? A matter of household management or menus, most likely, but we must keep the ladies happy."

"Indeed."

This was the opportunity Piers had been waiting for.

Once alone, he could search the man's desk, finish the business he'd come here to complete. Then he could announce his engagement to Charlotte and leave.

He moved to the desk.

Thud.

The noise gave him pause.

Probably nothing. Definitely nothing. A servant dropped something upstairs, that was all.

And yet even as he closed one drawer and noiselessly rifled through the second, his mind couldn't let it rest.

He didn't like the silence that followed that thud.

If an object was dropped, it ought to be picked up. Unless Charlotte was the one who'd dropped the object, in which case said object might remain on the floor for a year or more.

And with that, his mind was with Charlotte again.

He smiled a bit to himself, and before he even knew what he was doing, his eye had wandered to the window seat.

This was useless. He couldn't get her out of his mind. He couldn't be easy about that silence. And if he wasn't concentrating on the task at hand, he should wait for another opportunity. In his distraction, he would make a mistake.

He closed the drawer and left the library, turning to climb the stairs.

What he found in the corridor scared him bloodless. Here was the source of the thud.

Charlotte.

He dashed to her side.

"Charlotte." He gave her arm a gentle shake. "Charlotte. Are you well?"

No reply.

No response whatsoever. She was motionless.

As he turned and lifted her, her head lolled backward. Her lips had a bluish tinge.

A sick feeling rose in his gut.

"No." He shook her roughly, to no avail. "No, no, no."

This couldn't happen. Not this time. She would not be taken from him.

He pried open her eyelid to check her gaze, then turned his cheek to her pale lips.

She was breathing, at least. And when he pressed a hand to her throat, he found her heart to be beating—rapidly.

Maybe it wasn't too late.

Charlotte, Charlotte. Who did this to you?

"Ridley!" he called, suddenly hoarse. "Miss Highwood is ill."

Ridley joined him on the floor. "Shall I help you move her to the bed?"

"Don't touch her. No one else touches her."

He would be the only one to move her, to hold her. To gather her in his arms and carry her back to her bed. To smooth the hair from her mottled, feverish cheek.

"Find Sir Vernon," Piers said, barely restraining the edge in his voice. "Tell him to send for a doctor."

Ridley nodded. "At once, my lord."

Piers whipped the cravat from his neck and doused it with water from the washstand. Then he returned to her bedside and swabbed the cool cloth over her head and neck.

She stirred, and his heart leapt with hope.

"Stay with me, Charlotte."

He could almost hear her teasing him in return. *I don't like being told what to do.*

Wake, then. Wake up and tell me so.

If he needed to irritate her back to life, he would do it.

"Charlotte, stay with me. Do you hear? You can't leave me. I forbid it."

He held her, counting each of her shallow, precious breaths. When he dared glance away, he took a look about the room. Her breakfast tray sat on the table. It looked untouched, with the chocolate pot still steaming and the plate decorated with . . .

With a sprig of sinister greenery.

He knew it at once. Monkshood. One of the deadliest of nightshades. It didn't even need to be ingested. Mere contact on skin could prove fatal.

Charlotte hadn't merely fallen ill.

She'd been poisoned.

"Which hand?" he demanded. "Charlotte, you must wake. Tell me which hand you touched it with."

Her lashes fluttered, and she looked toward her right arm.

Piers turned her hand palm-side up. Christ. Her flesh still bore faint scrapes from where she'd clutched the reins on her wild ride the other day. An open door, and the poison had entered through it.

He reached for the ewer on her washstand and slowly poured the remaining contents over her right forearm, letting the water run down her palm, all the way to her fingertips before spilling onto the floor.

"Ridley!" he shouted.

Ridley appeared in the doorway, out of breath from his jog down and up the stairs. "The physician's been sent for."

"We can't wait that long. It's monkshood. Fetch the razor and basin from my washstand. I must bleed her to draw out the poison."

"Yes, my lord."

Piers tied his cravat about her upper right arm, cinching it firmly to serve as a tourniquet. She gave a faint moan of pain as he drew the knot tight. He ignored it. From this point forward, there was no time for emotion, no room for doubt.

His first objective was ensuring that Charlotte would live.

His second was learning who'd done this, and making him pay.

Chapter Nineteen

*S*he drifted in and out of consciousness for days, it seemed.

No matter when she woke, full daylight or dark of night, Mama was beside her, without fail. Pressing damp cloths to her brow or spooning her sips of beef tea.

When she felt well enough to sit up, her mother helped her wash and change into a fresh chemise. Mama sat behind her on the bed to brush and plait her hair.

"Thank you, Mama. You really needn't do all these things for me. I could call in a maid."

"Pish," she said. "I'm still your mother, even though you're grown. And mothers never fall out of practice."

"I have the vaguest memory of being ill as a child. I must have been two. Or even three . . . ?"

"Three. You had scarlet fever. Minerva, as well."

"Really? I don't recall being feverish. All I remember is that I was irritated at being kept indoors for so long afterward, and that you let me sip lemon and honey from a twisted handkerchief. Though I suppose you must have been worried."

She harrumphed. "My nerves have never been the same. Imagine it. I was recently widowed. We'd been cast out of our home when your father's cousin inherited, allotted only a paltry income. I was alone for the first time in my life, with three young daughters to raise, and two of you burning up with fever."

"What about Diana?"

"I had to send her away to the curate's wife. We didn't see her for a month." She paused. "Or was it two months? I remember she was still away on my twenty-fifth birthday."

"Lord." Charlotte knew Mama had been widowed young, but she'd never stopped to think about what that meant in such practical terms.

Her mother tugged on her hair. "Language."

"Sorry. I just can't imagine how you made it through."

"The same way every woman does, Charlotte. We aren't given the power or bodily strength that men have. We have to draw on the store of it within ourselves."

She divided Charlotte's hair into sections and

began to weave it into a tight plait. "Once all three of you were healthy and under one roof, I vowed that you would never find yourselves in such straits. You would marry well, to men who could offer you true security. I never wanted you to spend sleepless nights fretting over the butcher accounts."

Charlotte felt small for ever complaining about Mama's matchmaking attempts. No question, those attempts were ridiculous and mortifying—but hardship had a way of shaping people, the way boulders and wind could twist a growing tree.

Besides, she was fortunate to have a mother at all. So many children grew up without them. Piers, for one, and the poor man was the worse for it—walled off from the world, a stranger to his own emotions. At least Charlotte had always known she was loved.

She reached under her pillow and found her little bit of stitched flannel, rubbing its softness between her fingertips. "Why didn't you remarry?"

"I thought about it," Mama said. "And I did have offers. But I couldn't reconcile myself to the notion for many years, and by then it was too late. I'd lost my youth."

"You must have loved Father very much."

Mama didn't reply. She tied off the plait with a ribbon and came around the bed to sit beside her. Her blue eyes were moist as she searched Charlotte's face.

"Oh, Charlotte." She sighed.

A lump formed in her throat. "Yes, Mama?"

"You look like death. For goodness' sake, put some color into your complexion." She seized Charlotte's cheeks with her thumbs and forefingers, squeezing them hard.

"Mama!" Charlotte tried to wriggle away from her pinches. "Ouch."

"Oh, hush. When Lord Granville looks in on you, we don't want him to find you a disheveled horror. He might break off the engagement."

The mention of Piers made her heart twinge. She would endure a thousand pinches if it meant she could see him and be held by him again.

"Lord Granville wouldn't break off the engagement." She'd given him ample opportunity, and he'd refused.

I chose you, Charlotte. I'm not looking back.

"You *say* he won't, but don't grow complacent. You are a lively girl and tolerably bright, but your looks are your best advantage."

Charlotte fell back against the pillows. It was hopeless.

"Mama, I do love you." She said it aloud to remind herself, as much as anything. "Even though you are absurd and embarrassing, and you drive me utterly mad."

"And I, you. Despite the fact that you are ungrateful and headstrong, and have no respect whatsoever for my nerves. I suppose you want Delia to come up and read to you."

"No. Not right now. I want to see Piers."

"Lord Granville isn't here."

She sat back up. "He isn't here? Where did he go? And if he's not in the house, why on earth did you subject my cheeks to medieval torture?"

Mama shrugged. "He had some business to attend to. Great men often do, Charlotte. I know he is not quite a duke, but you must accustom yourself to the idea that your husband-to-be is an important man."

She sent up a prayer for patience. "Do you happen to know when my important husband-to-be will be returning?"

"I overhead him telling Sir Vernon that he expects to return tonight, but that it may be quite late. Just as well. By tomorrow, you'll be recovered enough to get out of bed."

This couldn't wait until tomorrow. She needed to see Piers. She had a memory of his arms about her in the corridor, and his grim face as he'd worked to find the cause.

She touched the bandaged incision on her arm. The last time he'd seen her, she'd been unconscious and weak. That was hardly the impression she'd hoped to create, when she vowed to convince him she could make a competent partner.

She'd begged for a chance to prove herself, and then she hadn't even made it through breakfast. At this point, she would be lucky if he trusted her to pour a cup of tea.

Piers pounded down the rutted dirt road like the Devil was breathing down his neck.

At times like these, he envied his brother. Prizefighting seemed the ideal career for beating back one's demons. When Rafe wanted to hit something—or someone—he didn't need an excuse.

Piers didn't have that luxury. The violence in his line of work was sporadic, at best.

Tonight, the best he could do was push his horse into a gallop as he turned down the drive, and hope the rush of cooling wind shook loose some of his rage.

He was angry with Sir Vernon and this genteel madhouse he seemed to be running. Furious with whoever had poisoned Charlotte. But most of all, he was livid with himself.

He dismounted his horse and handed the reins to a groom before striding through the doors of Parkhurst Manor. He didn't look for his host or make any effort at polite greetings, but blazed a path straight up the stairs.

He was tempted to head down the corridor to see

Charlotte, but he resisted the urge. He'd failed to protect her from being poisoned. The least he could do was leave her to her rest.

Once he'd conferred with Ridley and been assured of her continued recovery, Piers retired to his bedchamber and turned the key in the lock. He stripped off his waistcoat and pulled off his boots. His cravat unknotted, he cast it aside before yanking the hem of his shirt from his breeches and lifting it over his head. Then he went to the washstand and filled the basin, scrubbing himself clean and splashing water over his face.

"Are you going to leave this on the floor?"

He lifted his head and turned.

Charlotte was leaning on this side of his locked bedchamber door, dangling his cravat from one hand. A sly smile curved her lips. She looked like the beautiful assistant in a conjurer's act, poised for wild applause.

Voilà!

He wiped his face with a towel and stared at her in disbelief. "How did you . . ."

From behind her back, she produced a hairpin. "I've been practicing. You were right, it's not very difficult once you have the trick of it down."

"You should be resting."

"I've been resting for two days. I feel fine." She let his cravat slither to the floor and approached him, running her hands over his bared chest. "And I'm improving by the moment."

He closed his eyes, trying to shield himself from the temptation of her body wrapped in a silky dressing gown, with that thick braid of golden hair just grazing her breast.

But his attempt at distance failed. With his eyes closed, the intimacy of the moment only multiplied. He found himself reaching for her, lost in the pleasure of her soft touch. Her fingertips wandered over his bare skin, tracing the contours of his collarbones and tracing the furrow of hair that bisected his chest.

And then, when he couldn't have survived a moment longer without them, her lips touched his.

God, what this woman did to him. His lungs were emptied of breath. His heart pounded like mad.

Damn it, his knees almost buckled.

Buckling knees were a fiction of novels and penny dramas. It wasn't supposed to happen in real life, but here he was, weak with yearning.

His hands found her waist. Or perhaps her waist found his hands. It didn't matter. She wasn't getting away. He made fists in the silky, slippery fabric, tugging her close as he deepened the kiss.

How easy it would be, to carry her to his bed and lose himself in her sweetness.

She was fragile. But he could be gentle.

Perhaps. Somewhat.

Then she laced her arms around his neck, and he felt a light scrape. The bandage encircling her forearm.

It jolted him back to his senses.

His eyes snapped open, and he pulled her hands from his neck.

He couldn't allow this to happen. Not again. He could not let desire and emotion cloud his thinking. Not when her safety depended on his instincts remaining sharp.

"Who brought that breakfast tray to your room?" he asked.

She blinked, looking disoriented by his sudden change of subject. "What?"

"The breakfast tray with the monkshood." He led her to a chair so she could sit down, then sat on the footstool across from her. He propped his elbows on his knees and laced his fingers together. "Who brought it to your room?"

"A maid."

"Which maid?"

She shook her head. "I don't know. I barely saw her. She had ginger hair."

"None of the maids have ginger hair."

"Perhaps I was mistaken, then."

Piers doubted it. Memories weren't perfect things. They always had holes. But ginger hair wasn't the sort of detail someone's imagination tended to fill in the gap.

"Why don't you just ask?" she said.

"We have asked. Every member of the staff denied knowing anything about it."

"Well, naturally they would deny it. They're probably afraid of being sacked. Lady Parkhurst collects unusual plants. I'm certain it was only an honest mistake."

"Deadly monkshood does not end up on a breakfast tray by mistake."

She smiled a little. "Not in your line of work, perhaps. But this isn't a scene of international intrigue. It's a house party in the country."

"Don't be naïve," he said, his tone a bit more biting than he meant it to be. "You've been asking questions, pursuing your little investigation. Perhaps you've stumbled too close to a secret someone would do anything to hide."

"Piers, really. You must stop seeing conspiracies where there are none to find." She touched his brow, as though trying to iron the creases straight. "This is just another illustration of the differences between us. I'm an optimist. You always think the worst. I keep everything jumbled out in the open; you file it all neatly away. I see the glass half full. You see it riddled with poison."

"You would, too, if you were in my line of work.

Which is precisely why I'll never allow you to be in my line of work."

"You said you'd consider it."

He had considered it.

Despite his better judgment, he'd been intrigued by the idea of bringing her into the service. She wouldn't be skulking along any ledges or smuggling documents, of course. But Charlotte was perceptive and quickly gained people's confidence. He could see the two of them returning home at the end of a ball or dinner party to sort through their observations, share any bits of gossip or overheard words.

And then, make passionate love.

But when she collapsed in the corridor, all his plans had changed. Everything had changed.

"I can do it, Piers. I already have the temperament. When I return from traveling, I'll be more worldly, more polished. A capable partner to you, and able to fend for myself."

"I will do the fending. And you're not traveling anywhere."

Her gaze was wounded. "You promised to give me a chance to prove myself."

"That was before you nearly died in my arms. When I found you there, on the floor . . ."

He swore, more blasphemously than he'd ever cursed in the company of a lady.

"I know." She moved to the edge of the chair,

curling her hands over his trembling fingers and squeezing tight. "I know you were frightened."

No, she didn't know.

She could have no idea how deeply that sight had shaken him, and she never would. That secret—that crushing weight of shame—was his alone to carry. He'd borne up under it for decades, and he would shoulder it for decades more.

"I need to say something." She clung to his hands, though her gaze slanted to the carpet. "I've been wanting to tell you. Not that it will come as a surprise. You're certainly intelligent enough to have guessed by now. I mean . . . the meadow . . . you likely concluded it on your own."

He regarded her, perplexed.

"It's not something you'll be happy to hear, I'm afraid. You'll want argue against it, but it won't do any good. You're not the only one who can make an irreversible decision, and you know how I only dig in my heels when someone attempts to dissuade me."

Dear God. She wanted to leave him. He'd been a stupid braggart the other night, boasting of all the alternative ways he might have solved their little predicament. Now she was going to call him on it, ask to be released from the engagement.

And what was worse—he knew what his response should be. He ought to be decent enough to let her go.

But Piers would be damned if he'd do that now.

"Oliveview," she blurted out.

He blinked at her. "What?"

What the devil was Oliveview? A village? A person? An estate? Someplace she wanted to go on holiday?

"Goodness," she said, after a few silent moments. "I knew you were opposed to the notion, but I expected a bit more reaction than this."

"Charlotte, you're going to have to explain this to me. I am utterly lost. Where—or what—is Oliveview?"

She looked to the ceiling and sighed. "Not 'Oliveview,' you silly man. I said I love you."

Chapter Twenty

Charlotte grew more and more anxious as she waited on his reaction.

For long, unbearable moments, he only stared at her.

Perhaps she needed to say it again.

She slid to the edge of her chair, leaning forward until her knees touched his. "Piers," she whispered. "I said that I, Charlotte . . . with this beating organ in my chest commonly called a heart . . . love you. Most dearly. Does that make more sense?"

"No." He shook his head numbly. "Not really."

Lord, this was going even worse than she'd imagined it could. She knew he wasn't well acquainted with the emotion—not when it came to romantic attachments, anyway. But surely he grasped the general concept.

Then again, perhaps he did understand.

His expression was something different than confused. He looked resistant. Defiant. Forbidding.

"You can't say that, Charlotte."

"Why not? Do you think it's too soon?"

"A hundred years from now would be too soon. There are too many things you don't know. Things you will never know."

"You don't think . . ." She paused, gathering the courage to ask the question. "Surely you don't believe the poisoning was your fault."

"Of course it was my fault. I should have been more cautious. It couldn't have happened if I hadn't—"

"No, no. Not me. Not *only* me, at any rate. I'm speaking of your mother, too."

His eyes narrowed in defense. "What does my mother have to do with this discussion?"

"Everything, I think. How could it not influence your reaction? You found me slumped in the corridor. It must have provoked painful memories for you. Was it laudanum that took her, or something else?"

"Who told you this?"

She looked at him. "You did."

"No." He released her hands and slid back. "I told you she perished after a long illness. I never said anything about how."

"Not in words, but it only makes sense. It's common knowledge that women with variable moods are dosed with such things to subdue them. You're not ruffled by anything, and yet you went into a cold sweat when I was slow to wake from a nap. When I was poisoned, you raised all the walls again."

"Walls. What walls?"

"The walls around your heart, Piers. You lost so much as a child. As a man, you committed yourself to a dangerous, sometimes brutal profession. I can only imagine how that would change a person. Harden him to emotion. Make him reluctant to let anyone close."

"You're being absurd." He rose to his feet, pacing away. "There are fleas that jump from dog to dog with greater difficulty than your mind leaps from one conclusion to the next."

"Oh, no. Don't think you can shut me out now." She chased after him, sliding around him to block his path. "I know how long it took you to let anyone this close. For pity's sake, it's been more than a year since Ellingworth died, and you haven't even gotten a new *dog*."

He looked away and exhaled a slow, angry breath. "I know what you want. I told you from the first, I'm not the man to give you those things."

"Then we're equal. Because Lord knows, there are

ladies better suited to loving you. But I seem to be the woman who does." She touched his chest. "You told me yourself, it's too late. I'm on your mind, under your skin, in your blood. I will not be kept out of your heart."

"You need to understand this. My life has no room for uncertainty, no margin for error. I have to keep a clear head, or people get hurt. You'll get hurt." His hand encircled her bandaged wrist. "Damn it, you already have."

"What if I told you I know the risks, and I'm willing to take my chances?"

"It wouldn't change a thing. Those walls, as you call them . . . They're part of me now, and they are iron strong." He lifted a hand to her face, skimming his thumb over her lower lip. "Even if I wished to, I wouldn't know how to dismantle them."

"I know," she said quietly. "I know." She wreathed her arms around his neck. "That's why you need me. I'm going to burn them to the ground."

He started to reply.

She didn't wait to hear it.

Instead, she tugged on his neck, pulling him within kissing distance, and captured his mouth with hers.

He resisted at first, but she offered him no quarter. It wasn't fair, perhaps, to use desire against him. But it was the one weapon she had. This was a siege meant to conquer his heart. Charlotte would take any advance she could.

She sipped at each of his lips in turn, softening their stern set. And then she slid her tongue into his mouth, probing deep.

Taking the lead was a new experience. She liked it. She liked it very well indeed.

With a helpless sigh, she swept her hands down his back, then ran bold touches over his bare shoulders and chest.

"You're perfect. So beautiful all over." She kissed his chest, just to the left of his sternum. "Beautiful inside, as well."

He growled in warning. "Charlotte . . ."

"Yes?" she asked, making her voice sweet and innocent. She stepped back, looked up at him, and then let her satin dressing gown slither to the floor. "You were saying?"

From the hungry way his gaze swept her nakedness, she knew she'd gained the upper hand. He'd surrender to her now.

She took a step back, then another.

He moved toward her, as though he were pulled by invisible strings that stretched from her nipples to his eyes.

When the backs of her thighs hit the mattress, she reclined on the bed. His gaze still pasted to her bared breasts, he followed, prowling up her body on hands and knees.

"Not this way. Not this time." She hooked a leg over his waist and rolled them both, flipping Piers onto his back. "It's my turn."

As she leaned forward to kiss his unshaven neck, he muttered a curse. She trailed her tongue along his collarbone and down the center of his chest. She gave his small, flat nipples playful bites.

Then she sat up, straddling his thighs. She lifted her breasts with her hands, shaping and plumping them for his view. She circled her nipples with her fingertips, teasing them to tight, rosy peaks.

He made a strangled sound in his throat. "You'll kill me."

She only smiled.

She laid a single fingertip to his lips, then drew it down his chin, then his neck, then his chest. Down, and down . . . Until she found the bulge tenting his breeches and cupped it in her hand.

She reached for the buttons of his falls. Her fingers didn't falter this time.

He sucked in his breath as she reached into his breeches, freeing his swollen staff from the buckskin. She stroked his hardness up and down, then reached lower to cradle and caress the soft, vulnerable sac beneath.

Gripping his length in one hand, she bent her head and drew her tongue across the tip of his cock.

His hips jerked, and he muttered something in a language she didn't recognize.

When she lifted her head, he was staring down at her. Holding eye contact, she lowered her head and licked him again, this time swirling her tongue around the head.

"Christ."

His blasphemy didn't deter her in the slightest. To the contrary, she felt a surge of power that bordered on divine.

She sat tall. He reached for her, but she caught his hands, lacing her fingers with his. Then she pushed his arms back against the bed, pinning them to the mattress. As she leaned forward to brace him there with her weight, her hair came loose from its plait and tumbled about them both.

She moved a few inches, feeling his hardness slide deliciously against her most sensitive places. Then she sank down on him, one inch at a time, until she'd taken him all the way to the root.

Setting a slow, smooth rhythm, she rolled her hips, taking his fullness inside her again and again. She kept his arms pinned to the bed and stared into his eyes.

"You feel so good inside me," she whispered. "So hard and so deep."

She loved it when he said carnal things to her. Perhaps hearing them from her lips would excite him, too.

It would seem she'd supposed correctly. He began to arch his back, pushing up to meet her with each stroke. Urging her faster. As they moved together, her unbound hair brushed her nipples and his cheeks.

"Can't hold back much longer." He gritted his teeth. "Come."

She smiled down at him. "You first."

She released his pinned arms, leaning her weight on her elbows and tangling her fingers in his hair. His hands went to her hips, seizing her flesh in desperate handfuls. He guided her up and down, pushing her to ride him faster, harder. His brow furrowed with effort, and he bared his teeth.

Through it all, their gazes locked and held. His blue eyes penetrated her even more deeply than his cock. Searching, pleading.

"I love you," she gasped, feeling him swell even larger within her. "Love you, love you, lov—"

He kissed her. He might have stolen her words, but not the emotion. No force on earth could hold back the tide welling in her heart, or the bliss gathering at her center.

At last, he let go. With a harsh, guttural cry, he thrust deep, holding her hips in place. She felt a series of frantic spasms as he found his release.

His crisis unleashed her own.

She closed her eyes. She couldn't help it. The joy, the desire, the relief, the love . . . They all swirled and collided within her. White light sparked behind her eyelids.

She saw stars.

When her breathing calmed, she looked down at him again—and was heartened to find him gazing up at her. She smoothed the damp hair back from his brow.

"That"—she pressed a kiss to his lips—"was making love."

He closed his eyes. "Charlotte . . ."

She shushed him. "It's all right. I know this is new to you, and probably a bit overwhelming. It's rather new and overwhelming to me, too. But I love you, and it's important that you know that. Because no matter how you control your emotions, you can't control mine. I know what's inside you, behind all those walls. I'll keep chipping away until I get at it. Even if it takes years. Decades. I know you'll be worth the effort." She rested against his chest, burying her face into the crook of his neck. "I'm never giving up on you."

His arms went around her, clutching her so close and tight she barely had room to breathe. Nevertheless, she felt safe in his embrace. His heartbeat pounded in her ear, steady and strong, lulling her into a trance.

Someday, Charlotte told herself, she must learn how to make love without falling asleep moments afterward.

That day wouldn't be today.

"Charlotte, wake."

Her eyes snapped open. She sat bolt upright in bed. The past two times he'd tried to wake her had been disastrous. She wasn't going to give him cause to worry again.

"There's smoke," he said. "We must hurry."

No sooner had he pulled her from the bed than footsteps pounded down the corridor. Someone was running through the house, pausing only long enough to thump on each door.

"Fire! Fire!"

While Piers checked the corridor to make certain it was safe, she located her dressing gown and tied it about her waist.

They emerged from the room to find the house in an uproar. People in nightshirts hurried past them in both directions. She couldn't see any flames. However, a cloud of acrid smoke obscured the corridor to the right, blocking the way to the main stairs.

"This way," he said, taking her by the wrist and heading left. "The servant stairs. You go ahead, and be quick about it. I'll follow with your mother."

Oh, no. *Mama.*

She looked toward the streaming black smoke. Her mother's bedchamber was down the corridor that way. Just across from Charlotte's own.

Between Mama's age, her diminished eyesight, and her nervous condition, she would never make it out unassisted.

She pulled her arm from his grip and started toward the right.

Piers held her back. "No. You go downstairs."

"I can't. Not without her."

"Go, *now.* I can carry her if need be, but I can't carry you both. You'll be in the way."

"But—"

But who will carry you, if you're overcome?

Before she could respond, he'd vanished into the smoky corridor. She stood numbly for a moment, staring after him. Then the wave of smoke began to curl about her shoulders, stinging her eyes.

Her body's will to survive tugged her in one direction. Her heart pulled at her from the other side.

"Charlotte?"

She swiveled in place, turning toward the voice.

Delia stood in the doorway of her own room, coughing.

Charlotte rushed to her friend's side, sliding an arm under her shoulder. "Lean on me. We'll take the servant stairs."

Together, they hastened toward the dark, narrow staircase and fumbled their way down the steps. Delia faltered on a warped riser, but Charlotte steadied her. Once they reached the bottom of the stairs, they turned and stumbled down a narrow corridor. They kept at best two steps ahead of the smoke, which pursued them like a malevolent demon.

When they finally plunged into the night, they gulped the fresh, cool air like water in the desert, then hurried to join a huddle of servants and family in the back garden.

"Delia!" Lady Parkhurst ran to embrace her daughter, drawing her away from Charlotte's side and toward the bench where Frances sat trembling.

Sir Vernon held a torch aloft as he shouted to the footmen and grooms, organizing a bucket brigade to deliver water from the pump to the fire's source. Even young Edmund was pressed into service, bringing leather buckets out from the stables.

Charlotte turned back to look at the house. It was so dark, and the footmen running in and out made it even more difficult to see. With every moment her wait stretched, her heart climbed further into her throat.

The two most important people in her world were caught in that hell of smoke and heat.

If she lost them . . .

The tension was unbearable. She couldn't stand there any longer. She ran back toward the servant entrance, weaving her way around the manservants. If Mama and Piers were in peril, she would help them—or die trying.

Just as she reached the doorway, Mama emerged in a flutter of lacy white nightgowns, her cap askew.

Charlotte ran to her and flung her arms around her mother's neck, overcome with relief. "Mama. Thank heaven." Once she'd drawn her mother away from the house, she asked, "Where's Piers?"

"He turned back to help the men extinguish the flames."

Of course he had. Always the hero.

Oh, Lord. Charlotte pressed her hands to her mouth, holding back a sob.

"Come." Mama put her arm about Charlotte's shoulders. Her voice was steady. "Come sit down with me."

"I can't. I need to help him."

"He's strong and more than capable. You will help him best by keeping yourself out of danger. And in the meantime, we'll pray."

Pray? Charlotte's thoughts couldn't be settled enough for anything but the most desperate, inarticulate petitions. They went something like this:

Please, please, please, please, please.

After a few minutes, she noticed the pace of the footmen carrying buckets had slowed. A man emerged from the building and conferred with Sir Vernon, and then Sir Vernon came to join their group.

Charlotte rose from her bench. Mama rose with her, holding her hand.

"The fire is extinguished," he announced, making a calming gesture. "The men are a bit singed, but no one has been grievously hurt."

Charlotte's internal babbling immediately changed. *Thank you, thank you, thank you, thank you.*

"The flames were contained to one room, fortunately. The entire wing will need a good airing out to clear the smoke, but no further damage was done."

"What caused the fire?" Charlotte asked.

"I was planning to ask you that question, Miss Highwood. The fire was in your bedchamber."

"What?"

"From the looks of things, the flames started on the floor, in a heap of piled garments near the hearth. Then it spread along the carpet to the drapes and bed hangings."

Oh, no. Did he mean to say this was all Charlotte's fault?

Lady Parkhurst turned to her. "Did you tip over a candle, Charlotte? Fail to bank the fire?"

"I . . . No, I don't believe so."

However, she *had* rifled through a great many things in a quest to find her most alluring dressing gown. Perhaps a stocking or shift had fallen too close to the grate.

Sir Vernon frowned. "You must have some notion. Surely you noticed the flames, or you wouldn't be here."

"Do let her be," Delia said. "She's suffered a shock. Obviously, she was fortunate to escape with her life."

"It wasn't good fortune." Frances's gaze sent daggers at Charlotte. "And she can't tell you how the blaze started, Papa. She wasn't in her room at all. She was in Lord Granville's bedchamber."

Everyone stared at her now. Charlotte didn't know where to look. She drew her dressing gown tight around her body, holding it closed at the neck. For the first time since she'd escaped the house, a chill went through her.

Delia, good friend that she was, leapt to her defense. "You must have been mistaken, Frances. The whole house was in an uproar."

"I saw them clearly," Frances said. "Leaving his room together. I'm not mistaken. Am I, Miss Highwood?"

Charlotte swallowed hard. There was no use denying it. "No."

The ensuing silence was painful.

"Charlotte?" Delia's expression was wounded. "I thought we had plans. You said you wanted nothing to do with him."

"We do have plans. That hasn't changed."

"But then why would you . . . ?"

"Murder!" Edmund shouted. "It's murder! He's been trying to murder her for weeks now. I heard it myself. *Eek, eek, eek.* And then *grrra*—"

Lady Parkhurst clapped a hand over her son's mouth.

"Muh-urr," he insisted, despite the muffling.

"I tried to warn you," Frances said to her sister. "Gossip is always at least partly true. You saw in the *Prattler* how she is, but you wouldn't believe it. Now you know the truth. She's been using you."

Charlotte turned to Delia. "It's not true. Don't believe her. We *are* friends. The best sort of friends."

"Friends are honest with each other. You lied to me."

"I never meant to. This all began as a misunderstanding. I was trying to mend it on my own, and then somehow . . ."

"I've been so stupid." Delia turned her gaze to the distance. "I should have seen it. The shopping excursion. Your mysterious absences. I came to your room the night you claimed a migraine, but you weren't there. You must have feigned that silly poisoning episode, too. Just like the blackberries and the Satan spit."

"No. Delia, please. I know how it must look, but give me a chance to explain."

It was no use. Delia had all her guards up. Perhaps she'd be willing to listen and forgive her in time, but it wasn't going to be tonight.

"Don't worry, Delia," Frances said smugly. "The *ton* will punish her well enough. I suppose we know what name the *Prattler* will be giving her next. It's all too easy, given what rhymes with Charlotte."

"Scarlet?" Lady Parkhurst asked.

"No, the other one."

Sir Vernon interjected, "She means varlet."

"*Varlet?*" Mama echoed. "What on earth is a varlet?"

"It's a medieval term for knave or rogue."

Frances sighed. "Really, Papa. No one's going to call her a varlet, either."

"Well, then what can you be suggesting?" Lady Parkhurst said. "There's marmot, I suppose. But that's not even a true rhyme."

Charlotte couldn't bear this inanity any longer. "Harlot!"

The word quelled all chatter.

"That's what Frances is saying. They will be calling me Charlotte the Harlot."

A large hand settled on the small of her back. Its owner announced in a deep, authoritative voice, "They will address her as Her Ladyship, the Marchioness of Granville. My wife."

Piers.

Charlotte wheeled around. There he was, still bare-chested. His torso was streaked with soot, and ashes dusted his wild hair. He smelled like a bonfire.

In her eyes, he'd never appeared more perfect.

She didn't care what anyone thought of her in that moment. Let Frances call her all sorts of vile names.

She threw her arms around his waist and hugged him close, holding her breath until she could hear the comforting, steady thump of his heartbeat.

"I was so afraid," she whispered.

He ran a hand up and down her spine, soothing her in a low murmur. "It's over, darling. All's well now."

Frances wasn't mollified. "Surely you're not truly going to marry her, my lord. Don't be duped into preserving the virtue of a woman who has none. She and her mother are conniving wretches with—"

"I beg your pardon, Miss Parkhurst," Mama cut in. "I might be conniving, but Charlotte? Never. No matter how I tried to encourage her, the stubborn girl never cooperated."

Sir Vernon gave his eldest daughter a stern look. "Frances, calm yourself."

"Calm myself? Can't you see what's happened here?" Frances gestured at Charlotte. "She's been trying to trap him from the start. Now he's leaving soon, and she grew desperate. She set that fire herself. Then she slipped down the corridor to Lord Granville's room, hoping to cause a scandal when the alarm went up. I tell you, Papa. She could have burned our home to the ground."

"That's enough," Piers commanded. "I remind you, Miss Parkhurst, you are speaking of my future wife. I will not hear her accused of trickery or loose morals, much less slandered with accusations of arson. Our betrothal was settled well before tonight. The license has been procured, the contracts are signed, and the announcement will appear in tomorrow's edition of *The Times*."

Charlotte looked up at him. "You published a betrothal announcement, this soon? Without consulting me?"

He didn't even look at her. "She will depart with me, and we will be married from my estate."

Charlotte couldn't even begin to understand how this had happened. He must have been very busy while she'd been asleep.

"Well," Lady Parkhurst said, making an obvious effort to strike a light tone. "What fortunate timing. We're already having the ball tomorrow. We can celebrate your happy news."

Delia looked at her, eyes brimming with hurt. "Forgive me if I don't attend. I wish you both joy."

She turned and started back to the house.

Charlotte left Piers's embrace to dash after her.

"Wait! Delia, wait. Please, let me explain. The things Frances said—they aren't true, I swear it. I wanted nothing more than to travel the Continent with you. I . . . I'm just so sorry."

"So am I," Delia said. "I'm going to walk away now. Do not chase after me."

"But—"

"Don't, Charlotte. It isn't fair. I'm too easy to catch. At least give me the dignity of a dramatic exit. You owe me that much."

Charlotte wanted to argue, but she knew it wouldn't help. So she nodded, reluctantly.

Then she watched her best friend walk away.

Chapter Twenty-one

*I*n the morning, Charlotte went upstairs to her bedchamber, to gather anything that might be saved. She stood in the middle of the room, looking around at the soot and ashes, and gave a small, mournful whimper.

It could have been worse, she told herself.

Thanks to the quick response of the men, the flames had been contained to the heap of belongings in front of the hearth and the hangings toward the foot of the bed. The soot and smoke would never be aired from her frocks or shawls, however.

"I'll buy you all new things."

She turned to see that Piers had quietly joined her.

"We can visit the shops today," he said.

"Some of my clothing was collected for washing

yesterday. My best gown had been sent down for pressing, too. I won't be completely without."

She set her valise on the charred dressing table and opened it. She went through the trays and drawers, keeping whatever could be salvaged.

"Nevertheless, I'm sure you're upset."

"Why should I be upset?" She turned a soot-streaked bracelet over in her hands. "It's not as though my life was decided while I slept, my best friend won't speak to me, and I nearly burned down a house." She eyed a burned, soggy pelisse on the floor. "Much as it pains me to admit you were right—perhaps I *had* created a death trap. I suppose I've learned my lesson now."

"We'll announce our engagement tonight, and depart immediately thereafter. I've made all the arrangements."

"Yes. I recall. A license and announcement and everything." She looked up at him. "What did you mean, the contracts are signed? I didn't sign any contracts."

"Your mother signed them."

"My mother?"

"You're not yet one-and-twenty. She's still your guardian."

She let the bracelet drop. "I can't believe you did that. Do I need to appear at the church and recite my vows, or have you seen to that, too?"

He took a step toward her. "Charlotte, you must understand."

"I'm trying. Perhaps you can explain why you intend to trust me with your homes and your children, but you couldn't trust me to sign my own betrothal contracts."

He spread his arms, gesturing at the destruction around them. "Look at this. I am removing you from this madhouse and taking you to my home. Where I will know you are safe."

"You are just as excitable as Edmund." She shook her head. "This fire was my fault. The monkshood was an accident. Delia closed my window that night. No one is trying to MUR-DER me."

"Perhaps they are, perhaps they aren't. Considering that achieving certainty on the matter would involve a chance of you ending up dead, I'm not interested in performing any experiments." His eyes flashed. "I'm not going to risk coming upon your lifeless form in the corridor."

Charlotte winced in regret. She ought to be more understanding, less churlish. It wasn't as though he'd planned it this way. She'd gone to his room. If not for the fire, they wouldn't have been caught together. He wouldn't have made a dramatic announcement in the garden.

Once again, she had no one to blame but herself.

"I'm sorry," she said. "I know you mean well, and

I don't wish to argue. The important thing is, we are all safe, and there was no irreparable damage." She only wished she could say the same for her friendship and reputation. "Everything in this room can be replaced."

Everything except . . .

"Oh, no. My bit of flannel." She rushed to the head of bed, pushed aside the singed, damp bed hangings and began tossing back the pillows and smoky quilts. "It should still be here somewhere. I keep it under my pillow at night."

But it wasn't there. She searched the bedding, but she couldn't find it.

"Where could it be? If the pillows weren't touched by the fire, how could it have burned?"

Piers came to her side and put his hands on her arms. "Don't worry. You're fatigued and overwrought. Go downstairs to rest, and I'll search for it."

"I'm not going to rest. I can't rest until I've found it."

She went to the chest and began opening the drawers to rifle through them. Had she put it away somewhere else? When that search yielded nothing, she rushed to the closet and thrust her hand into the pockets of her capes and cloaks.

Nothing.

The fatigue and fear of the night's ordeal began to catch up with her. She felt a weight of despair settling on her shoulders.

She would not cry, she told herself. Considering what could have happened last night, she was fortunate to have escaped with her health, and her mother's, and the Parkhursts', and Piers's. It was only a bit of fabric and ribbon.

"It's here."

She turned around. Piers was at the hearth, withdrawing her scrap of flannel from the wrought-iron tinderbox on the mantel.

"You are an angel." Charlotte ran to seize it, running her fingers over the familiar, comforting softness. She lifted it to her nose. It didn't even smell of smoke. "How did it get in the tinderbox, of all places?"

"Does it matter?"

"I suppose not." She clasped it to her breast. "I'm just glad it's undamaged. So strange, though. I know *I* wouldn't have placed it there, and yet that was the safest place for it to be. Almost as though someone knew that . . ."

Her voice trailed off. A knot twisted in her chest.

There was only one person who could have possessed both the ability to set a fire in Charlotte's bedchamber *and* the knowledge to secure her most prized possession first.

She looked up at Piers. "You set the fire. You did this."

* * *

Piers didn't attempt to deny it. She might as well know.

"You came here while I was asleep in your bed," she said, blinking as she looked about the room. "You heaped my belongings on the floor and set them afire."

"I was careful to contain it. It was all smolder, little flame. It never would have spread beyond this room."

"Why would you do such a thing?"

"You're a clever woman. You don't need me to tell you."

She stared at him. "You wanted us to be discovered. You knew I wanted a long engagement. And you decided to force my hand."

His silence served as his confession.

"You bastard." She flung her arm toward the window. "I stood in that garden last night, terrified. Not knowing if I'd ever see you alive again. I prayed to God for you."

"Then you wasted your time. In the future, you would do well to save your prayers for someone else."

"Why would you do this? Why lie to me?"

"Come now, Charlotte. I've been lying to you since the night we met."

"If you're referring to your career . . ."

"There's so much more than that." He walked

to the opposite side of the room, giving them both space. "The mystery tuppers, to begin. It was Parkhurst, that night in the library."

She frowned. "Lady Parkhurst? But . . . but I had clues. She doesn't fit them."

"Not Lady Parkhurst. Sir Vernon. He was the tupper. I'm still not certain of the tuppee."

"Sir Vernon? But it hardly seems like him. He's so traditional, and his only passion is sporting. He doesn't seem at all the sort of man to toss a mistress on the desk and . . . grunt on her."

"He's the reason I'm here. He's been bleeding money. Taking mysterious, unannounced trips from Town. A mistress or natural child was the most likely explanation, but I needed to rule out blackmail."

"So you've known this from the first. Even before you offered to marry me."

"I suspected it, yes."

"And Sir Vernon knew, too. The whole time. He let take us the penalty for *his* indiscretion."

"That's the way secrets work. People will do anything to hide the truth. I should never have indulged your attempts at an investigation. But I never imagined you'd—"

"Be any good at it?"

He shrugged. "I underestimated you. I freely admit that much."

She turned away. "I can't believe this. I've been skulking along window ledges, riding demon horses from Hell, risking everything to mend my reputation in Sir Vernon's eyes so I could travel the Continent with Delia. And now you tell me that Sir Vernon was the culprit, and I did it all for nothing?" Her voice was edged with anger. "This wasn't a game to me, Piers."

"It wasn't a game to me, either. Looking into Sir Vernon's indiscretions was my duty to the Crown. The man's going to be given a sensitive post overseas."

"Where overseas?"

"Australia."

She put a hand to her brow. "Australia?"

"If there's any chance a man in his position could be blackmailed, England's interests would be at risk. Lives could hang in the balance."

"And so you decided to sacrifice mine."

"That's a bit overdramatic, Charlotte."

"Not by much. Last night cost me a friendship and any shred of respect I might have regained. You betrayed me. I can't believe you would do such a thing."

"Can you not? How do you think a diplomat convinces despots to surrender territories? How does he force invading armies to retreat?"

She dropped her gaze to the scorched carpet. "By leaving them no other choice."

"Got it in one," he said. "I did what was necessary to protect you."

"Oh, please. You were protecting yourself. You can't tell me that what we shared"—she gestured at the wall, the bed, the bath—"was all in the line of duty. It's grown too real for you, too intense. Too close to your heart. I told you I loved you, and it scared you to death."

"You don't love me. You don't know me. If you think this comes close to the worst I've done, you have no idea. You've been telling yourself a pretty little story. That I'm an honorable man at my core. I've been trying to warn you—crack me open, and you'll find darkness inside."

"I refuse to believe that. I know there's love in you."

He moved toward her. "I have trespassed and stolen. I have traded secrets and brokered exchanges that caused blameless people to be killed. I have spilled blood with my own hands, and I have left battered men to die alone."

"England was at war," she said. "Good men had to do unspeakable things."

For God's sake. Piers rubbed his face. "It wasn't the war, Charlotte. It's who I am. I have deceived every person in my life since I was seven years old."

"Well, that's hardly evidence. Who *doesn't* tell lies at seven years old?"

"Not this kind of lie. I concealed the truth of my mother's death. From everyone. For decades."

Her brow furrowed. "So it wasn't too much laudanum."

"Oh, it was too much laudanum. And it wasn't an accident. She took her own life."

"But . . . you were a child. How could you know that?"

"Because I was there. I found her in her bed, just before she breathed her last. I heard her final words."

"Piers." She stepped toward him.

He stayed her with an outstretched hand. This was not a plea for pity. Quite the reverse.

"I couldn't let anyone know it was a suicide. Especially not my father. I was young, but I understood that much. He would have viewed it as a stain on the family legacy." He paused, looking into the distance. "So I hid the truth. The bottle had slipped from her hand, shattered on the floor. I mopped up the spill, gathered every sliver of glass. I carried it all to the pond in a bundle and sank it with a stone."

He could still see the reeds clustered at the water's edge, feel them grasping at his boots as he waded out. He heard the sound of birds singing. And the frog that leapt out of the way as he pitched the stone into the deep, greenish water.

"I didn't breathe a word of it to anyone," he said. "I meant to pretend surprise when she was found.

It would only be a matter of hours, I thought. What I didn't consider was that my father might delay in breaking the news to me."

"Delay for how long?"

He inhaled slowly. "Months."

"Oh, no."

"I suppose he thought it would be too great of a shock. Rafe was too young to even understand. He said she'd gone to a spa for a cure. Every week or two, he told me she'd written a letter. She missed her boys, but the cure wasn't taking. Finally, he told me she'd succumbed. I found her dying in May. I wasn't taken to visit her grave until winter. By then, I'd been concealing the grief for so long . . . I couldn't have shown it if I tried."

It wasn't merely the grief he'd hidden. It was the shame. The shame of lying to his father, of denying his mother her rightful mourning.

The shame of not being enough to make her stay.

A mother was supposed to live for her children, wasn't she? But Piers hadn't given her sufficient reason to carry on.

I can't. I can't bear it.

He pulled away from the painful memories. "Suffice it to say, deceit has come easily to me ever since."

She looked at him with those clear blue eyes. "I'm very sorry for what happened, Piers. I'm glad you told me the truth. I hope you'll talk about it more.

With me, or Rafe, or someone else. But I don't see how this excuses what you did last night."

"I'm not offering excuses. Or apologies. I don't desire forgiveness. I did what needed to be done."

"What needed to be done?" Her eyes widened in disbelief. "You gave me that speech about being a powerful man with every option at his fingertips. Am I to believe you couldn't come up with any other idea besides setting fire to my undergarments in the middle of the night?"

He gestured at the burned floor. "Those undergarments had it coming to them. They attacked me first."

"Good Lord." She stood back a pace. "I can't decide if you've gone completely blockheaded, or if you are trying to make yourself detestable."

"You tell me." He gestured at the left side of his face. "I thought the eyebrow oracle revealed all."

"Yes, well. It's difficult to look at your eyebrow when your head is so far up your arse."

He firmed his jaw. "It's done now. There's no undoing it. We're leaving tonight, and we will be married soon thereafter. There isn't any choice."

"Oh, I still have a choice. Even if the consequences have changed, I always have a choice. If my alternatives are social ruin or a loveless marriage, I will take ruin. At least that would leave me the chance to find happiness somewhere else."

He spread his hands. "I don't know what you want me to say."

"I want you to tell me, in simple terms, just what I'm getting if I marry you. Are you offering me love and partnership? Or a cold, elegantly appointed prison?"

He sighed heavily. "Charlotte . . ."

"Don't give me that exasperated sigh. You know this is important to me. I want to hear, from your lips, that we will have a marriage built on respect and laughter and abiding devotion. Either you make me believe that, right here and now, or I will leave this house alone. Or let you leave it alone. We won't be leaving it together, that's my point."

Apparently, he wasn't the only one who could be a ruthless negotiator.

She crossed her arms. "I'm waiting."

"I made it clear from the beginning that I can't offer you that."

"*Love*, Piers. That's what we're discussing. And I know you're not accustomed to it. You can't even bring yourself to utter the word."

"Words. Words are meaningless."

"Gah." She made a motion as though she would strangle the air. "The very purpose of words is to mean something! There are entire books dedicated to listing nothing but words and their meanings. They're called dictionaries; perhaps you've seen one."

He gave her a dry look.

"It may be just a word," she said, calming. "But hearing it would mean a great deal to me."

"I do not countenance ultimatums. From anyone. And I cannot afford distracting attachments. I haven't made such declarations since I was a child."

"Perhaps you just need practice."

"Perhaps *you* need to grow up."

The words were sharp and aimed to wound, and Piers knew at once they'd hit the mark.

"I won't do it," she said quietly. "I've already lost my friend. There'll be no recovering my reputation. Thanks to Frances, the gossip will reach London faster than we do. I'll be called every vile name there is, whether it rhymes with Charlotte or not."

"No one will dare." If nothing else, he could promise her that. "Not if they wish to avoid the barrel of my pistol or the point of my sword."

"Men can call each other out. This is enmity among ladies, Piers. You cannot shield me from it, and believe me—a woman's tongue can be rapier-sharp. The ladies will cut me to my face. They will slice me to ribbons when my back is turned." She pressed a hand to her chest. "I could endure it all, if I knew you loved me. If we shared a life together that went beyond dinner parties and procreation. But without that . . ."

His heart twisted. "Charlotte."

"I can't," she said. "I can't bear it."

She ran from the room.

And there it was.

All her sweet words last night . . . Vowing to chip away at his defenses. To work for years, even decades, if that's what it took. Because, she'd said, he'd be worth the effort.

I'm never giving up on you.

And yet she had. It had taken her all of one night. One glimpse at what he truly was, and what he was capable of doing—and her naïve promises went up in smoke.

Just as he'd known they would.

Because now she finally saw the truth. If she broke through the walls, there was little inside him but a dark, empty space.

It wasn't worth the effort. Not at all.

Chapter Twenty-two

*C*harlotte spent the day in a trance, unable to sleep or take anything more than a few sips of tea.

When the maids came up to her newly designated room, she let them dress her in freshly washed underthings, cinch her stays tight, and help into her blue silk gown. She sat perfectly still as they dressed her hair in a pile of curls atop her head, bound with a silver ribbon.

She stared into the mirror.

Oh, Charlotte. You've been such a fool.

From the beginning, she'd been insisting that their match defied all logic. No one could fail to note the vast gulfs between them in class, education, and experience, not to mention their wildly different personalities.

But somewhere along the way their match had come to make perfect sense—to Charlotte, at least—no matter how implausible it might appear to the world. She unsettled him; he anchored her. Together, they could be more than they were apart.

She'd dared to hope that he felt the same. That he was in love with her, too. Even if saying so didn't come naturally to him, his willingness to support her dreams, to wait for her, to treat her as his equal, would prove it to be true.

But instead of supporting her, he'd thrown her under the carriage wheels.

She didn't know what to do. Delia wasn't speaking to her. And though Mama had been her strength last night, she couldn't ask her for advice today. Charlotte knew what the answer would be.

Of course you will marry him. He's a marquess! Have you no regard for my nerves?

Just as the maid finished tying a cameo choker about her neck, someone rapped lightly on the door.

"Charlotte?" The door opened a crack. "It's us."

She knew that voice. Her heart leapt, and she ran to fling open the door.

Her sisters stood in the doorway, dusty and rumpled from travel.

To Charlotte, they looked like angels.

"Oh, this is wonderful. I'm so glad you're here."

She hugged her oldest sister, then turned to Minerva and clasped her tight.

"Of course we're here." Minerva adjusted her spectacles. "Colin was invited to a party. He's not going to fail to appear."

Colin was invited? That must have been Piers's doing. He'd asked the Parkhursts to invite her family. So they'd be present for the announcement of the betrothal. Thoughtful of him, that.

"We decided to make it a family trip." Diana glanced at Minerva. "We thought you might need us."

"I do. I need you desperately." Charlotte pulled them into the room. They all settled onto the bed. "I seem to have found myself betrothed to a wealthy, handsome, unfeeling marquess."

Diana smiled. "And what's wrong with him, precisely?"

"Aside from him being everything that Mama would want, of course," Minerva said.

Charlotte sniffed. "I don't even know where to begin."

Minerva plucked a biscuit from her untouched tea tray. "Try the beginning, then."

So she did. She told them everything. Or rather, *nearly* everything. She didn't betray any hint of Piers's secret work, of course, and she was purposely vague about any episodes that involved clothing removal. As she related the episodes of the locked room and Lady the Demonic Mare, her sisters laughed.

Four biscuits and one tearstained handkerchief later, Charlotte finally came to the end. "And then he told *me* I needed to grow up."

"He didn't," Diana said. Her gasp of shock and dismay gave Charlotte some cold satisfaction.

"He's so walled off, so stubborn. The man doesn't know the slightest thing about love."

Minerva smiled. "As opposed to . . . you?"

Her older sisters exchanged a look. A how-sweet-she-sounds look.

Charlotte found it maddening. "I know it must sound ridiculous. He's a worldly, educated peer, and I'm young and inexperienced. But when it comes to emotion, I'm leagues ahead."

"Men can be taught," Minerva said. "Even the worst-behaved ones, like Colin."

"And if I'll be forgiven for saying it," Diana added, "you may have some things to learn, too. I know I did." She squeezed Charlotte's hand. "Do you love him?"

"Yes." She sighed. "But I told him that, and he still betrayed me to force my hand."

"Well, there's the problem," Minerva said. "You *told* him you love him. That doesn't mean he *believed* it. Most likely, in some desperate, shortsighted, arsonist way, he meant to test you. It would be just like a man."

"Perhaps."

If it had been a test, Charlotte had failed it. He'd revealed his deepest, most shameful secret, and she'd received it with cold indifference. Despite all her promises to wait him out, knock down his walls . . . she'd walked away.

"I do think he cares for me. When he can get out of his own way, he's so tender and passionate. But maybe I *am* too young. Maybe it *is* too fast. If we marry like this, it will be for all the wrong reasons."

"I'd like to know who marries for the right ones," Minerva said. "I all but kidnapped Colin, and we were nearly to Scotland before he gave in."

"And there's a reason the twins were born less than eight months after I married Aaron," Diana said. "Sometimes love unfolds gradually. But more often than not, life hurries it along."

Charlotte smiled a little, and it eased the knot strangling her heart. Her sisters were the best medicine.

Still, she picked at the edge of her handkerchief. "I'm just afraid."

"Of what, dear?"

"Of becoming Mama."

There it was, out in the open at last.

"I'm not a scholar like you, Min. Or as patient as

you, Diana. If I marry without love, with little experience of the world and nothing to occupy my time . . . What will prevent me from becoming a ridiculous woman with a nervous condition?"

Minerva looked to Diana, and they shared another of those older-sister looks. "Should we tell her?"

"I think we should," Diana replied.

"Tell me what?"

"You *will* become Mama," Minerva said flatly. "It's inevitable. Once babies come along, you don't even have a choice."

"It's true." Diana sighed. "All the things I swore I'd never do, never say . . ." She buried her face in her hands. "The other day I told Aaron to consider my nerves."

Minerva rose from the bed and went to her traveling satchel. "Do you want to know what's even worse?" She reached into the bag and withdrew her evidence. "I've started carrying a fan."

"Oh dear." Charlotte laughed.

Diana gave her a smile. "The truth of it is, it's only now that we can fully understand. Mama loves us, and in her own, misguided way she tried to secure us the best possible future she could imagine."

"I know," Charlotte said. "And we didn't give her an easy time of it, either."

"At least *we* will not have such a narrow idea of what our daughters' futures can be," Minerva said, returning to the bed. "Colin and I have already started putting aside money for Ada's university education."

"University? But there aren't any colleges that admit women."

"Not yet. But we have some time to change that, don't we? If it comes to it, we'll build our own."

"And if Ada doesn't wish to go to university?"

Minerva looked at her over her spectacles. "Don't be absurd. Of course she will want to go to university."

Charlotte had a mental image of Min storming the gates of Oxford and demanding a college for women—with Ada standing several paces distant, cringing behind her hand.

Perhaps every generation of Highwood women was destined to be an embarrassment to their daughters. If it happened to Charlotte, at least she wouldn't be alone.

"If you don't want to marry this marquess, you don't need to," Minerva assured her. "You'll always have a home with us. Once things are smoothed over and the gossip is forgotten, you can start afresh, pursue the future you want for yourself."

"Scandal's like a fire," Diana added. "It only burns so long as you give it fuel."

"Doesn't love need fuel, as well?"

Could she and Piers keep that fire burning for

a lifetime? After the events of last night and their argument in the morning, Charlotte wasn't sure. She wasn't strong enough to be the only one carting coals. He would have to supply at least a few.

But he'd refused her even that much.

Diana patted her on the knee. "Minerva and I had best go wash and dress for the evening. We'll leave you to think."

Sir Vernon invited Piers to join him in his library before the ball, for a brandy.

Piers accepted, naturally. The irony was irresistible. They were returning to the scene of the crime.

"Too bad about that unpleasantness in the back garden last night. But it's all worked out in the end, eh, Granville?"

He handed a brandy to Piers before taking a seat behind the infamous creaking desk.

"You needn't worry about any scandal," he said. "My daughters understand it's in their best interests not to sully the virtue of a close friend."

The nerve of the man.

Piers took sole responsibility for wounding Charlotte. But he never would have hurt her at all if Sir Vernon Parkhurst were the honest, upright man he pretended to be.

Atop this very desk, he'd committed adultery.

He'd had weeks to confess his indiscretion, but to this day, he would allow his daughter's friend to pay the price for it. Which was a loss, of course, to Delia as well.

Piers tossed back a scalding swallow of brandy. He'd been sent here to find answers. He was tired of dodging around the questions.

Forget stealth and searches. He was going to outright ask.

"Sir Vernon, how long have you been married?"

The man frowned in reflection. "Three-and-twenty years this August, I think?" He counted on his fingers. "No, twenty-four." He laughed. "If my lady asks, I answered you correctly the first time. Without hesitation."

"Of course."

"I'm not so handy with numbers, but I recall everything about the evening we met. It was a masquerade. She was dressed as a cat. Tail attached to her skirts, little pointed black ears. Fur edging her bodice." He raised an eyebrow and leaned back in his chair, propping his boots on the desk. "I'm a hunter, Granville. A sporting man, through and through. I knew then and there, Helena might lead me a pretty chase—but in the end, she would be mine."

What a charming story.

Piers sat up in his chair. "We are friends, are we not?"

"I certainly hope so."

"Then I hope you'll permit me a personal question. The answer will be kept in the strictest confidence, of course."

Sir Vernon waved his brandy glass in invitation.

"As you say, you're a sporting man. In twenty-three years, have you never caught sight of a different quarry? Been tempted to give chase?"

His host's grin faded. He let his boots fall to the floor and set his brandy on the desk. "I know what this is about, Granville. What you're truly asking."

"Good." That would make this all the easier.

"We're men. We understand each other."

"Yes, I believe we do."

"Then let's get to the heart of the matter." Sir Vernon regarded him gravely. "You're getting cold feet."

Stunned, Piers found himself at a loss for words. "I . . . You've . . ."

"No need to be ashamed of it, Granville. You needn't make excuses to me. I felt the same on the eve of my nuptials. Spent a sleepless night convinced I was making a mistake. In the morning, I thought I'd be sick all over the vicar's vestments." He tapped the desk blotter thoughtfully. "But I'll tell you God's honest truth. Once I caught sight of my Helena walking down the aisle of that church, all my doubt vanished."

"Vanished?"

"Gone." The man's eyes were unwavering, solemn. "Never looked at another woman after that day. Well, I'll be honest. I'm a man. I've *looked*. But I've never felt restless, never been tempted to stray. I've never even given it a thought."

Piers regarded the man.

Most people were exceedingly poor liars. He'd long ago learned to tell a truth from a falsehood, unless the liar in question was very, very good.

And he'd be damned if he didn't believe, to the soles of his boots, that Sir Vernon Parkhurst was telling the truth. The man was devoted to his wife.

Which meant Piers knew even less than he'd thought.

It didn't make any sense. The missing money. The strange journeys to seedy row houses and country inns. What on earth could be behind it, if not a mistress or illegitimate child?

Some other agent would have to find out, apparently. Because Piers was at a loss.

Sir Vernon rose from his chair and came around the desk to give him a hearty slap on the back. "You'll be fine, Granville. A bit of doubt on the bridegroom's part is only natural—but don't be fooled. You're not truly worried she won't be enough for you. You're worried you won't be enough for her."

Piers reached for his drink and downed the remainder in a single swallow.

"You never will be good enough, you know," Sir Vernon went on, chuckling. "For some unfathomable reason, the ladies insist on loving us anyway. Sometimes I even think they like us the better for it."

With another resounding thump to Piers's back, Sir Vernon left the library—leaving Piers alone with an empty glass, a mind awhirl with thoughts, and a heart full of regret.

He stared at the window seat. He remembered clasping Charlotte to his chest as she laughed herself to tears against his shirt. He recalled watching her smile as she conversed with his brother. He thought of making love to her in a sunny meadow.

He thought of Oliveview, and of ranking solidly in her top quartile.

He'd likely plunged to the bottom of those ranks today, hovering somewhere just above the dullards who rarely bathed.

Who was he fooling? He'd sunk beneath them, too.

Damn. He'd been so stupid. Beyond stupid. He'd had a lovely, sweet-natured woman naked in his bed, vowing to love him forever. And the minute she fell asleep, he'd decided to go play with matches. All in some stupid attempt to prove her wrong.

Now—thanks to Sir Vernon Parkhurst, of all people—it was clear to him that he'd been not only an idiot, but an ass, as well.

Of *course* Charlotte was wrong.

Every woman was wrong. They had to be, or else humanity would have died out long ago. If they could hear the vilest thoughts in a man's head, see the craven darkness lurking in his chest . . . they would never allow men anywhere near them.

And chances were, it worked the same for women, too. Charlotte doubtless had flaws or some insecurity she'd rather swallow tacks than let him see. It wouldn't make a damn bit of difference in the way he felt. He didn't love her for being perfect, he loved her for being Charlotte.

Good God.

He loved her.

He *loved* her.

Of course he did. She understood him. Reached out to him, no matter how many times he pushed her away. She'd found a way inside his heart, and if she left him now, he would be more hollow than ever.

Naturally he would realize this *after* he'd set her room on fire. And humiliated her in front of several people. Then caused her best friend to reject her. Pity about that tearing-her-dreams-to-shreds bit, too.

Bloody hell.

Piers braced his hands flat on the desk and pushed back in his chair, drawing to his feet. He was a man of action. He couldn't sit here, doing nothing.

He'd deservedly sunk to the level of pond scum. Somehow he had to scrape and claw his way back up. Beg Charlotte's forgiveness, confess his true emotions.

No, no. He had the steps out of order.

First, admit to *having* emotions.

Then confess what they were.

Convince her he would make all her dreams come true, plead with her to be his wife . . . Flowers probably wouldn't go amiss. All of that in—

He glanced at the clock.

Five hours. Give or take. No small task, and the stakes couldn't have been higher. Even if he succeeded in setting the stage for a grand apology, there were no guarantees Charlotte would accept it. He was in danger of losing her forever.

He tugged on his cuffs, pulling them straight. Well, was he a top agent of the Crown, or wasn't he?

Danger was what he lived for.

Chapter Twenty-three

For Charlotte, it was an all-too-familiar scene.

The orchestra warmed their instruments, the quadrille began . . . and she found herself a wallflower once again. Delia sat in the opposite corner of the ballroom, refusing to look her way.

At least tonight she had her family surrounding her. Mama stood chatting—or more likely, boasting—with Lady Parkhurst and her friends. But Diana and Aaron, Minerva and Colin . . . they all kept Charlotte company.

"You needn't stand about with me," Charlotte said. "You should dance."

"I'm not much for dancing," Aaron said.

"Neither am I," said Minerva.

Charlotte turned to Colin, who had seldom encountered a dance or a partner he didn't enjoy.

"I'll save my strength for the waltz," he said. "I'm getting to be a grizzled old man, you know. A touch of the gout perhaps."

Her lips curved in a bittersweet smile. They were so transparently trying to console her—and she loved them for it.

Diana sidled close to Charlotte and took her arm, squeezing it in a reassuring gesture. "What time is the engagement due to be announced?"

"Lady Parkhurst asked us to wait until the end of the midnight supper. Everyone will be gathered in one place. Sir Vernon will raise a toast."

Minerva tilted her head. "Have you decided what you'll—"

"No," Charlotte said. "Not yet."

She was waiting to see Piers. Desperate to speak with him. But as yet, he hadn't made an appearance in the ballroom. This time, she wasn't going to chase after him.

Colin firmed his jaw. "If he doesn't come up to scratch, Dawes and I will call him out. Won't we, Aaron?"

Aaron crossed his big blacksmith's arms over his chest. "Absolutely."

"You don't want to do that," Charlotte warned. "Lord Granville's handy with a pistol. And his brother would be his second."

Colin considered this. "That's the heavyweight champion bare-knuckle fighter brother, is it?"

"Yes."

"Just confirming that he didn't, you know, have another, smaller, less violent brother." Colin sipped from his drink. "We'd still do it, of course."

"Absolutely," Aaron said, sounding a shade less absolute about it than he had been a moment before.

"We'd hold our own. Dawes here is brawny, and I've been in a brawl or two. We were Spindle Cove's finest militiamen, weren't we? You know, the finest not counting Bram. Or Thorne."

"Susanna," Minerva added. "Susanna ranked above you too, I believe."

Colin's mouth pulled to the side. "Yes, can't deny that. But we're no slouches."

"Solidly in the top quartile," Charlotte said.

Her heart pinched in her chest. Where on earth could Piers be? She scanned the room, leaning to either side to peer around the pairs of dancers. A glimpse of a tall man with dark hair propelled her a few paces to the left.

It wasn't Piers.

But something else caught her attention.

A hint of perfume, wafting behind her.

The perfume.

Poppies, vanilla, and black amber. No doubt in her mind. The aroma took her directly back to the library window seat, where she'd laughed in Piers's arms as the desk creaked and lovers groaned.

She turned in place, striving to appear nonchalant as she searched for the perfume's source. Her path was obstructed by a pair of gentlemen, who parted for her cordially—but maddeningly slowly—causing her to lose precious seconds. She began to work her way along the edge of the ballroom, sniffing as deeply and frequently as she could without prompting inquiries on the state of her health.

Then her heel caught on something slick, and her foot nearly slipped out from beneath her. She turned to look down at the floor. A folded piece of paper lay in the shadows where the damask silk wall-covering met the inlaid parquet.

Charlotte discreetly crouched to pick it up. As soon as she had it in her hand, she could smell it. It wasn't a perfumed person she'd detected, but a perfumed note.

Her pulse drummed in her ears, and she concealed the note in her gloved hand.

She didn't dare open it here.

Without stopping to give a word of explanation, she slipped out of the ballroom and headed directly upstairs to her bedchamber. She locked the door behind her and lit a small lamp before unfolding the paper with trembling fingers.

The note contained only a simple, four-line poem,

written in florid script. She held it close to the lamp
to make it out.

> *Where true Love burns Desire is Love's pure flame;*
> *It is the reflex of our earthly frame,*
> *That takes its meaning from the nobler part,*
> *And but translates the language of the heart.*

—S. T. Coleridge

A pretty enough verse, but utterly unhelpful. No
salutation, no signature. Her heart deflated with
disappointment. She turned the paper to the reverse
side, scanning it closely. Nothing there, either.

Then she returned to the verse. She decided to
read it aloud, slowly. Perhaps there was some sort of
message within.

"Where true Love burns Desire is Love's pure
flame," she read aloud. "It is the reflex of our
earthly—"

She stopped and blinked. Now she was seeing
things. She could have sworn that words were dancing between the lines of the verse.

She held the paper closer to the lamp, directly
over the flame. As she watched, a word materialized
on a blank space of the paper, darkening to sepia
one letter at a time.

l—a—t—e

Late.

Invisible ink!

There was a message hidden between the lines of the poem.

Exhilarated, Charlotte pushed through the jumble of hairbrushes and ribbons on her dressing table until she located the curling tongs. She used them to hold the paper over the flame, letting the heat touch every corner, as if she were toasting a slice of bread. The tediousness of the exercise tried her patience to its limits, but she didn't dare risk letting the paper catch fire.

When at last she'd heated every inch of the paper, she smoothed the note on the flat surface of the table. The invisible message read:

> *The ladies will meet Tuesday next*
> *Please bring in the conserves and crumpets*
> *Both are obligatory at midday nuncheon*
> *Such damp nights of late.*

Crumpets?

Crumpets and humidity.

This was the mystery message. Of all the inconsequential, nonsensical lines to inscribe in invisible ink and perfume with rich scent.

Whoever these mystery lovers might be, Charlotte was annoyed with them both. Midday nuncheon, indeed.

She rubbed her eyes and read it again. Then she ran the paper over the flame once more. Nothing new appeared.

Perhaps it was some sort of code? She tried reading it backward, reading every second word, every third or fourth letter . . . none of these methods yielded any comprehensible message.

She was on the verge of crumpling the thing and tossing it into the fire in disgust, when she noted a tiny dash of sepia where she wouldn't expect it to be. She'd dismissed it before as a stray droplet of invisible ink, but now she noticed that it was centered perfectly beneath one word of the poem: "frame."

With her fingertip, she scanned the paper for any other small, overlooked markings. She found another dash; this one directly beneath the word "heart."

Frame and heart.

Heart and frame.

On a hunch, she found a scrap of paper, trimmed it to match the size of the note, and then folded it down the middle and made a swooping cut with a penknife, removing a heart-shaped piece from the center. Then she laid her makeshift valentine over the note, sliding it around until it seemed centered.

The frame blocked out nearly all of the hidden message. The still visible parts read:

will meet
in the conserv
atory at mid
night

"Oh, Lord." She rose from her chair, jumping back in disbelief. "I . . . I've done it. That's it. 'Will meet in the conservatory at midnight.' " She laughed aloud. "I, Charlotte Highwood, have decoded a secret message, and I've done it all by myself. Take that, Agent Brandon."

Now she felt like dancing. But there wasn't time. Someone was expecting a clandestine lover to arrive in the conservatory at midnight, and Charlotte had been working at this for ages. It had to be getting close to the hour.

She checked the mantel clock.

Oh, no. Five minutes past!

Charlotte rushed downstairs.

She crept to the door of the conservatory and opened it silently before sliding inside. The space was dense with the misty fragrance of a thousand blossoms. The glass windows were fogged.

Weak, flickering light spilled from a distant corner of the indoor garden.

A trail of rose petals on the tiled floor led into the conservatory, then disappeared around a bend some ten feet ahead. Perfume, poetry, rose petals . . . ? Whoever this lover was, he or she was truly a romantic.

She paused, suddenly hesitant.

Did it even matter who waited at the end of this trail? It was too late to redeem her reputation, and it wouldn't change her dilemma with Piers. But it would mean so much if she could regain Delia's friendship. Finding the lovers would mean a great deal to her pride, as well. By society's standards, she wasn't accomplished. This was her chance to prove them all wrong.

In any event, she'd come this far. The mystery would haunt her forever if she didn't take these last few steps.

She held her breath as she followed the trail of red, velvety petals. When she turned the corner, her heart pounded in her chest.

The fragrant mist of the hothouse parted to reveal a dark, tall figure.

There, standing in a leafy, candlelit alcove was . . .

"Piers?"

He made an elegant bow. "Good evening, Charlotte."

"What are you doing here? Did you find a note, too?" She looked around. "Were they here already? Did you see them?"

"Did I see whom?"

"The mystery lovers! Or tuppers, or whatever they might be. I found a perfumed note in the ballroom, in code. It took me ages to decipher it, until it was almost too late, and then I hurried down to—"

As she spoke, she took in more details of the scene. The brass candlestick fitted with a beeswax candle. The bottle of champagne chilling in a silver ice bucket. The picnic hamper.

The sly smile on Piers's face.

"It was you." She slapped a hand to her forehead. "You left the note. For me."

"The rose petals were Ridley's idea." He reached for the bottle of champagne and popped the cork. "Did you enjoy your investigative work?"

"You tricked me."

"No, I didn't. You're here, aren't you? That means you weren't tricked at all." He handed her a glass of champagne and nodded at the paper in her hand. "That message used the same methods, more or less, as General Benedict Arnold employed to send intelligence during the rebellion of the American colonists. You deciphered it. Well done." He raised his glass to her, then drank from it.

Yes. She had deciphered it, hadn't she?

She took a well-earned sip of champagne. "See, I told you I could be a spy."

"Perhaps. But you'd need some work to be a successful one. Arnold *was* caught, you know." He picked up a half-eaten sandwich from the picnic hamper and gestured with it. "I brought supper. There are lemon tarts."

She looked at the basket of sweets and sandwiches. "You tricked me, *and* you started the picnic without me. I don't know which is the greater offense."

"I wasn't certain how long it would take you to puzzle it out."

She stole the half-eaten sandwich from his hand. "That settles it. I am definitely most angry with you for doubting me." She took a large bite.

"Next time, I'll make it more of a challenge."

Next time?

Despite the teasing, pride was apparent in his gaze. He was quite pleased with himself, and with Charlotte.

Moreover, he was having fun.

And so was she.

She had a vision of the two of them, leading one another on mysterious late-night treasure hunts through his darkened mansion, a secluded, romantic scene waiting at the end.

Could they have a life like that? One built on playfulness and seduction and just a hint of mystery? Her heart warmed at the thought. But it all depended on whether he felt that warmth, too.

"I love you, Charlotte."

She nearly choked on her bite of sandwich.

"Now?" she protested through a mouthful of bread and sliced cucumber. She swallowed. "You tell me this *now*. You couldn't wait until I'd finished my sandwich?"

"No. I planned to, but I couldn't."

"Well, I hope you mean to say it at least once more."

"Of course I do, darling."

Darling. She loved it when he called her that. In his deep, aristocratic voice, it sounded equal parts suaveness and affection, with a current of danger running beneath.

After setting aside his champagne, he closed the distance between them in slow, determined strides. Oh, but he looked magnificent tonight. Smoothly shaven and turned out in a black tailcoat with a white vest and cravat. Perfect.

He laid his hands to her arms, cherishing her with a gentle caress. "You're exquisitely beautiful tonight. Did I mention that yet?"

She shook her head, thrilled despite herself. "I wish I could honestly say that flattery will get you nowhere."

"It won't get me far enough, I know. I owe you more than compliments. You're due a great many apologies."

Well. She wouldn't make any argument there.

"After you were poisoned, I told myself that by taking control of everything, I would protect you. But you were right. The only person I was protecting was myself. The thought of losing you gutted me. There was no thought in my mind but to keep you, make you irrevocably mine. No matter what villainy was required."

"How could you have worried I might leave you? After all we'd shared? I told you I love you, Piers."

"How to explain it?" He paused. "I didn't think it could be enough. I didn't think that I would be enough."

What?

This beautiful, strong, loyal man worried he wouldn't be enough? Charlotte could have laughed at the absurdity of it, but perversely, a tear burned at the corner of her eye instead.

She blinked it away. "Why would you think that?"

"Past experience. Mothers delight in their children, so they say. Mine didn't find sufficient delight to stay around. My first engagement ended when my betrothed grew tired of waiting." He shrugged. "I haven't been very successful convincing women that I'm worth a lifetime."

She slid her arms around his neck. "You're more than enough for me."

"You don't have to feed me platitudes. I'm hard to know, and even more difficult to love."

"But you must understand how my mind works by now. That only makes you more tempting. I love knowing there's so much more to you than it seems on the surface. And that while a good bit of it is pure brilliance, some of it's dark and twisty, too. You're a puzzle. One that will take ages to solve, and you know how stubborn I am. I'm not one to give up."

He slid his arms around her waist and pressed his brow to hers. "Promise me."

"I promise you." She closed her eyes. "I'm sorry I gave you reason to doubt it. I never will again."

"I will never give you cause."

She lifted her head. "You know, you still haven't said it again."

He gave her a sweet, slow kiss that tasted of champagne. "Oliveview."

She growled in playful protest.

"Teasing, teasing." He looked deep into her eyes. "I love you, Charlotte. Somehow you worked inside my heart, detonated there, and left it an untidy shambles. I don't know if I've pieced together enough of it to love you as well as you deserve. But I swear to you, so long as I live I'll never cease trying."

"Much better, thank you." She swayed in his arms, staring up at this man who belonged to her. "We're going to have the grandest time. Capering about the Continent, stealing secrets . . ."

He shook his head. "That's the one thing I can't

give you. I can send you and Delia to travel the Continent. I'll wait for you as long as you like. But my work requires at least the appearance of detachment. It's too dangerous otherwise. Anyone who wished to hurt me would know the shortest path is through you."

"I understand," she said, trying to mask her disappointment. "I won't complain if you seem distant or unfeeling when we're in public. I . . . I'll just think of myself as working under cover."

"No, darling. I can't risk it. That's why I mean to resign at once."

Chapter Twenty-four

"Resign?" Charlotte's face fell. She pulled away from his embrace, leaving him bereft.

"Yes," he said. "I must. As soon as possible."

"Piers, you can't. You can't give it up. The Crown needs you, and you need your work. I've seen you in moments of action. That's when you truly come alive."

He touched her cheek. "I come alive with you."

"But the challenge, the danger. I know how you enjoy it."

"Oh, I'm not giving up either of those." He smiled. "Love is, by far, the most dangerous thing I've ever felt. Marrying you will be like jumping off a cliff. I feel approximately as secure in my ability to deserve you as I do in my ability to fly."

"I think you could do most anything. Including the flying."

"The truth of it is . . . ever since you walked into my life, my skills have been slipping. To stay in my post would be irresponsible. My instincts are dulled. I've missed clear signs of danger. I'm no closer to completing my mission than I was the day I arrived, and I've lost any talent for prevarication." He searched her lovely face. "Why is it I can't seem to keep anything from you?"

"Because you don't want to."

He frowned. What she'd said didn't make sense.

She'd already destroyed his composure and his defenses. Perhaps she had addled his brains now, too.

"You don't *want* to lie to me," she repeated. "You've been dying to tell someone all your secrets, I think. For whatever reason, you chose me."

He looked to the fogged window for a moment, considering.

Could it be that she was right?

Maybe some deep, visceral part of him had recognized at once this affinity they shared. Perhaps he'd intuited that he could be open with her. That if a crack in the walls around his heart happened to unleash a flood of guilt or melancholy . . . Charlotte would be too lighthearted to sink, too stubborn to drown.

If so, it was damn ironic.

He'd spent the past fortnight in a near-panic, terrified that he was losing his edge. Perhaps he'd worried for nothing, and his instincts were functioning better than ever.

Maybe he was at the top of his game.

"But I still haven't the faintest idea what's been troubling Sir Vernon," he said. "I was so certain he must be having an *affaire*, and that his mistress tried to frighten you off with the monkshood incident. But as of this afternoon, I'm convinced the man is devoted to his wife."

"And none of the women on my list matched the clues. They weren't even consistent. Does she have ginger hair or dark hair? Is she the maid who brought in breakfast, or a lady who buys rich perfume?" She frowned in concentration. "It's almost as if it couldn't have been the same person."

Piers went still. Something sparked in the corner of his mind. A theory. Then a memory. Within the space of a heartbeat, conjecture became conclusion.

"Charlotte." He took her by the shoulders and kissed her soundly. "You are brilliant."

"What do you mean? All I said was that it couldn't have been the same . . ."

He watched as the same realization dawned in her eyes.

"No," she said. "You don't think it was—"

"It must have been. It all fits, doesn't it? The money, the trips, the clues that don't match . . . the reason he didn't own up to the truth."

"It does." She thumped him on the chest. "I *told* you they were mystery lovers, not tuppers. Admit it, I was right."

"Very well, you were right."

She grinned. "I'll never let you forget it, either."

Piers wouldn't have it any other way. She must always remain the optimist to his cynic, the laughter to his silence, the chaos to his order, the warmth to his cool. Their hearts would meet in the middle somehow.

"Do we tell them we know?" she asked.

"What would be the purpose?" He looked toward the door. "We're due to announce our engagement at any moment. That is . . . if we *are* engaged. I don't mean to presume, if you—"

"Good heavens." She put her hand in his and pulled him toward the door. "Of course we are. Let's not start that again."

Piers was exceedingly glad to leave that question behind them, forever.

They left the conservatory and rushed hand-in-hand down the corridor, heading for the dining room. Piers took the lead, weaving through the doorways and navigating the turns.

They were halfway through the entrance hall

when his ankle caught on something. A thin cord, stretched across the room.

He had the presence of mind to release Charlotte's hand immediately, so as not to take her with him. He stumbled toward the floor shoulder-first, hoping to transform his hapless fall into a debonair roll-and-recovery motion. But the moment he hit the parquet tile, he was smothered by something that dropped from above.

A net. A heavy one, made of knotted rope.

"Oho! Caught you now."

Piers groaned softly. He knew that voice.

Edmund.

Bloody hell. This was a new low. He'd been snared by an eight-year-old boy.

Piers tried to maneuver onto his back so he could fling off the net. "Now, Edmund. Let's discuss this like gentlem—augh."

Edmund crossed his arms and plopped his arse atop Piers's stomach, pinning him down.

"You dreadful boy." Charlotte tugged on Edmund's arm. "Get off him."

"Don't hurt him too much," Piers told her. "The Foreign Office may be offering him a post in ten years."

"MUR-DER! MUR-DER! MUR-DER!"

Delia hurried into the hall. "Edmund! What are you doing? Release Lord Granville at once."

"Not until the magistrate comes. He's got to be brought up on charges. Of murder."

Guests began filtering in from the dining room, drawn by the clamor. The servants, too.

Wonderful.

"That's not even possible," Charlotte said. "For there to be murder, there must be a victim. No one has died."

"Well, he *tried* a murder." Edmund replied stoutly. "Tried to strangle Miss Highwood with a rope. His first night here, in the library."

A murmur went through the assembly.

"Edmund, don't be absurd," Delia said. "You must have been mistaken."

"No, I weren't. I heard it all."

"Delia, please listen," Charlotte whispered. "I've been trying to tell you. The night of the ball, there was a misunderstanding."

"First," Edmund declared, pleased to have a rapt audience, "I heard a squeaking. *Eee-eee-eee-eee.* Then . . ." He paused for dramatic effect. "Screams."

The quiet in the hall was unanimous. The crowd of people hung on the boy's every sordid word.

"And last," Edmund said, "there was a noise like the very Devil groaning. Like this: *Grrrrraaa—*"

"*Grrrrraaaagh.*"

"That's it!" Edmund bounced on Piers's chest. "See? It was him."

"Edmund, that wasn't Lord Granville just now," Delia said. "That noise came from the closet."

"The closet?"

Everyone in the hall went silent.

A series of distressingly familiar noises emanated from behind the closet door.

Thump. Thump. Thump.

Piers tried to look at the bright side. Judging by the frantic rhythm, at least this time the lovers were well under way.

Thump.

"Oh!"

Thump.

"Urnph."

Thump-thump-thump-thump.

And one last:

"Grrrraaaaaagh."

After the noises mercifully ended, Edmund leapt to his feet, leaving Piers free to disentangle himself.

Fists at the ready, the boy started to charge toward the closet door.

Piers caught him by the back of his coat. "You don't want to do that."

"Let me go!" he said, punching the air.

"Miss Delia," Piers said in a low voice, "please take your brother upstairs to the nursery. Now."

"Yes," Charlotte agreed, grabbing Delia's free

hand. "Let's all leave the hall, as a matter of fact. And be quick about it."

"But the murderer!" Edmund cried.

It was too late.

The closet door opened, and out tumbled a pair of red-faced, panting lovers with their hair mussed and clothing askew.

Charlotte tried to cover Edmund's view, but he dodged her hand. His eyes widened to saucers in his round, boyish face.

"Father?" he asked in a small voice. "Wh-what were you doing to Mama?"

Minutes later, Charlotte sat in the empty salon, staring blankly at her folded hands as they waited for Sir Vernon and Lady Parkhurst to make themselves presentable.

"I've just realized something," she said to Piers. "We are never, ever going to be able to tell our children how we met."

"We'll come up with a convincing story," he replied. "I've some experience with that."

"I suppose you do." She looked up at the ceiling. "At least now Delia believes that I didn't betray her. She'll start speaking to me again."

She was looking forward to a good, long laugh

about this with her best friend. Over generous glasses of sherry, ideally. There was so much to tell.

"Poor thing," she said. "She's probably upstairs talking to Edmund about peaches and aubergines."

Piers tilted his head. "What is all this about aubergines, anyway?"

Before Charlotte could explain, Sir Vernon and Lady Parkhurst entered the salon, closing the door behind them.

Piers rose from the settee, waiting for Lady Parkhurst to settle into a chair before retaking his own seat. Ever the gentleman, even on an occasion so wildly bizarre as this one.

"We first met at a masquerade," Lady Parkhurst began. "I suppose it started then."

Sir Vernon broke in, gregarious as always. "I'm a sporting man. I can't help it. I live for the hunt, a good chase."

"And I enjoy being pursued."

"Gets the blood pounding."

His wife briefly closed her eyes. "So we . . . play roles. Over the years, they've grown more elaborate. Vernon gives me a purse full of money, and I use it to create a new identity. New name. New gowns. Wigs, jewels, even servants. I write him a letter in the character's voice, telling him when and where to find me, and then . . ."

"And then you enjoy each other's company," Piers finished.

Thank you, Charlotte silently replied. Beyond that, she had no desire for details.

Lady Parkhurst went on, "Sometimes it's gentleman and lightskirt, or travelers stranded at an inn. Lovers having a secret affair . . ."

"Butler and chambermaid," Charlotte supplied.

"That, too."

"So it *was* you who brought the breakfast tray to my room that morning," Charlotte said. "You were wearing a maid's costume and a wig."

"Yes," Lady Parkhurst confessed. "And I'm so sorry about the monkshood, dear. It was an accident, and it wasn't my fault." She slid a cutting glance at her husband. "The 'butler' did it. He mistook the flower for an iris."

"What do I know about flowers? It was purple and pretty."

"It could have killed her, Vernon."

"But it didn't, now did it?" Sir Vernon gestured at Charlotte. "Look at her. She's well enough now."

Charlotte squeezed Piers's hand. She could sense him struggling not to unleash a tirade.

"It's true," she said. "I am fully recovered. And I always assumed it was an honest mistake."

"Why didn't you tell me the truth that first night?" Piers directed his question at Sir Vernon.

"I would have gladly done so, Granville—in private, away from Edmund's ears. But you leapt so quickly to offer for the girl, I didn't have a chance. I thought perhaps there *was* something between you. After all, you were hiding behind the drapes together."

Charlotte exchanged a look with Piers. "That's true, we were."

"And you weren't mistaken, Sir Vernon." Piers held her gaze. "There was something between us from the start."

Lady Parkhurst gave a relieved sigh. "I'm so glad it's all worked for the best. Can we hope for your forgiveness?"

"Yes, of course." Charlotte rose and went to Lady Parkhurst, kissing her on the cheek. "You even have my thanks."

And, she admitted to herself, no small amount of her admiration.

It was heartening to see a couple so clearly in love—and lust—after many years of marriage. She found it sweet, that they were still finding ways to surprise one another. It gave her hope for her own marriage to Piers. Whether they married tomorrow or years from now—settling down didn't have to mean being settled.

As for Edmund's shock . . .

Well, there were worse things for a child than confronting the evidence that his parents were in love.

"Everyone's returned to the dining room. They've likely lost their appetite, but one way or another—supper will nearly be over by now." Lady Parkhurst smoothed her hair and skirts. "Considering the events of the evening, perhaps we should skip Vernon's toast and proceed straight to your announcement?"

Piers stood. "That would probably be best."

They followed their hosts down the corridor, but Piers stopped her just outside the dining room.

"As I see it," he said, "there are two ways we could handle this."

"Oh?"

"I could make a staid, proper announcement of our intended nuptials, kiss the air above your hand, and engage you for the next minuet."

"Hm. Very lordly. What's the second?"

His left eyebrow quirked with wicked intent. "It involves declarations of mad, passionate love. Ample application of lips. Multiple waltzes where I hold you indecently close. Your brothers' mild displeasure, a possible swoon from your mother's quarter . . . and enough gossip to fill the next three issues of the *Prattler*."

Charlotte pretended to think about it.

"What will it be, my love?" He offered his arm. "Shall we make a few stitches in your tattered reputation? Or do you want to start a scandal?"

She threaded her arm through his. "With you? I'll take the scandal any day."

Epilogue

Three months later

They rolled away from each other, collapsing on the pillows and bed linens, slick with sweat and panting for breath.

For the moment, they were mutually sated—but only for the moment.

Three months of abstinence couldn't be undone in one go.

Charlotte nestled her head on her husband's bare chest. His strong arm wrapped around her, cinching her close. A gentle caress up and down her arm sent warm ripples of comfort through her languid body.

There was nowhere else in the world she would have wished to be.

He squinted up at the chandelier. "How the devil did my glove get all the way up there?"

"I've no idea."

She looked about the bedchamber. Discarded garments were *everywhere*. His shirt and waistcoat had been flung over the dressing table. Her stockings hung from the bedposts. Pools of petticoats lay on the floor, tangled with a pair of gray trousers. Her silk wedding dress with the delicate lace and seed pearls had been reduced to an exquisite heap on the carpet.

"I promise, I will make an effort to be tidy," she said. "But only after we spend the honeymoon tearing apart every room in your house."

"First, darling—it's now *our* house. Second, I feel obligated to warn you that Oakhaven has forty-six rooms."

"I'm up for the challenge if you are."

He rolled to face her and swept her naked body with a slow, desirous gaze. "Have no doubt. I will rise to the occasion."

She laughed. They'd seen each other regularly in the months leading up to their Christmas wedding. There'd been flowers to choose and menus to sort out and Mama's lavish tastes to appease. They'd even managed to attend a few balls and make two appearances at the opera. However, they'd never been without a chaperone. Aside from a stolen kiss here and there, they'd been reduced to clasped hands and longing glances.

How she'd missed this—not only the carnal pleasure he gave her, but simply cuddling and talking with him in bed.

"Perhaps we'll take on the bathing room next." He rolled to a sitting position and dropped a sweet kiss on her lips. "But first, we could do with a bit of sustenance."

As he rose from the bed, Charlotte collapsed back on the mattress.

Forty-six rooms. Lord.

The scale of this bedchamber alone was palatial.

Soon, she would have to reconcile herself to this grand house and the intimidating duty of being its mistress.

However, for tonight, she need only pay attention to Piers. Her husband. Her friend. Her dearest love.

Her expert tupper, on the right occasion.

She rolled onto her side, propping herself on one elbow to watch him. She'd missed this sight, too. His lean, masculine body was a thing of beauty.

She eyed him with possessive, shameless interest as he walked away from her—loving the way the muscles of his thighs and backside bunched and flexed—and stared with even bolder interest when he started back, bearing a silver tray laden with champagne and refreshments.

A sigh escaped her. She was a lucky woman indeed.

And, suddenly, a ravenous one.

She sat up and tucked her feet beneath her thighs, and they enjoyed a sort of picnic in the center of the bed. Sandwiches, iced cakes and currant-studded scones, an array of cheeses and fruits. How did his cook find ripe, sweet apricots in December? A marvel.

"I almost forgot." He set aside a roll stuffed with butter and wafer-thin ham. "I have presents for you."

Charlotte swallowed the last of her champagne. "Wedding presents?"

"Wedding presents, Christmas presents. However you wish to think of them."

"You have my interest piqued."

He stretched to open the drawer of a bedside table and rummaged through it. "Well, first there's the expected one." With a bored, careless air he drew a gleaming rope of gold and jewels from the drawer and held it out to her.

Charlotte was almost afraid to touch it.

Almost.

Her fingers did tremble a bit as she took the necklace into her own hands, turning it over to catch the light. A cluster of exquisite sapphires, each as big as her fingernail, hung from a diamond-studded chain.

"My goodness. Piers."

She held it to her décolletage, and he helped her

fasten it in back. She craned her neck to catch her reflection in the mirror across the room. Even at this distance, the necklace flashed and sparkled like a night full of stars.

"I don't know what to say. It's beautiful."

"It's made beautiful by you wearing it. But as I said, it's the expected thing."

"*I* certainly didn't expect it."

"There are a few more gifts, less traditional."

Charlotte reluctantly tore her gaze from her own reflection. "More?"

"See that bureau?" He nodded toward an immense burled-walnut chest with inlaid flowers, taking up one full corner of the room.

"It's difficult to miss."

"It has fourteen hidden drawers. And no hints. I suspect it will take you years to find them all."

"Hah. I suspect you just want me to learn the usefulness of drawers."

"Perhaps. Now, for the last. And best, I hope. Close your eyes and hold out your hands."

She obeyed, sitting up straight and cupping her hands in front of her.

"Open."

Charlotte opened her eyes to find a small finger of brass, dangling from a velvet fob. "A key? To what?"

"A secret passage, located somewhere within this house."

She gasped with delight. "This house has a secret passage?"

"It does now. One that ends in a secret room. I had a team of architects and builders add it in. And even I don't know where it is, so don't think you'll get the answer out of me."

He knew her so well.

And he was right, this was the best of all.

She clutched the key in her fist. "This is the most perfect gift I've ever received. Thank you. And now is the moment where I confess that I've only one gift for you, and it's nowhere near so wonderful."

"Charlotte." He reached for her, cupping her cheek in his hand. "Mere hours ago, you vowed before God to be my wife. I love you so completely, you've already filled every hidden chamber of my heart and every dark, secret cupboard of my being. You need never trouble with presents. I consider myself full up on gifts for the rest of my days."

Oh, this man. How could she have ever believed him to be cold and unromantic?

She smiled and blinked away a silly tear. "Well, then. Perhaps my gift is appropriate after all."

She hopped down from the bed, rummaged through the baggage the footmen had carried up until she found the right hatbox, and hurried back with her small present.

"Here." Before she could lose her nerve, she thrust it into his hand. "It's just a portrait. Of me."

Excellent, Charlotte. As if he couldn't see that for himself?

"Delia painted it before she left with her family," she explained.

"She captured you well."

"Do you think so?"

In answer, he set aside the portrait and took her mouth in a passionate kiss. "I adore it," he whispered against her lips. "I adore you."

He bent his head to kiss her neck and her ear, cupping her breast in his hand and gently stroking his thumb around her nipple.

"Delia wrote that she's painting us a landscape now." Charlotte sucked in her breath when his hand dipped between her thighs. "A view of the rolling hills and groves. She says the Italian countryside is almost as inspiring as the frescoes."

"Glad to hear it."

She tangled her hand in his hair as he rolled her onto her back. "Did I thank you for using your influence to change Sir Vernon's appointment?"

"Mm-hm," he murmured, flicking his tongue over her nipple.

"And for promising we'll visit the Parkhursts this summer, stopping over in Paris and Vienna on the way?"

"Only few dozen times."

"It just means so much to— Oh."

He drew her nipple into his mouth, teasing the sensitive peak with his tongue and teeth. By the time he released it, she'd lost the thought entirely.

In a flash, he'd moved atop her, pushing her thighs apart and hooking her knees over his shoulders. Then he grasped her hips and yanked her toward him with a flex of his arms, spreading her most intimate places for his kiss.

The move was brusque, commanding.

Anything but proper.

And the way he set about using his tongue was devilish indeed.

"Piers." Several breathless, writhing moments later, she tugged on his hair until she caught his gaze. "You didn't really resign, did you?"

"The truth?"

"Always."

He gave her a slow, wicked smile. "Spies never truly retire, darling. They just go under very deep cover."

With that, he drew the quilt up to her waist and disappeared beneath it.

The next morning, Charlotte slept like a stone.